Filthy RICH

Filthy RICH

BLACKSTONE DYNASTY BOOK ONE

RAINE MILLER

This is a work of fiction. Names, characters, organizations, places, events, and incidents are either products of the author's imagination or are used fictitiously.

Published by Montlake Romance, Seattle

www.apub.com

Amazon, the Amazon logo, and Montlake Romance are trademarks of Amazon.com, Inc., or its affiliates.

ISBN-13: 9781503939639
ISBN-10: 1503939634

Cover design by Damonza

Cover photograph by Specular

Printed in the United States of America

For Luna, who is someone very special.
"No friendship is an accident."

–O. Henry, Heart of the West

PROLOGUE

Caleb

My father always said I would know when the right woman came along. He was such a wise man. When it happened, I didn't even question it because the process was so effortless. I just fell into her . . . because my heart knew her right away.

Knew she was the one for me.

I'd known her for years actually. She came to Blackstone Island to live with her grandmother after her parents were killed in a car crash. A devastated fifteen-year-old trying to adapt to a new life in a new place, trying to find where she fit in a world so different from where she'd come—a forty-square-mile resort island off the Massachusetts coast where her grandmother ran the household at Blackwater, the family ancestral home.

Should have known *of* her, that is.

Our paths didn't cross that I am aware of, but it's possible. I rarely visited the island in those days because I was a twenty-three-year-old junior executive fresh out of Harvard Business School, learning everything I could about the family business. I traveled the world, enjoying the excitement of international boardroom deals by day and socializing at off-hours business affairs by night. I worked hard at both. Affairs, liaisons, one-night stands had all come and gone without a backward glance. Nameless faces and unremarkable encounters filled my nights whenever I wanted them to. The hopping nightlife of the big cities with even bigger players vying for a piece of the pie became my normal. I embraced every aspect that came with the lifestyle. Wealth, sexual favors, a certain celebrity born out of my name, all collected with barely any effort. For the next eight years, I had the world in the palm of my hand as I went about amassing a personal fortune in addition to increasing the family coffers.

Or so I thought.

I didn't yet know what was missing from my life. Until her. And then, when I realized exactly *who* she was, and how fate had gotten the last laugh on me, it was already far too late. She'd bewitched me utterly. And furthermore, I knew she had no idea who I was or what ties connected us.

Maybe that's what made her so intoxicating?

I didn't know and I didn't care because it made absolutely no difference to me. I wanted her with a primal desire I could barely understand, yet I embraced that desire wholeheartedly because I was incapable of doing anything else with it. How could I not? She had enchanted me.

However, once my brain managed to catch up, it wasn't quite so effortless to accept this new and unfamiliar reality of feeling something for a woman beyond the unquestioning curiosity of when and if we might fuck.

I struggled against the idea of her at first for a few reasons. She was too young. My mother would never approve of us together. Others in my world would probably chew her up and spit her out, destroying her sweetness. But I soon found out my heart didn't give a flying fuck about any of those reasons. The heart wants what it wants, and I'd discovered that for *my* heart, *want* was all wrapped up in the package that was Brooke Ellen Casterley.

The death of my father from the evils of cancer was an eye-opener for my siblings and me. Money can buy a lot of things, but it can't stop the Grim Reaper from calling on you if it's your time to go. Death is called the great equalizer. And it truly was. Wealth is a trivial thing when it's only extra fuckin' zeros on a balance sheet that makes any difference between lives lived. Doesn't matter if you are rich or poor when you die, because none of it counts at the end. You leave this life the same way you come into it. You go out alone and take nothing. "There has to be more to life than making money, son," he told me at the end. He took hold of my hand and squeezed as hard as his frail strength could manage so as to make me understand the importance. He had regrets and wanted to share with me what he'd learned to prevent me from making the same mistakes. I understood him clearly.

The most essential value my father tried to teach me along with my brothers and sisters was the idea of family. Family took precedence over money. "Take care of the family first and the wealth will grow, Caleb," he said.

A strong family moving forward was the only thing that truly meant anything at the end of the day.

The Blackstones had been here on the island since the days when the *Mayflower* made its treacherous journey to the untamed American shores. As the eldest son it was my duty to make sure the Blackstones would still be here a hundred years from now.

My plan to fulfill my duty included her. It wouldn't work any other way for me. I knew it the first time I ever felt the heat of her eyes as they burned me from across the room.

I knew it down in my bones.

I was going to marry that lovely, beautiful girl from England, and she would be mine.

Caleb

September
Boston

I rolled off her and knew it was the last time we would ever fuck. No use in trying to fake it and pretend there would be a next time. Janice and I were done even if she didn't know it yet. Sex happened when I needed some, and the rest of the time, it was work, work, and more work. I'd been busy anyway, traveling all over the world since I'd taken over the reins at Blackstone Global Enterprises eighteen months ago when my father became too ill to continue.

Janice purred up against my neck and rubbed her tits into the side of my chest. I fought the urge to push her away but stripped off the condom instead. In the beginning we both seemed to be on the same page with expectations that our connection didn't really extend beyond the bedroom. She was a successful model in the fashion industry and traveled as much as or more than I did, so I hadn't found her to be clingy before. If she had been, then there never would have been a "thing" at all between us, because I knew all about women who cling. The line of females looking for a rich man to make all their dreams come true was as long as it was easy to spot, and I'd fielded so many attempts over the years, I was an expert at avoidance.

But now I sensed Janice wanted so much more from me than I was able to give her, and I dreaded the confrontation that was coming. Some sort of commitment to the future was never going to happen, and it annoyed me that she still pushed. I thought I'd been clear when we started out.

She'd come to my father's funeral six months ago with her family, and in my grief I'd turned to her offer of comfort, even though I'd said I probably couldn't give her more than an infrequent night at a time. After a few weeks of regular sex, I'd suggested we be exclusive, which was completely new territory for me. Not having to play the field in order to get laid was convenient, and we came from the same world, having grown up privileged in the Boston area, attending the same private schools, vacationing at our beachfront homes on the island. Being with someone who understood the ins and outs of New England society just made for an easier time of it, so I decided to give the girlfriend thing a shot with her. We both had to be in Boston at the same time in order to be together anyway, and that wasn't always easy. As much as I'd made the effort to work toward my first real relationship in the hopes maybe I'd feel *something* for Janice, it was time to face up to the fact there was nothing deeper than an orgasm or two going on between us, and there never had been.

My mother would be devastated when she found out. Probably even more than Janice would be. Our families were close and I accepted that it would be awkward between her people and mine once our breakup was announced.

Note to self: don't fuck friends of the family ever again.

And there was also the suspicion Janice was cheating on me. The fact that I wasn't bothered too much was telling in itself, but she was the only woman I'd been with for the last six months. If we couldn't even be honest with each other about who we were fucking, then it was hopeless for us anyway. Not contracting genital herpes would be an additional plus.

I wished I could lay that bomb on my mother when she started in with the guilt trip over our demise as a couple. But it wouldn't do for Madelaine Blackstone to hear the word *fuck* or any variation of it in a conversation with her son. Ever. What a pity that was. I'd love to see the horrified look on her face—

"What are you smiling about?" Janice asked, her hand sliding down my stomach on a direct path to my cock.

"Was I?" I stopped her hand from gripping me at the last second and disentangled myself from her body. I rested my forehead in my hands as I sat up on the side of the bed.

"Yeah, Caleb, you were." She sounded annoyed. "What's the matter with you anyway? Why don't you want to go again?" She draped herself over my back and shimmied the whole naked length of her body into mine while I tried not to shudder. "You know once is never enough for me," she said with a very noticeable touch of desperation thrown in to hopefully change my mind.

You're a motherfucking idiot for ever getting involved with her. Learn from this, moron. Learn!

I was pretty sure Janice was a nymphomaniac, and while it had been a bonus in the beginning for a guy who needed to have his brains fucked out to bear the loss of a beloved parent, now not so much. I reached for my pants and dragged them on, desperate to put a barrier between my cock and her as quickly as possible. I really needed a shower, but my conscience couldn't go another five minutes without delivering the news we were finished—fucking—forever.

The three *f*s that became an eventual reality for every woman I'd ever been with.

I knew it made me an asshole for having sex with her first. I shouldn't have and I wasn't proud of it, but to be fair, Janice initiated the sex tonight, starting with the elevator ride up to my apartment. She would have happily blown me on security camera if I hadn't insisted we wait. Public fucking was her thing, not mine.

Tonight I'd needed her on my arm for a charity dinner because at five grand a plate it was downright cheap if you went solo. Ten thousand dollars to cancer research was a lot better than five for the charity. I wouldn't have minded writing a check for ten times that amount and skipping the dinner altogether, but that would be a socially retarded thing to do. Benefitting cancer research in my father's name was something I would support generously for as long as I lived. My check would always have the extra zero at the end of it anyway.

"So you're really all done for the night." I could hear the disdain in her voice. "Caleb, I'm leaving for Hong Kong in the morning. It'll be at least a week before we can be together again."

Try never.

I sighed and turned to face her.

"Janice, we need to talk."

Thirty minutes later I was minus my first "girlfriend" and in possession of a very noticeable shiner. For a hundred-pound woman, Janice could throw down. It helped that she took me by surprise and I never saw it coming. It would also be fair to say she was unhappy about our breakup.

I checked the bruise on my left cheekbone and the accompanying black eye in the entryway mirror. It would look so much worse in the morning. Going into the office would be fun tomorrow. When I asked that her key to my apartment be returned, the crazy bitch had punched me right in the face.

With her motherfucking shoe.

The crying came a minute later, accompanied by hysterical accusations of me leading her along to think we were heading toward marriage and a future together. I knew exactly where that idea had come from the second she screamed it at me in a rage.

Fucking crazy talk. I told her there was only one Mrs. Blackstone alive in my family and that was my recently widowed mother, the person responsible for planting such a ridiculous notion into her head. She'd told me to fuck off before storming out my door, calling me every name in the book as she cat-walked her way toward the elevators. The neighbors would've had to be dead to miss her not-so-subtle show.

God.

My phone buzzed and I was afraid to look to see who was messaging me. I wasn't up for discussing Janice with Mom right now, or any time for that matter.

James. I guessed what he would say before I even started reading because he only lived two floors down from me. She hadn't had far to travel.

J: Hey man, Jan is here crying b/c u broke up w/ her. That true?

I shook my head as my fingers flew.

C: Yeah.

J: So . . . u don't care she's here?

The poor bastard was playing with deadly fire. Like soaking a huge pile of dry leaves with gasoline and blasting it with a blowtorch.

C: Nope. Thx for checking w/ me first but we are over.

J: Ok, man.

Christ, James was gonna go there with Janice.

C: Hey, James?

J: Yeah.

C: Be careful. Don't die tonight. Jan is a goddamn nympho if u didn't know already.

J: Yeah I got that impression when she showed up here and said she wanted 2 suck my cock. I won't die u fool. Talk later—

C: Safe sex, James, and wrap that shit up tight.

J: Yep.

C: Suggest u only go one night. She's a clinger.

J: <middle finger emoticon>

I went to get a Sam Adams from the fridge. What a cluster of a night. Did it make me a horrible person to be worrying more about what was happening to my friend than my ex-girlfriend right now? James Blakney was in for a night of crazy sex with an even crazier Janice. I couldn't help but feel grateful for dodging an immediate bullet with her, but knew this shit couldn't possibly end well for me, or for James. I had to remind myself he was a big boy and he had been warned. He'd find out exactly what Janice was like soon enough.

I needed to put in an order to have my locks changed. I quickly sent a text to my PA, Victoria, to set that up. She'd take care of it tomorrow.

A shower was calling my name. Burning hot with lots of Dial soap—the hard-core yellow stuff that just about took your skin away with the dirt.

I flipped on the light to my bathroom and flinched at the sight of what greeted me.

"Jesus. Christ."

Janice had been upstairs trashing my bathroom while I thought she was getting dressed to leave. *Fucking Bastard* was scrawled on the mirror in her red lipstick. She'd smeared shampoo, toothpaste, and God knows what else everywhere from the walls to the countertops to the floor. Towels had been shoved into the toilet. The contents of the drawers had been dumped out and thrown around. Utter mayhem and destruction. I checked the cupboards but the stuff there appeared untouched, somehow miraculously escaping The Wrath of Janice. I was almost expecting a severed horse head or a dead bunny rabbit to be behind the doors when I opened them to check. The whole thing was straight out of *Fatal Attraction* and creepy as fuck.

I shut off the light and headed for the guest room to take my shower, draining my beer as I went. I felt sorry for Ann having to clean it all up tomorrow, but the mess was too much for me to deal with right now. I'd be sure to thank Ann with an extra paid day off during the week for her trouble. I felt my phone vibrate in my pocket.

Oh goody, a picture. From Janice. Of her sucking what I assumed was James's cock no less. She even added a message to go along with it. You will be so sorry you ever fucked with me, Caleb Blackstone.

I was already sorry. And Janice was seriously unhinged.

I did three things before powering off my phone for the night: Deleted the photo. Blocked Janice's number. Texted James to tell him she was posting pics of his dick in her mouth. His father, a judge for the

First Circuit Court of Appeals, wouldn't be too keen about it should the picture get leaked. Well, four things. I went back for another beer and downed it before going to the guest room for my long-overdue shower.

As the too-hot water poured over my skin, I made a promise to myself to stay away from women for a while. Dating certainly wasn't doing me much good, and I'd had it with all of the crazy females who only wanted to use me for open access to my money or trap me into marrying them.

Where were the normal women of the world?

Were they only a myth?

I remembered something Dad had said to me before he'd died. "When you find whatever it is that makes you happy, Caleb, hold on to it with everything you've got. Your heart will let you know."

I wanted to believe what Dad had told me was true, but the fact of the matter was my heart hadn't told me a thing in a very long time.

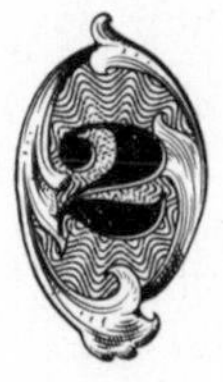

Brooke

Blackstone Island, Massachusetts

Living on an island had its perks, but the hour-long commute on the ferry into Boston wasn't one of them. There were other reasons for being here, though. Good reasons, I reminded myself as I pulled my coat a little tighter against the autumn chill breezing over the water.

My nan needed me now, and there wasn't anything I wouldn't do for the woman who'd taken me in at fifteen after Mum and Dad were killed. I don't really remember a great deal about when I first came to live on the island with Nan. I must have blocked it out due to the terrible shock of what had happened to my parents and being so suddenly uprooted. The high-end, touristy retreat called Blackstone Island couldn't be more dissimilar from the place I'd previously called home. From the suburbs of London to a swath of colonial America separated from the mainland by Massachusetts Bay. Well, at least the language was the same.

Sort of.

"Oh, you have an accent." *No, you're the ones with the accent.*

"You're from Australia, right?" *Wrong hemisphere.*

"Hey Brooke, say something in your English accent for me." *Something.*

I had heard every joke and had been asked nearly every question imaginable, but it didn't bother me. Not really. I knew people were merely curious about how I'd come to be here and tried to be friendly.

In time I came out of my shock. I went on to finish what they called high school here on the island, and then later attended university at Suffolk where I earned my degree in interior design. I didn't realize it then, but those were the happy times.

Then I met someone and made a terrible mistake, and had to leave Nan on the island while I lived far away in Los Angeles. I suffered through my terrible mistake for a year and a half until the day came that I didn't have to endure the suffering anymore. Not physically at least. The sorrow was still with me and probably always would be, but I was determined to keep moving forward in a positive way. And I'd made a promise to myself not to let the bad parts of my past hurt me anymore. It was a goal and I planned to stick to it.

Five months ago I left LA and came back to Boston and then went about the process of getting my life back. Nan was still in her darling cottage on Blackstone Island where she had come to live all the way from England as a young bride. Many a time I've heard the locals tell the story about how my grandfather had brought home an *English girl* for a wife, as if she'd come from an alien planet. Nan and I had our citizenship in common—both British born but called America our home.

I'd lived in the US for so long now it *was* home in my mind.

"Penny for your thoughts, young lady."

I turned toward twinkling blue eyes that regarded me kindly and smiled. Herman was a dedicated flirt. Since he had to be pushing seventy and was also the mayor of Blackstone Island, I gave him a pass. He was rumored to own most of the property on the island and to be worth millions. You'd never know it, though. He lived what appeared to be a modest life in a small house, with a really big oceanfront view—probably what constituted the millions he purportedly had—and was one of the most cheerful people I'd ever met in my life. He always greeted me warmly and asked about Nan. I'd wondered if he might be a little in love with my nan, actually.

"Good morning, Mayor. What has you heading off-island today?" I asked, suddenly curious. I'd never seen him on the morning ferry to Boston before.

"County council quarterly meeting in the city." He looked out at the view of the shoreline and seemed pensive as he studied it. "One of the few reasons left to get me to leave, otherwise I wouldn't."

"Ahh, well I don't blame you a bit. I'd choose the island over Boston any day."

"Why don't you then?" he asked quickly.

"Herman, you are the mayor so I know you are fully aware there is no thriving interior design business on Blackstone Island for which I might be employed."

He stroked his chin thoughtfully before replying, "I'll have to work on that one then, but you never answered my question."

"What?"

"I offered you a penny for your thoughts, but I guess you've raised your rates." He pretended to sulk. The man could still flirt like a champion and his handsome features hadn't been erased by the years, either. He must have been quite a specimen in his younger days, breaking hearts all over the place. I'd have to ask Nan about his past sometime.

"For you, no charge." I nodded toward the trees rising majestically along the rock cliff and the rocky beach below as the ferry moved around the horn of the island toward the open bay. "I was thinking about how happy I am to be back here. I do love that view so much."

He admired the scene along with me for a minute. "Glad to have you back, too. I know your grandma is thrilled." Was that a flicker of something I just saw pass through his deep-blue eyes? I waited for it. "By the way, how is your grandma doing since her surgery?"

As dependable as clockwork, dear Herman Blackstone was when it came to my nan.

"Thank you for asking. She is recovering well, but between you and me, I don't think she was ready to retire from Blackwater when they closed the house. She loved her job, and now I think she's a bit bored." There were other things I left unsaid because I didn't want to offend Herman in any way. It was his family who'd employed my grandmother for more than three decades before abandoning the property two years ago. Nan had been the housekeeper at the Blackwater estate for thirty-five years when it was boarded up for good and now sat empty along the western cliffs of the island. The family didn't come here anymore. I'd heard it was only the father who loved it so much, but after he became ill they didn't return again.

"A lot changed while you were away."

"As things do," I replied softly, sensing his sadness but not wanting to pry.

"Yes indeed, but that doesn't mean there's no room to improve the situation," he said, "and remember where you've come from." Clearly he was unhappy with his family giving up on the island.

I put my hand on his arm. "I am so sorry for your loss, Herman. Nan told me about your brother's passing." I'd heard Mr. John William Blackstone had died of cancer not long before I returned five months ago. "I only met him one time when Nan first took me in, but he was always a very good employer to her and she thought the world of the family." That was mostly true. Nan never said a word against her, but I don't think she held Mrs. Blackstone in the same esteem as her husband, and she'd stopped coming to the island for holidays years ago, once her children were grown. I guess not everyone could love the rich beauty of the island in the same way.

He turned his wise eyes on me and covered my hand with his. "I'm sorry for your loss as well, Brooke. Your grandma told me when it happened. She was worried sick about you, and she needed—well, I think she needed to talk to somebody about it at the time or she would have lost her mind."

Kindness can induce an outpouring of emotions I had found. This wasn't the first time it had happened to me, either. My friend Zoe's heartfelt condolences had done the same thing when we first met up after I returned. Same with Eduardo. When someone showed they cared about you and expressed it in a kind way, that very kindness held the power to bring all of those experiences and hopes and dreams and memories rushing right back up to the surface again like they had happened yesterday. Even when I believed I'd buried it deep, my hurt was really just hovering at the surface, barely covered by the thinnest of sheets ready to blow away in the breeze.

My eyes filled with tears before I could stop them. I gave in and let them fall. Sometimes I was weak and couldn't help remembering what I'd lost . . . and I cried.

"Oh, hell, I've upset you—I'm so very sorry, Brooke," he sputtered.

I could tell Herman was absolutely horrified by my outburst, the poor man. I heard it in his voice. Awesome! I'd freaked out a sweet old man, and the day was barely underway. I'd bet money he'd go straight to my nan and tell her about it the minute he returned from his meeting in the city. Then she would be worried. And she didn't need to be worrying about me right now as she healed from her knee replacement. I was fine. And nothing would change the past no matter what people said or didn't say to me. The whole experience of grief was rather an unending cycle, and so damn exhausting; I just wanted off the ride at this point.

I shook my head and stared down at the decking below my feet. "It's okay, please. This happens to me sometimes and I—do this—" I used my knuckle to brush away a tear and took in a slow, deep breath to help bring my emotions back down to a functional level. "I'll be fine. Sorry, Herman."

"Don't you apologize to me when you've every right to grieve," he scolded. Then he presented a pristine white handkerchief to my hands. I took it gratefully as Herman drew his arm around me and pulled me in against his shoulder. The soft leather of his jacket cushioned my cheek as I accepted his offered comfort. "Of course you'll be fine, Brooke. You have your whole life ahead of you and wonderful things will come, you'll see."

We stood like that and watched the island grow smaller and smaller until the ferry turned southward and she slipped out of sight. I knew I'd be back to this same exact spot in the ocean when I returned on the five-thirty after work. I'd wait for that moment when the island appeared on the horizon, after the captain made his northward turn. I'd breathe a sigh of relief when she came into view, and my heart would settle. It was a weird ritual with me, but it happened every time I came and went from Blackstone Island. It hurt a little to leave her each time, but the tiny thrill I experienced when I returned had never failed me, either. The safety of the island provided sanctuary for my troubled heart.

As I pulled myself together and indulged in my Zen moment with Herman, I thought about what he'd said . . . about wonderful things being ahead for me.

I wanted it to be true.

I so wanted it to be true.

Brooke

Harris & Goode was tucked away on Hereford Street where it was a bit quieter than the foot traffic of Newbury Street. It didn't matter that the location was quieter, though, because clients looking to hire a designer in this neighborhood usually weren't walk-ins. The interior-design business relied on word of mouth, mostly the coveted referrals from prior clients to their friends with the money to pay for such services.

When I felt like walking, I got off at the Copley Station and followed Newbury Street down to where I worked. If the weather was unpleasant, I took Hynes because it was a lot closer. Today wasn't unpleasant, though. A sunny and dry autumn day was always appreciated.

My small emotional breakdown on the ferry this morning with Herman had strangely helped.

In a way.

So I had let my guard down and remembered my sadness for a moment.

I'd become emotional.

I'd cried and scared poor Herman.

But we both survived it, and when the flurry of my sadness had passed, I'd felt much better. And I think Herman did as well. It wouldn't be weird when we saw each other next time because now we'd sealed our friendship. That, as I pondered further, was a good thing.

I stopped at Starbucks to repair my makeup, and more importantly to supply my coffee addiction, before heading inside Harris & Goode at the next doorway. God, I loved that we had a Starbucks next door. One of the nicest perks about my job. There was a queue for the loo so I checked my messages while I waited. The one from Martin was unexpected. He wanted me to work a reception cocktail party this evening, six to nine.

My side job serving for Jonquil Catering was not my favorite, but it paid pretty well when I could fit a job in. I loved working at Harris & Goode, designing rooms for clients based on their visions, but couldn't quite make the ends meet on a junior designer's salary. Not yet anyway. So I took jobs serving on weekends and evenings *if* I had proper notice. Nine hours wasn't enough time for me to arrange anything, and Martin knew that. I had to have a place to stay the night for one thing, because the last ferry left the dock at 8:30 p.m. on the dot, and if I wasn't on it, then I was stuck in Boston for the night. I'd stay over with Zoe, but my friend was out of town for her sister's wedding for at least another week. I didn't have clothes for the following day of work at Harris & Goode or my black-and-whites for serving. There was no way I could work for Martin tonight.

I texted him my reply: Sorry, can't do, Martin. I'm already on the mainland for the day. I need some notice to arrange where to stay, clothes, etc. –B

He'd be pissy with me now, but what could I do about it? Living on an island made for some challenges and I couldn't control the ferry schedule. There wasn't a lot of demand for a boat to Blackstone Island in the middle of the night.

I fixed my face in the mirror at Starbucks and thought I'd pass for normal. If Eduardo didn't notice I'd been crying, then I'd call the whole thing a success. Straight blonde hair and very light brown eyes—that I'd been told were amber—had been inherited from my mum. Nan reminded me frequently that I looked just like her. I thought my mum had been very beautiful, so when Nan told me I could be Mum's twin, it made me feel good inside.

I studied myself thoughtfully and came to the conclusion that I didn't look bad, just a bit . . . sad.

Because I was.

It was no coincidence my favorite character from the movie *Inside Out* was Sadness. She was necessary—an important part of your life—and if you tried to keep Sadness out completely, and didn't let her in once in a while, then the rest of the parts of you started to break down from the pressure of trying to deny yourself the right to be sad. It all made total sense to me. Maybe I'd watch it tonight after I visited Nan at physical therapy.

"Good morning!" Eduardo lambasted me with his standard greeting. "Looking very sexy today, *mi condesa*. Those boots are screaming 'do me 'til I can't take it anymore' you know."

I set my coffee down on the reception counter and unbuttoned my coat. "Good morning to you, too, and they are not screaming anything of the kind."

"They so are, darling. I bet you didn't notice the hunk in the sunglasses checking you out either, hmm?" Eduardo waved toward the full-glass front doors of the building where a *hunk* was indeed peering in as he took a call. Six-two, maybe six-three, with dark hair, a very nice wool coat in camel over an expensive gray suit, and aviator sunglasses was all I could make out through the window. But even through the glass and shadows, his handsomeness was apparent. There were men like him everywhere in Boston's business center, though. I saw them every day, hurrying from one corporate deal to another. Trying to get ahead just like everyone else.

"He's talking on his phone, Eduardo, not looking at me, you tit-head."

"He did. You passed by and he checked you out real good, honey. He liked what he saw, mmm-hmm," he informed me with a straight face, "and I love it when you talk dirty English to me." It was all I could do to keep from laughing at him outright. Eduardo Ramos was good for my soul. I'd only known him since I'd started working at Harris & Goode four months ago, but we had clicked right away. He knew all about my past, and was nothing but supportive and compassionate about my situation. He loved the fact I was British and called me *condesa* most of the time—Spanish for *countess*. The thing with Eduardo was you had to overlook the outrageous and inappropriate comments he made on just about any off-limits topic for a place of business—*and* always at the most inappropriate times—because it was simply part of the package. A gorgeous Puerto Rican gay man with a mouth, and absolutely, perfectly lovely.

I shook my head at him slowly. "Do Jon and Carlisle know that you fantasize about the foot traffic when you should be working?"

He sniffed and frowned. "They do the same thing when they come through the front. But it's right there, Brooke, right in front of me."

"What is right in front of you?" I looked back toward the glass and noticed the hunk had moved on.

"Man heaven," Eduardo sighed dreamily. "Big . . . hard . . . cocks . . . just walking—walking past us all day long. *Ay, Dios mío!*" He fanned his face with both hands flapping.

I lost it and had to either laugh out loud or explode. "Probably not so hard as you imagine if they are walking. I think it would be quite painful to walk around with a stiff cock all day."

"You have a point there, *condesa*, and please say *stiff cock* for me again in your pretty accent."

"No, I will not say it again, and you can stop being cheeky with me."

Eduardo knew I wasn't annoyed. It was a game we played for fun. Jon and Carlisle, the owners, didn't give a toss, either. It was part and parcel of working with three gay men who were interior designers. It came with the territory, and the setup worked for me just fine.

$$$

"MARTIN, I've already explained why I cannot do it. I do not live in Boston. I have no place to stay overnight nor do I have clothes to wear tomorrow. If you want me to work for you, then you will have to give me at least twenty-four hours' notice next time."

Seriously, the man was dense. What did he not understand about the situation? More likely he just didn't care.

"Why can't you stay the night with your friend?" Martin suggested.

"Zoe is away, and even if she was here, there's still the matter of clothes." I wanted to smack him.

Eduardo, who had the habit of listening in on all conversations in the office if he was at all able, spoke up. "You can stay with me if you need a place to go tonight." Too bad he said it rather loudly.

"I heard that," Martin informed me. "So it's settled, then?"

I stayed quiet and glared at Eduardo. He would get payback in a minute.

"Brooke?"

"Yes, Martin?"

"So I'll see you at six. I'll text the address when we hang up."

"Wait. I don't have my black-and-whites with me."

"What are you wearing right now?"

If Martin were in my line of sight, he would be writhing in pain from my death stare. "I have on a chartreuse-and-emerald-green blouse with a black skirt and over-the-knee boots. Totally inappropriate for serving. I can't do it as I've said."

"So you go buy a white blouse on your lunch hour and wear the boots. It's some sort of corporate celebration and most of the guests will be men. I'm sure they'll appreciate the boots over your beautiful long legs."

Ewwww. What a grotty little arsehole. "I'm going to pretend you didn't just make a sexually suggestive comment about my performance on a job and move along to payment, shall we, Martin?" Serving in heeled boots wasn't going to be easy, plus I'd be out the cost of a new shirt as well. If Martin didn't like it, then he could fuck on off.

Eduardo giggled and gave me two thumbs up.

"Double time, Brooke, just be there."

As much as I wanted to decline, the extra money would be helpful right now. "Fine, I'll do it, but Martin, if you want me in future—give me some notice so I can make arrangements for the night." If there would even be a next time. Maybe a job search was a good idea.

After I ended the call, I pointed a finger at Eduardo and gave him only a slightly less violent version of my death stare. "You are in trouble in case you didn't realize. You are to go tell the bosses we are leaving to shop for a blouse for me and will return with their lunch. And you get to pay for mine today." I then smiled sweetly before getting up from the desk to put on my coat.

"Yes, my *condesa*," Eduardo sang before bolting up to the second floor to get Jon and Carlisle's lunch order.

While he was busy upstairs, I needed to let Nan know I wouldn't be over to see her tonight. She would get a kick out of me having a sleepover at Eduardo's place, though. I tried to see her every evening for a short visit and didn't want her wondering where I was when I didn't show. My call went through to the front desk, which wasn't a surprise.

Nan rarely stayed in her room, especially when there were activities going on.

"Blackstone Therapy Center, Lilah speaking. How may I assist you?"

"Hi Lilah, this is Brooke calling."

"Your grandma is in a painting class right now, working on a seascape."

"Ah, sounds lovely and I can't wait to see it. Can you please let her know I'm working for Martin tonight? She will understand, and tell her I'll visit tomorrow as usual."

"Sure thing, Brooke, and thanks for letting us know so she doesn't worry, because she would you know."

Placing Nan in a temporary nursing facility while she recovered from a knee replacement had been our only option. She couldn't be left alone in the cottage all day trapped in a wheelchair while I was working in Boston. She never complained, but I knew she would rather be at home, as anyone would.

I wished she could have in-home nursing care and that I could provide it for her, but it just wasn't possible on her very fixed income, or mine. Once the Blackwater estate closed and she was forced to retire, her money had to be carefully managed to make ends meet. She wasn't old at only sixty-one, and I suspected she missed her job very much, as well as the camaraderie with her workmates. In fact, the fall that resulted in the need for her knee replacement had happened after she'd lost her job, while she was bored stiff all alone in her cottage. Thank God her friend Sylvie was due for tea later on that day and discovered Nan at the bottom of her cellar steps—frightened and in terrible pain.

I often wondered if the Blackstone family who'd employed my nan bore any kind of conscience at all to dismiss a loyal servant after more than three decades with hardly a thank-you and good-bye. No pension or departure compensation—nothing at all. *Deplorable* came to mind.

Selfish arseholes did as well. There was no defense for their behavior. None at all.

Blackstone Island was primarily a place where a few very rich people, with oceanfront vacation homes worth millions of dollars, came to play at summer holidays. Unfortunately, it was also a place where a great many poor people worked very hard to serve those same rich people and had little to nothing to show for it.

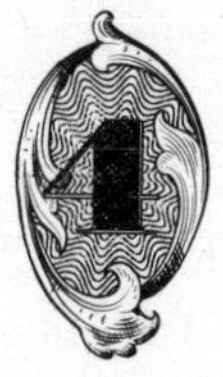

Caleb

The last thing I wanted to do at the end of my day of shit was go to a client appreciation reception for cocktails and hors d'oeuvres with my face looking like it did from being smacked by Janice's Valentino. All day long I'd fielded the concerned inquiries from people who weren't assholes along with the jokes and harassment from the people who were most definitely assholes. I don't think many of them bought my lie about slipping in the shower and colliding with the marble soap dish. What they didn't know was I couldn't care less what they thought of me in my personal life. As long as they respected me in business, I was good. I could make money grow from just about anything. So what if I had terrible emotional skills when it came to relationships with women. I just didn't feel anything for those women like I probably should if I cared about them for more than sex. But I'd never felt anything beyond an admiration for their beauty, along with the desire for some shared pleasure if they were interested in the same.

I wasn't stingy, either. Before we were done, I made sure they were well satisfied. I didn't know how to operate any differently, and until I figured my shit out, I should just stay away from women altogether. It made the most sense.

The fact it was my father's law firm hosting this gathering was the only reason I'd set foot inside the door. There was a part of me that still wanted to make him proud, even though I'd made my own successful career apart from his. Now that he was gone, I'd taken on his business as well, and I knew his peers were watching closely to see how I would do. My brothers had their own interests and money, as well as a share in Dad's holdings, but they weren't involved in the day-to-day management like I was. Lucas lived like a hermit on the island, designing game systems, and Wyatt divided his time between LA and New York doing his thing, which nobody seemed to know much about. Being the oldest child, followed by identical twin brothers, and then five years later by another set of twins, but this time girls and fraternal, I was the odd man out. Willow was engaged to her Ivy League professor, and Winter was in grad school, so everyone was focused on their own goals as they should be.

My mother was very proud of the fact she'd given my father five children and only suffered through three pregnancies. And Mom made sure we all knew it was *suffering* of the worst kind to give birth to every one of us. Maybe that was why she resented me. All that effort only produced one baby—me.

My relationship with my mother was just the start of my women troubles. I'd had a not-so-pleasant conversation with her on the phone earlier today. Janice had gotten to Mom quickly, crying out a sad tale of disrespect and broken promises on my part. I didn't tell her that within five minutes of leaving me, she was deep-throating James Blakney. Thinking my mother didn't need that visual, I didn't say much in response except that Janice wasn't the girl we all thought she was, and she definitely wasn't going to be anything more than a friend of the family to me from here on out. Mom then took the opportunity to tell me I'd made things very difficult for her friendship with Janice's mother. I offered her the advice that a generous donation to their non-profit would probably smooth things over. I suppose she didn't care for my suggestion because she ended our call quickly after.

I would give this thing two drinks max before I was outie.

Nodding and saying the right things, I shook hands with the colleagues who'd known my father and accepted condolences from others. I made a mental note of the people who'd made the effort to mention his name to me, and I would write their names down with the event and date as soon as I got home.

I'd worked my way through the room, as I had been taught by my dad—by the best to ever work a roomful of potential deals—when I decided I'd accomplished what I'd set out to do tonight. It was time for me to go. After setting my glass down on an empty table, I started for the door . . . until I saw *her*.

Just like that. She appeared in my line of sight and I couldn't take my eyes off her.

The beautiful girl from this morning at the Starbucks on Hereford Street.

I knew it was her because how could anyone forget those sexy boots? Her blonde hair wasn't down like it had been this morning, though. She'd pulled it back into a sleek ponytail . . . but she was serving at this event? I'd seen her go into that design studio next to Starbucks. She probably had two jobs. Industrious . . . beautiful . . . sexy.

I quickly returned for my half-empty glass and snatched it up from the table. I suddenly felt like an appetizer or two.

She saw me approaching and moved closer with her tray. "What are these called?" I asked without sparing her tray a second glance. Bad move on my part, but I was too busy taking in her golden eyes and hair, and everything else I could now see up close. Perfect skin, dark lashes that framed spectacular eyes, and a scar along the hairline of the right side of her face. Something had hurt her at some point in the past, and I found it utterly insane that I was disturbed by it.

She rolled her pink lips together as if she was trying to suppress laughter. "Well, they've told me it's something called a . . . *meatball.* Very unusual gourmet creation. You should try one. They're said to be quite delicious."

That voice of hers was . . . fucking beautiful.

"Okay." I picked up a meatball and popped it in my mouth. Didn't taste a thing. I could have been chewing slaughterhouse by-products and I wouldn't have known. My brain had shut off everything except her beautiful voice.

"You are either messing with me or that blow to your head must have been devastating. I would wager you've had a meatball before."

"I am."

She lost her smile. "You are messing with me?"

"No, I am devastating—I mean devastated—by the blow to my head." What in the mother fuck was I even saying to this girl? I sounded like Rain Man minus the IQ. I needed to stop talking.

"I'm sorry to hear that. It looks painful."

"It doesn't hurt me now." I thought I smiled and shook my head but couldn't be sure. Just call me the village idiot because I knew I was acting like one. I did love the sound of her voice, though.

"Another rare and precious meatball?" She offered her tray and studied me this time. She had to be disgusted by my appearance and turned off by my behavior, but she didn't show it if she was.

"Yes, please." I took another meatball but I didn't eat it. "You are British."

"You are American," she said with a fast wink, before turning away to serve other guests.

I watched her walk away from me and felt the pounding of my heart vibrating throughout my entire body.

Something had just happened to me.

I wasn't completely sure what exactly, but I was crystal clear on the reason.

Her.

$$$

I did not leave as I had planned to do.

I stayed in that ridiculous meet and greet so I could stalk a girl I did not know.

I, Caleb Blackstone, became a stalker in that moment and was not apologetic about it in the least, either.

Oh, for the next hour or so I put on a good show and kept schmoozing with people I hardly paid attention to, so I could watch her walk around the room, serving meatballs in her tight skirt and fuck-me boots. I even managed to paint an image of her wearing nothing *but* those boots in my head. My thoughts were downright filthy, to the point my cock wanted in on the action.

Badly.

This wasn't happening to me in a roomful of business associates. My dick was not getting hard from watching a pretty girl offer up food.

Yes, it was.

I also figured out I wasn't the only one looking at her, and those boots weren't exactly helping her fade into the background at an event like this one, made up of mostly men thinking about sex once every fifty-two seconds. Seeing her, it was impossible to think about much of anything else.

"I'd take my time tapping that tight ass nice and slow—with the fucking boots on."

Kevin Aldrich was a dipshit investment banker with a receding hairline, an expanding waistline, and a big trust fund inherited from his old-money grandfather. He also had a wife, two or three teenage kids, and a drinking problem. The sad truth was he probably did get beautiful women like her to fuck him because he had the money to help them get over the fact he was a complete and total douchebag.

I said nothing, but I felt my blood start to boil. In that instant I truly understood the meaning behind the expression "it made my blood boil." Mine was going nuclear.

Aldrich lifted his drink and all but drooled in her direction to call her over. She noticed him and came forward with her tray of what I knew were individual shrimp cocktails. I'd not make the same mistake again.

"Shrimp cocktail strike your fancy, gentlemen?" she asked pleasantly.

"You strike my fancy, Sexy Boots," Aldrich said with an obvious leer. Okay, the guy was worse than a disgusting douche. He was a moron with the social skills of a cockroach.

"Clever. I've only heard that fourteen other times in the last hour and a half," she said smoothly. "Can I offer you a shrimp cocktail?" she repeated, clearly not amused and her golden eyes showing it.

Aldrich was either too drunk or too stupid to catch the clues, however. "How about your number instead? I'll take you somewhere where we can eat all the shrimp we want." He flicked his tongue at her, and I just about lost my shit. Forget my boiling blood, I wanted to kill him.

"No fucking way, Aldrich, you did *not* just do that!"

He did two more really stupid things nearly simultaneously. He reached his arm around to drag her body against his and said to me, "Don't cock-block me and Sexy Boots here. We're just getting acquainted, and she looks like she can use a long slow ride in those b—"

Aldrich didn't finish his sentence however, because he received an immediate and skilled defense move of an elbow to the front of the nose. *Her* elbow. His nose. Too bad I tried to get in there first and push him off her. The back of his bulbous head caught me on the chin and he went down hard, taking me with him, along with tiny glasses of cocktail sauce and airborne pink shrimp that sprayed out in an arc, catching anyone within a ten-foot radius.

Silence ensued as all conversations ceased and focused their attentions on us.

"You fucking cunt! You broke my nose," Aldrich bellowed from behind the hand trying to stem the gushing blood pouring from his mean little face.

"You put your hands on me. Nobody does that and gets away with it *anymore*," she told him in a steely voice before bolting off in the direction of the kitchen.

"Get the fuck off me, Aldrich!" I shoved him away and got to my feet. "Stupid goddamn shit you just pulled, man. Very goddamn stupid," I said as I removed a lone shrimp stuck to my jacket by its tail.

"But she assaulted me. You saw it happen, Blackstone," he yelled. "I will sue that bitch for damages, the fucking whore!"

I grabbed him by the collar and dragged him right up to my face. "You will do nothing of the kind or you'll live to regret it. Go home to your wife and family if they'll even have you at this point."

"Fuck you, Blackstone." But it came out sounding more like, "fung gew, Blaxsdone," on account of his broken nose. Lost a lot of its impact that way, too. Arrogant asshole.

"And make sure you take a cab to protect the populous of the city from yourself," I added. "You're too fucking drunk to stand right now, let alone drive anywhere." Then I let go of him and watched as he fell back down to sprawl on the floor, soaked in his own blood and a shitload of shrimp cocktail.

I found her having it out with her boss in the kitchen.

"Why in the hell did you hit him?"

"Sexual assault is against the law, you idiot. Why in the hell did you put me in this situation tonight, Martin, and then abandon me to that pack of dogs out there? Hmm? Do you have any idea what I've had to put up with tonight?"

Ouch. I dearly hoped she didn't lump me in the same category as the rest of the dogs in the room tonight.

She reached into the front pocket of the red apron wrapped around her hips and pulled out a handful of business cards and tossed them at her boss. "That's how many of the dogs want to get to *know* me better and show me a banging good time, emphasis on the *bang*! I shouldn't have to deal with that sort of thing when I am trying to do a job." *Jesus Christ, she's right.*

"Oh, for fuck's sake, Brooke, it wasn't that bad out there. You totally overreacted."

She really didn't. "He put his hands all over my arse and flicked his tongue at me, and you think I overreacted?"

Her boss had the brains to keep quiet about her last comment at least, I'd give him that. "Go back out there and get names and numbers, apologize, and clean up the mess. We'll have to cover the dry cleaning at least. Do that and you can keep your job." *I don't think you know your employee very well. She's done with you, asshole.*

She gaped at him in shock for a moment, then put her hands down and began untying her apron. It took a few seconds for her to get the crisscrossed ties free, but the passage of time only seemed to increase the anger coming off her in waves. Her idiot boss just stood there watching her, waiting for her to drop the apron.

Which she did. Right at his feet to lie with the scattered business cards the dogs had given to her. *Good girl.*

"No, thank you, Martin. I quit this hideous job, and don't you *ever* try to contact me again." *Smart girl.*

"Brooke," he yelled after her, "who is going to pay for all of this?" *I think that would be you, Martin.*

But Brooke had already grabbed her things and was at the door when she turned back one last time, her long blonde ponytail whipping around her neck from the force. She was so very angry, but her composure was a thing of magnificence—and her words spoken in that accent of hers, awe-inspiring. I couldn't take my eyes away for anything.

"Take it out of my final pay. And then you can fuck off." *My dick is so hard for this girl right now.*

Then Brooke was really gone.

"I'll cover any damages, but I sincerely doubt there will be any. The guy who grabbed her was way out of line and I witnessed the whole thing. I'll cover the dry-cleaning bills, too." I handed the fool my card and left him standing there in the kitchen with his mouth hanging open like a goldfish gasping its last breaths.

I caught up to her out on the street where she was in line for a cab. She looked me over as I walked up but she didn't say a word.

"Hey, those were some impressive self-defense moves you've got," I said.

"Sorry you were in the line of fire in there." She indicated her head toward my suit, which was pretty much trashed with shrimp cocktail sauce.

I shrugged. "It'll clean. How about you? Are you all right after that disaster *in there*?"

"I'll be fine as soon as I can get home." Her voice didn't sound as strong as before, and I sensed the adrenaline was wearing off. She was upset and rightly so.

"Can I give you a lift? My car can be here in five minutes and I'd be happy to take you wherever you need to go."

She shook her head. "That's not possible unless your car can float on water." She checked her watch. "Besides, I don't know you and I would never get into a car with a man I don't know."

"Fair enough," I said. Although I was disappointed she wouldn't take me up on my offer, I had to agree with her superior logic. A girl who looked like her definitely shouldn't go with any man she didn't know. It would be dangerous. For some reason I hated the idea of her in any kind of danger. "I'm really sorry you had to endure that crowd tonight. I hope I didn't do anything to offend you—"

"I saw you stand up to him, and I thank you for that. And no, you didn't offend me with your ignorance of meatballs. I'm happy to have helped sort out that little problem for you. Now you are an informed connoisseur of the rare delicacy called a meatball, and you owe it all to me," she replied with a hint of a smile.

She was so awesome, trying to joke around with me when it was apparent she was still upset about the clusterfuck that had happened to her inside that reception tonight. She looked beautiful, but very . . . sad. If I had to choose a word to describe how she appeared to me, it would have to be *sad*. And that bothered me greatly.

"Thank you for the meatball tutorial. I enjoyed it very much. I'm Caleb by the way. Caleb Black—"

I was interrupted by her phone chiming out the unusual but unmistakable ring tone of Ricky Martin's "Shake Your Bon-Bon." Interesting choice I thought, as she turned away to take the call.

"Fucking hell, I'm so glad you called me back." *The word* fuck *in that accent—damn . . .*

"I can still catch the eight-thirty ferry if I hurry so I'm going home after all. I won't be staying over." Ah. *That's not possible unless your car can float on water.* Got it.

"Long, dreadful story. Suffice to say I'm looking for a new second job." *She needed a second job?*

"I'll see you tomorrow." *The offices on Hereford Street.*

"I love you, too." *Boyfriend or just friend?*

My stalking skills were improving by the second if I was now capable of listening in on entire conversations and deciphering them. I'd caught every word she'd spoken. A cab pulled forward for her, and she said clearly, "Blackstone Island Ferry Company," to the driver as she got in.

I watched her cab pull into traffic and drive away until it was out of sight.

She never looked back to say good-bye.

She hadn't told me her name, either, but I knew it was Brooke. Brooke who lived on Blackstone Island and worked in the design studio on Hereford Street next door to Starbucks. She was beautiful and witty and feisty. I was more than impressed by her no-nonsense attitude throughout the night with her boss and the patrons. Brooke was no shrinking violet, plus she had the most amazing voice I'd ever heard.

That was all the information I had been able to gather about her, but it was enough to find her again if I wanted to. There was no *if*. *When*.

And it was more than plenty.

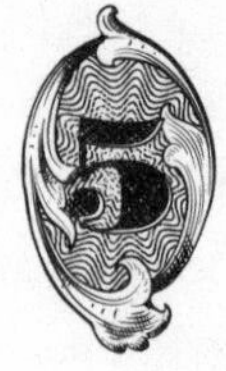

Brooke

"Thank you, Will. I was racing to make it in time," I said to the captain as I boarded the final ferry crossing to the island for the night.

"Two minutes to spare." Will Darlington, who ran Blackstone Island Ferry Company, never failed to mention how much time I had left before departure. It was our little running joke. I think he would've let me on late if he saw me running for the dock, but so far I'd never missed my boat.

"Ages of time, Will. Two minutes to spare and with running in heels, I feel I've been a complete success."

That earned me a shy smile and a slow shake of his head. "Glad to have you on board, Brooke." Will was not much of a talker, but he was kind and very serious about captaining his boat. Another one of those hardworking islanders who put in long hours to make a living in a challenging economy. If you loved your work, as I supposed Will did, then all the better.

Once I found a seat inside where it was warm, I let my guard down for the first time in the past three hours. I became suddenly very sleepy, not wanting to think about the arsehole who'd grabbed me, or the fact I'd just left a shit job, or the lack of money, or any of my problems.

So I folded my arms on the table and rested my cheek on the arm of my wool coat.

I closed my eyes and allowed the sway of the boat to rock me to sleep.

A gentle hand to my shoulder and my name being called woke me one *very* fast hour later.

"Everything okay, Brooke?" Will's green eyes looked down at me in concern. "We're here and I have to close her down for the night. Everyone is off the boat."

"Oh! I crashed. I'm so sorry," I began. "I'll get going." I rushed to get up and gathered my bag.

"No worries at all," he assured me in that kindly shy way he'd perfected. "You take care driving home."

"Goodnight, Will."

"Night, Brooke."

I sensed that if I'd given any encouragement to Will Darlington beyond friendship, I could've had him. He didn't come on to me and he was always a gentleman in every way, but a girl knows the signs when someone is interested. Will was nice, really good-looking, hardworking, and an excellent catch for any girl, but he wasn't for me. More accurately, I wasn't for any man right now. Too soon. Too much. Too hard to imagine being with somebody again when I was still working on finding the person I'd been before. The person I'd been before I'd allowed *him* the power to nearly destroy me.

He'd very nearly accomplished just that, and I couldn't—*wouldn't*—make that same mistake again.

I made my way to the parking lot and started up Nan's 1980 Jeep Cherokee, lovingly named Woody due to the faux wood paneling trim on the outside and within. I was always grateful for Woody's reliability, because even though he wouldn't deliver the smoothest ride over four miles of bumpy lanes in the dark, he would get me there safely. You had to know where you were going, or you'd be lost in the middle of a meadow or a wood with only one wrong turn. I always took it easy because little creatures had a tendency to leap out in the night and it wrecked me for days if I accidently hit a rabbit or a night bird.

Nan's cottage stood solid and cozy on her perch at the top of a gentle hill overlooking the sea. It was dark now, but the Fairchild Light illuminated the cape below. The island had a lighthouse for each port—Fairchild Light at the southern end, and West Light on the western shore where most of the mansions and estates were built between the shelter of the island and the mainland, protected from the harshness of the open ocean.

As I parked and went inside, I got that little flip of panic down low in my belly. It was worry about how much longer Nan could remain here in the cottage. I didn't know that answer. I did know she owned it outright and that it was the only thing of value my grandmother possessed from her marriage to my grandfather. He'd died when my mum was a baby, so even my mum had never known her father. Nan never remarried after my grandfather died, but instead gave her life to her work at Blackwater estate. Unencumbered with a mortgage and given the land value on a resort island with an unobstructed view, it had to be worth a significant amount. But it was a very small property, and it wasn't in the exclusive area where the luxury hotels and private estates were located. I couldn't imagine selling and moving Nan somewhere else. Where would we go? But the money situation wasn't going to get better and I needed to at least make inquires. I'd make a point to visit Herman and ask for his advice. If anyone would know, it was him. Maybe Nan could take out an equity loan on the cottage and that would get us through.

Who was I kidding? Get us through our financial troubles until we won the Massachusetts State Lottery? Yeah, right.

Frustrated, I set off to the kitchen to make a cup of tea. The hour was far too late for caffeine now, and I needed sleep after the shit day I'd had. I peeled off the boots first. It bothered me that my beloved boots were what prompted my problems this evening. They'd certainly brought me unwanted attention while I was serving. Hadn't Eduardo greeted me with "those boots are screaming 'do me 'til I can't take it anymore'" just this morning? This morning seemed like it had been ages ago now. If I'd been working tonight in my regular uniform clothing, would that heinous man still have grabbed me and said those horrible things to me? I shuddered at the remembrance. The harsh movement and possessive touch of his mean little hands on my body had just brought it all back so quickly. My only thought was to get him off me, because I couldn't bear being touched roughly anymore.

It was too close to the way *he* had touched me. And I would never forget how that felt. I wanted to forget . . . I just didn't know if it was possible for me to forget.

There was a spot of cocktail sauce on the collar of my one-day-old white shirt. Crap. I treated it with a bleach pen and set it to soak in the bathroom sink but figured it was probably ruined since it was white. Something in the sauce made it next to impossible to get out of clothing. I'd ruined clothes before from shrimp cocktail sauce. My stomach took another dive as I realized there were several expensive suits splattered tonight, and my pay from the job wouldn't come even close to covering the cleaning of designer suits. Hopefully the dry cleaners had a magic solution to remove the stains. It was Martin's problem anyway. He could find the arsehole who'd caused the whole mess and have him pay.

You broke a man's nose tonight. Yes, I did. And I would do it again in the same situation—in a heartbeat.

I looked down at my legs.

The scars on my right calf and knee were the reason for the boots or tights when I wore skirts. The scars were ugly, yes, but mostly I just didn't want to have to see them and . . . remember.

$$$

"YOU have an admirer, *condesa*, look what's been delivered for *Brooke*." Eduardo strolled up to my work area with a gorgeous pot of dark red peonies and set them down on my desk. The flowers were a stunning cranberry red with most of the stems still in the round-bud stage. They would become huge blooms when they opened. Striking and unusual, and totally unexpected.

"Who from?" I couldn't imagine who would send me flowers. Martin? No, he was too cheap for flowers. These looked expensive, plus it was a plant and not a vase of cut flowers. I could plant it in the ground in Nan's garden eventually and enjoy them for a long time.

"Read the card, *ay Dios mío*, what are you waiting for?" He plucked it from the bouquet and shoved it at me. "I will die before you tell me who sent this to you."

"You really should have been an actor, Eduardo," I told him as I opened the envelope and read the card.

Brooke,
Please accept these flowers as a token of my appreciation
for the meatball lesson last night.
It was unforgettable.
Caleb

The guy with the black eye. Unforgettable? He'd made the effort to be nice even after he'd been knocked down by the arsehole who'd put his hands on me. Why? Why send me expensive flowers, and furthermore, how did he even know *where* to send them? He knew my name. I wondered if he'd asked Martin, but that would be a really low blow for Martin to disclose my information to a stranger. Also illegal.

I handed the card to Eduardo so he could read it.

Remembering our conversation from last night, I recalled how he'd offered me a ride, which I hadn't accepted, but he hadn't turned nasty when I'd declined his invitation. I appreciated that part of his personality most of all. A man who understood the word *no* wasn't that easy to find in my limited experience. They seemed to be few and far between. I was tempted for a moment, to call the number written in bold black pen on the back of the card that I could now see clearly visible from Eduardo's hand. But what would I say?

Caleb. I couldn't help smiling when I remembered how cute he'd been with me over a tray of meatballs. Surely the most ridiculous conversation ever, yet he'd gone to the trouble to send me flowers that even looked like a meatball while in the bud stage. I studied the flowers again. The color was spot on. So pretty. Wow.

What a very clever man this Caleb was.

Incredibly handsome, too. Even wearing the results of that devastating blow to his head.

I endured the teasing of the peonies sitting prettily upon my desk for the next two hours before I said to hell with it and gave up the struggle. My excuse? I'm a woman and my curiosity won out. I sent him a text.

> Caleb, thank you for the beautiful flowers in meatball red. Very lovely gesture . . . but . . . how did you know where to find me? –Brooke

My phone rang about one minute later, and I couldn't help but smile for a second time.

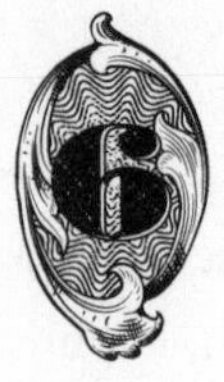

Caleb

"Yes," I said when her text came through, maybe a little too enthusiastically, but what the fuck did I care? I owned the company, and Brooke had just given me her number.

Victoria stopped her rundown of my schedule and looked up from her notes curiously.

"I need to make a call—we'll finish after lunch," I told her, knowing she understood what I really meant. Which was, "get out and give me privacy." Victoria Blakney was no dummy, and that was why she was my PA. She was also my best friend's little sister and the perfect candidate for the job as my personal assistant. I'd known her since she was a toddler, and she knew the world in which I moved as well as or better than I did. Since it was the same world for her.

"The red peonies?" she asked as she got up from her chair.

"Maybe." I added *Brooke* into my contacts and ignored Victoria.

"Thought so." I could hear the smirk in her voice as she went out, closing my door with a soft click.

I hovered my finger over Brooke's number for just an instant, realizing I was making a conscious decision to pursue her. So much for my vow to swear off women for a while. There was something about her I couldn't turn away from. I had to know more.

My finger tapped the green circle.

It rang five times before she picked up, and with each ring I think my grip on the phone grew a little tighter.

"Hello, is this Caleb calling?" Ahhhh . . . that voice of hers had power . . . over me. She spoke and for some reason I *lost* the ability to speak. It was insane.

"Yes, Brooke, it is."

"You have excellent taste in flowers. I've been enjoying them all morning, but why did you send them?"

"I thought you needed some cheering up after what happened last night."

"Ah, that's very kind of you, but how did you know I worked here?"

"I'd say it was fate, Brooke."

"And how's that?" I couldn't tell if she was getting ready to tell me to get lost or not, so I figured I had nothing to lose by telling her the honest-to-God truth.

"I saw you yesterday morning getting coffee at Starbucks, and then you walked into the offices next door. When you showed up at the cocktail party serving, your boots reminded me that I'd seen you just that morning. I had to take a call and stepped under the eaves of your offices to be out of the way of sidewalk traffic, and I could see you through the front glass."

"That was you?" A shot of something hit me painfully right between the chest, and I had to bring a hand up to rub it.

"Uh-huh, it was me. Why do I get the feeling you saw me as well, Brooke?"

"You were wearing sunglasses on account of the blow to your head?" Yep, she saw me.

"Yes. I was devastated by it, remember?"

She laughed and I wished I could see her. "Oh yes, I remember very well just how *devastated* you were, Caleb. You had absolutely no recollection of what a meatball was."

"Right. I think my memory was slightly damaged from the devastating blow to my head, but thankfully you were there to clear up my confusion. I was lucky."

"How is your injury today?" The fact that she asked was nice.

"Looks worse, but it doesn't hurt a bit."

"Well, I am happy to hear that, but Caleb, how did you know my name was Brooke?"

"I heard your boss call after you when you left the room."

"You're quite the Sherlock Holmes, aren't you?"

"Not really, but my hearing is pretty good. For example, I heard you tell your cab driver to take you to the Blackstone Island Ferry Company, so using my superior powers of deduction, plus the fact you said you were going home, I am guessing you live on the island."

"Are you stalking me, Caleb?"

Yes. "Not at all, Brooke, just being observant and taking note of some things we have in common."

"Such as?"

"Blackstone Island, of course. My family has a home there near the West Light, and my brother lives there, too, but he has his own place a few miles down the western shore. It's a great house with a private beach—perfect for a weekend away from the city." Okay, that was a lie. I'd never been to Lucas's place on the island because I hadn't set foot on the island in nearly a decade. I only knew of it because he'd sent me the realtor link when he bought the property two years ago.

"Your brother's home sounds lovely, but I can assure you we don't have much in common as far as the island goes."

Was that sarcasm in her voice?

"What do you mean?" I sensed displeasure, and doubt had started to creep in to kill the happy buzz I'd had when we first started this conversation.

"Not everyone who lives on the island has a mansion with a private beach, Caleb. In fact, most of the permanent residents struggle to find work that will keep them housed and fed year-round. The tourist trade is seasonal, and it's a very different reality for the rest of us who don't live on the western shores."

"Oh . . . where do you live?" I asked hesitantly.

"In my grandmother's cottage on the hill above Fairchild Light, where there are no private beaches and no estates. And no job for a woman who gave thirty-five years of her life working for one of those fine west-side mansions before they closed it down and dismissed everyone."

"That's a terrible thing to do. Was that your grandmother who worked for them?"

"Yes, she was in charge of the housekeeping and general management of the house."

"I'm so sorry to hear she lost her job."

"Why? It's not your fault, Caleb. You can't help it if your family is west-side and mine is south-end."

Awkward silence stretched out between us and I wasn't sure how to respond. Brooke took care of it and saved me from having to think of something to say.

"Listen, that was rude of me and I apologize for the rant. I forgot myself for a moment, sorry. I do want to thank you for the beautiful flowers. They really are so lovely, and I don't think I'll ever look at a meatball in quite the same way again."

"You're very welcome for the flowers, and please feel free to think of me whenever you see a meatball. I am so honored."

She laughed but it wasn't the same as the first time. The magic had gone and been replaced by something vaguely unpleasant.

"Good-bye, Caleb."

"Take care, Brooke."

I sat on my ass and pondered where that conversation had taken a wrong turn. Because it most certainly had. Was I attracted to her only because she was beautiful and spoke with a sexy accent that turned me on? Had I indulged in preconceived ideas about her because she appeared so confident and intelligent? Had I evaluated her status and assumed she came from money because of where she lived and because she worked in a professional office? *And had I believed that would be the only necessary criteria to continue my pursuit?*

I didn't think I'd done any of those things, but maybe subconsciously I had. I couldn't recall what I'd thought when I discovered she lived on the island, but it never occurred to me she might be—what—poor? I didn't think about it at all because such an idea wasn't in the scope of my realm. I dealt in money, and making sure that money grew into even more money. *Poor* wasn't part of my vernacular, and it never had been. *Never would be.*

I was guilty of letting my dick lead me again. A pretty girl had caught my attention because she spoke in an oh-so-sexy English accent. I must be losing my goddamn mind. *Wake up, fuckhead, and pull yourself together.*

I texted James to see if he wanted to meet for lunch. I still needed to get the recap on Janice and maybe hanging with my bestie would straighten my stupid ass out.

$$$

October

"YOUR suit came back from the cleaners with a note. He can't get the stains out, and since the fabric is gray, they still show. Something in the cocktail sauce makes the stain set permanently he said." Victoria held my Brioni Colosseo on a hanger underneath a dry-cleaning bag. "What do you want me to do with it?"

"Donate it to charity I guess. Someone must be able to make use of a five-thousand-dollar suit stained with cocktail sauce." I wondered how long it would be before Brooke's dipshit catering manager came calling for the cleaning bill for the rest of them. "Anything else?"

"A guy named Martin called and said he needs to talk to you about damages you agreed to pay for an event he catered."

Bingo. I could predict this shit like clockwork. "Let me guess—several light-colored suits need to be replaced because the stains are permanent."

"He mentioned seven or eight suits, yes. It was hard to follow his explanation to be honest. Something about the enzyme in the horseradish, blah, blah, blah," Victoria said with a shrug.

"I don't want to talk to that asshole. Just tell him to collect the claims with the receipts and send them over, and I'll see they are paid."

"I'll tell him." She walked out of my office with the dry-cleaning plastic covering my favorite-but-now-ruined suit fluttering behind her.

If all those suits combined came in at a dime under fifty grand, I'd be surprised. Yeah, well, a promise was a promise, and my word was good. I'd said I'd cover damages, and eight ruined designer suits certainly constituted as damages. Fucking waste of good money. It wasn't the damages being out of my pocket that bothered me really, it was the cause of the whole thing—an arrogant prick taking advantage of a nice girl just because she was pretty and he'd decided he wanted to fuck her.

That was how it went down. I was there. I saw everything happen almost as if it were in slow motion. If Brooke had just taken Aldrich's abuse, as he assumed she would, then no flying shrimp, no ruined suits, no damages—just another example of SOP in the after-hours corporate world. The number of hits she'd received that night alone were proved in the business cards she'd tossed at the feet of her shithead boss. That must be a horrible thing to have to put up with while you're trying to do your job. She shouldn't be in that situation at all. I wished I'd never gone to that fucking reception in the first place.

And I wouldn't know her name was Brooke, or that she lived on the island with her grandmother, or that she needed a second job because she didn't make enough money at Harris & Goode as an interior designer to pay the bills. Oh, I'd had plenty of time to think about Brooke over the last few weeks. The things she'd said to me on the phone. How much she resented the people who had fired her grandmother. The regret in her apology when she realized she'd said too much to the wrong person. And maybe even the same disappointment I'd felt when we both realized our little attraction—or whatever the fuck it was—wouldn't be going anywhere because we came from different sides of the tracks.

I'd gone to the Starbucks twice, hoping I might bump into her accidently.

No sign of her.

I'd come close to calling just so I could hear her voice again, but what would I say? "Your voice is so sexy I get hard like a teenage boy when you speak. Wanna go out with me?" She already suspected me for a stalker, and it would barely put me above Aldrich if you really got down to the brass tacks of what I wanted from her. And what in the mother fuck was that exactly?

I don't think I'd yet figured out what I wanted from Brooke. Sex? To be her boyfriend? Something even more than that? I'd only cared about the sex in the past. Oh, I'd love to take my time with her in bed, and I'm sure it would be spectacular, but for the first time since I could remember, sex was not my main motivation. Why the fuck was that? What made Brooke unique in that way? Why was Brooke so tantalizing to me I couldn't get her out of my head?

I remembered something else, too, and I suspected it was a biggie. What she'd said to Aldrich right after she broke his nose. "You put your hands on me. Nobody does that and gets away with it *anymore*."

It made me crazy that Brooke had been hurt badly by some guy in the past. *Who the fuck would touch her with anything other than respect? Adoration?* The fuckwit certainly hadn't deserved her. *Did I?* Was it important to me that *I* deserve her? I'd never had to entertain that thought before and it confused me. I didn't really have a handle on what I was doing in regards to Brooke . . . at all.

Taking time I really didn't have, I considered my options.

And then I called my brother Lucas.

"Caleb, long time, no talk. To what do I owe—"

"Lucas, who is the girl named Brooke with an English accent living on the island with her grandmother?"

"Umm . . . bro, don't you remember Ellen Casterley, the housekeeper at Blackwater? She worked there for our whole life."

"Ellen Casterley, our sweet British housekeeper, is her grandmother?" I felt the hair on the back of my neck stand straight up.

"Yeees. Brooke came to live with Mrs. Casterley after her parents were killed in London. Brooke was like fifteen at the time, and it was kind of big news on the island. I remember everybody talking about it—why don't you know this?"

"That's a fucking good question, little brother. When did this happen?"

"Oh, probably eight or so years ago. Sylvie, my housekeeper, would be the one to ask if you want better details. Sylvie and Mrs. Casterley are good friends, and she knows Brooke very well."

I did the math. That would make Brooke twenty-three now. Eight years ago I was twenty-three, and I don't remember visiting the island for holidays. I hadn't been around when Brooke came to live with her grandmother. "Okay, but why would Brooke say Blackwater was closed and all of the staff dismissed? That's not true."

A long pause preceded the heavy sigh from my brother on the other end of my phone, and I knew something was terribly wrong. "Caleb, do you ever speak to Mom? She closed it down nearly two years ago when Dad got sick. The place is boarded up and for sale. When a buyer comes along, it's gone."

"No. No way would Dad ever allow Blackwater to be sold off from the family holdings. He loved it there."

"When was the last time you were at Blackwater?" My brother's question felt like a metal spike in my heart. He was right. Our father had loved it there. And we'd enjoyed our summer holidays there when we were kids. But then we grew up and lost interest. Or maybe it was just me who lost interest and never went back.

Too fucking long ago.

"How do you feel about putting your clueless brother up for the weekend in your fancy beach house?"

"Plenty of empty rooms for you to choose from, Clueless Brother. You taking your chopper or do you need me to send mine over there to get you?"

"Funny. I always take my own chopper, asshole."

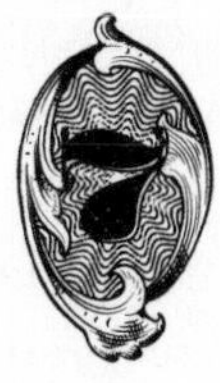

Caleb

"Victoria, can you bring me the files for the Blackwater estate? I want everything: property tax records, payroll, employee pension payouts, back through ten years."

"You want me to request copies through your mother's office?"

"My mother's office? No, I want the original files on everything." Mom retained a separate business office for her own personal interests and private accounts apart from the family holdings. I'd never questioned it before because my father set it all up for her, and it was basically keeping with the status quo after he died. I'd been so overwhelmed since I'd had to step up to take over the bulk of Dad's business when he got sick, that I'd not paid attention to what seemed insignificant at the time. Funny how the passage of time can change that.

But was a historic property that had been in my family for generations insignificant? It shouldn't be. My father loved it and I couldn't imagine him wanting it sold to strangers. He would have wanted his kids to enjoy it with their young families. Families. None of us were even married yet, or had families of our own. But some day we would. My sister, Willow, was the closest in line for kids since she was already engaged. To a guy who taught history at Brown University, and I'd only met one time. *One time.* Dad sure as hell would've met him more than once if he were still alive. *Put the family first, Caleb.* I decided I needed to get a little more involved with my family.

A pang of regret hit me hard right in the chest as I realized my dad would never know a single grandchild from any of his five children. What kind of legacy was that to pass down if the family estate was sold off before he was barely cold in his grave? Christ, my mother was a piece of work. She'd never said a word to me about it.

"I'll go down and see Myrna in the file room and she can point me in the right direction hopefully. You know ten years is going to be a lot of files, Caleb."

"I realize that. Box them by year and have Spence help you get them up here to my office. He can line the boxes under the window."

"And when Myrna wants to know why we're emptying her file room?" she asked.

"Good point. Just tell Myrna we need them for an internal audit because the property is looking for a buyer. I don't want my mom to know, okay?"

Victoria nodded once and that was our code for, "Got it, boss," which was just another reason why she was an excellent PA. She was all business with no drama, but most of all, I could trust her. "Victoria," I called her back as she was almost out the door, "did you—did you know Blackwater was up for sale?"

"Yes." Her dark-blue eyes were full of compassion for me. That feeling a person gets when they understand you are the last to know what is really going on, and feel sorry for you. "My parents mentioned it to me a while back."

"What did they say?" I needed to know.

"That it was a shame for such a magnificent place as Blackwater to go to people who wouldn't have the connection to the island."

"Your parents are right." Blackwater wasn't going to go to strangers. I knew that much. It might be sold, though . . .

To me.

"I also need Spence to get the chopper ready for seven tonight, so set that up with him, please. I'm staying with Lucas this weekend and visiting Blackwater for myself."

"Lucas," she said quickly, "tell him—please tell him I said . . . hi."

That was weird. Victoria always kept her emotions in check, but seeing she'd just lost that careful composure the second I mentioned my brother's name meant something was going on. Lucas was a touchy subject for a few people. His twin, Wyatt, and our mother were at the top of that short list. I stayed out of it since it wasn't my battle.

"Will do, Victoria," I said with a smile—something I rarely gave, but sensed she needed right now. Which just goes to show I'm not always an asshole.

$$$

IN the car I had time to ponder, and more importantly, to *digest*, what I'd learned about the Blackwater estate and its management. Much of it didn't sit well with me, with the most disturbing revelation being the letting go of employees who had no retirement compensation in place. How had that been allowed to happen? I was still in disbelief over what I'd discovered in those files. My father had never been mercenary like that. He took care of his people, and loyalty was always rewarded generously. There hadn't even been any health insurance. It took some major self-control on my part to keep from confronting my mother, but I managed to hold myself back.

All I could hear was Brooke. "And no job for a woman who gave thirty-five years of her life working for one of those fine west-side mansions before they closed it down and dismissed everyone." Every ounce of her bitterness justifiable. Mrs. Casterley deserved so much more than what she'd received. It was now on me to fix it.

"Isaac, take me to Harris & Goode on Hereford Street."

"Yes, sir. Will you be wanting Starbucks as well?"

"Not this time. I need to engage the services of an interior designer."

It was just after five o'clock on a Friday so traffic was all jacked up. People were hurrying to get a head start on the weekend and to beat the rain, which couldn't decide if it wanted to piss down or not. Isaac stopped at a red light on the corner of Massachusetts and Newbury, and in the twisting mass of humanity crossing the street . . . I saw her for the third time in my life.

Brooke.

Brooke whose last name I didn't even know yet.

Beautiful Brooke walking full-on in my direction, toward what I guessed would be the Convention Center T stop. From there she would take the train to get off at Aquarium, where the ferries transferred people and cars to the different outlying stops: Cape Cod, Provincetown, and Blackstone Island being the main destinations. I had a perfectly clear view of her, too.

I didn't have to worry about being caught staring because of the window tint. Thank fuck for window tint.

So I enjoyed every second of her walk across the street right in front of me, from her approach, to her passing the car, to her retreat.

My heart pounded mercilessly as I devoured her. Completely and utterly devoured every detail I could see of the girl who had infected me with desire from the first moment I laid eyes on her, and then sealed the deal when she spoke to me in her beautiful, sultry voice.

Her hair was down again, but this time she had on a soft black hat. She stood out in the crowd because of the baby-pink military jacket she wore, with the same high black boots over tight-fitting leather pants. Brooke possessed goddamn amazing legs. Legs I wanted to have wrapped around me with my hands free to touch the rest of her. I'd kiss every inch of those legs first before I moved on to the part where we fucked good and sl—

No, not *fucked* because it wouldn't be like that with her. Would it? I didn't want it to be . . . I was so confused about what I wanted at this point; I'd talked myself out of pursuing her several times already just to shelve that plan the second I saw her walking across the street.

Jesus Christ, I was in major powerful lust with this girl. Lust? It was a different feeling for me, though. It wasn't like the lust for sex I'd known in the past. It was more of a need. A raw, unfiltered, almost frightening need—that quite honestly scared the ever-loving shit out of me. I couldn't explain why, but I felt like I just needed her. Brooke was like a breath of fresh air into my very narrowly constrained life. Refined, yet not haughty. Strong, but wielding her strength with a careful sense of purpose. Fiery, but not with anger, just wickedly intelligent sass on the tip of her tongue ready to fly. Someone who knew who she was, but not through entitlement and prestige. In other words, a complete anomaly in my world.

She had a leather bag over her shoulder and a Starbucks in her hand. Her expression was what I remembered from the cocktail party—beautiful but with that same touch of sadness. I kept on taking in my front-row show until she was swallowed up by other bodies moving in front of her once she stepped onto the sidewalk.

She was going home after the end of her work day. Home to Blackstone Island where she lived in a cottage above Fairchild Light at south-end—a place I probably hadn't been since my high school days when James and the rest of us drank beer under the lighthouse in the summer and indulged in general teenage mayhem.

I would be on the island in a few hours. Maybe I could see her this weekend. I reached for my phone and pulled her number up on

Messenger . . . and just stared at it with absolutely no idea of what to say. The light turned green and the car moved on. I closed the Messenger app and put my phone away.

She was so young. The weird thing was she didn't seem as young as her years. Losing her parents at fifteen probably had something to do with it. That would certainly make a kid grow up fast. But there was also the evidence of a life lived and the maturity of experience in how she handled herself. The scar on her face possibly? The comment about "nobody puts their hands on me *anymore*"? I'd bet those two clues meant her life experience had been painful and she'd been hurt, so maybe that was the reason she appeared older than twenty-three.

No, I wouldn't try to see her this weekend. That wouldn't work for what I had planned over the next two days. I had to be patient so I could fix the mess with Blackwater first. I had to take care of family business and do what I knew my dad would if it were him.

"Harris & Goode, sir," Isaac announced as he pulled up to the curb.

I'd had Victoria make a late appointment with the owner in the hopes that Brooke wouldn't be there, and so far everything was working in my favor. I wanted this deal done before she was informed on Monday morning. In a few minutes I'd know her full name.

"I'm here to see Mr. Harris," I told the guy at reception, not quite able to process his dark-pink leopard scarf—or was it a shawl?—as office attire. The thing was fucking huge and draped down past his knees. I was in a design studio after all, so maybe he knew something I didn't.

"Welcome. I'm Eduardo and you are Mr. Blackstone?"

"Yes."

"Right this way, Mr. Blackstone. Mr. Harris is expecting you. His office is upstairs."

Eduardo led me through to the back where I caught a peek at Brooke's office as we passed by the doorway. I knew it was hers because

I saw the red flowers I'd sent to her. I was glad she liked them enough to still have them in her office weeks later.

It dawned on me she'd just been in there a few minutes ago, and I liked to think I could still smell her perfume lingering. It was hard to tell because all kinds of scents seemed to be swirling around in this place. Starting with Eduardo's cologne. I had a suspicion he was her phone call out on the street the night of the clusterfuck cocktail party. Which was good news for me because he was one hundred percent certifiably not her boyfriend.

Yeah. Eduardo knew about a *lot* of things I didn't.

"Ah, Mr. Blackstone, it's a pleasure to meet you. Jon Harris." He shook my hand and asked if I'd like some coffee before we got started, the usual pleasantries exchanged. "How can we help you here at Harris & Goode?" he asked.

I decided to skip the bullshit and let him know exactly what I'd come for. "My 1920s penthouse just a few blocks from here needs a complete renovation. More specifically, a woman's touch as far as the designing goes—that point is essential, Mr. Harris. I hope you understand that I know exactly who I want working on my project. I need some help transforming a bachelor apartment into something a family could be comfortable in, and it definitely needs to be a woman doing the designing." I smiled pleasantly before casually glancing at my watch to check the time, just to help nudge him along a little bit.

"I see." He eyed me curiously, probably wondering what planet I'd dropped in from. "What would be the budget for your renovation?"

There we go. The universal language that everyone can speak fluently. "Oh, I think five million ought to be sufficient for my needs, but open to upward adjustment, of course."

He bowed his head slightly, as if to suppress his elation at realizing what a contract for that amount of money could do for his business, even without the future referrals he might gain through me. "I am absolutely certain we can help you, Mr. Blackstone."

"Excellent. Just the words I wanted to hear, Mr. Harris." And that was how it was done.

$$$

IT had been so long since I'd needed casual clothes, it threw off my usual routine of packing for business trips. That should tell me something. Only thirty-one years old, and I couldn't remember the last weekend I'd had away.

I really couldn't remember when or where, and it annoyed me. Because it brought back what my dad had told me on his deathbed in full-on Technicolor. I could see him saying the words to me. "When you find whatever it is that makes you happy, Caleb, hold on to it with everything you've got. Your heart will let you know."

Did I even know what my "happy things" were?

No, I did not.

I did, however, know what didn't make me happy. And that was being so fucking confused about my feelings for a girl I barely knew. My feelings? I scowled at that thought, and threw the last of my shit into my bag and zipped it closed.

Just enough time for a quick shower before heading back to the offices where the heliport sat at the very top of Blackstone Global Enterprises.

I stripped off everything and let the hot water roll over me for a minute before I went for the soap. I wasn't sure about a lot of things at the moment, but one mystery had been cleared up for me. Brooke Ellen Casterley. I was also in possession of her design bio, and had an appointment to meet with her late Monday afternoon.

So, it was happening, and I'd have to deal with it Monday when I walked into her office to let her know about her new project, and hopefully relieve her financial stresses. She didn't need to find a second job any longer. The retainer fee I'd deposited tonight, payable directly to her, would take care of any urgent debts. I'd made sure.

My plan might flop if she decided she wanted nothing to do with me, but I felt confident she would accept. And if she did accept the job, at least she would be working for me for as long as it took to renovate the penthouse. That meant I would have access to see her and talk to her . . . for a long time. What did I care if the styling cues weren't to my taste? What did I know about the interior design of a home? Nothing. Everything I'd given input on before was for business offices.

Just thinking about her even a little drew a reaction out of my aching cock. Remembering how she looked walking across the street in her pink coat and leather pants had me rock hard in seconds. Some soap applied under the steaming hot shower spray to just the right places . . .

My hand reaching down to grip the heavy weight was inevitable.

I needed to release some tension, and it felt far too fucking good once I started to even consider stopping. I wouldn't stop pumping my fist up and down the length of my cock. *Couldn't.*

The sound of my hand as it fought for friction against the tight skin of my dick sounded almost brutal. Root to tip, twisted, and then slammed back down all the way again. Over and over the motion was repeated, all while images of her bombarded me. Some real, some fantasy—mixed in together to make such an erotic concoction I nearly went down in the shower at one point when my knees buckled. Only one thing would end it. And that would be when I came furiously hard from picturing the image of Brooke beneath me, surrounding me, and in my arms as we did this together.

It took about three more seconds after I imagined how beautiful she'd look while we were fucking.

Beautiful is how Brooke would be with my cock buried deep inside her. She would be mine when that happened.

I called out her name when cum shot up hard from my balls and out through the head of my now-abused cock. It kept coming in punishing spurts to mix with the steam and the hot water, draining me in a way that felt unfamiliar because everything was different now.

Her name on my lips as I came would have happened whether I wanted it to or not. Brooke and I were inevitable.

Inevitable.

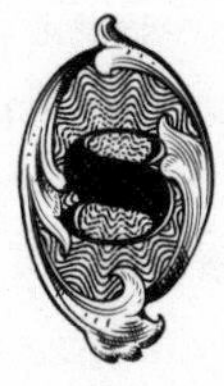

Brooke

On Fridays I had my dinner with Nan at the therapy facility. She told me what was going on with the other "inmates" as she referred to them, and I ate cafeteria food served on a tray complete with a boxed juice and a chocolate pudding for dessert. I didn't mind; it was just food. You put it in your body when you're hungry.

"Hi, Brooke," Lilah called from the nurses' station, "there will be three of you for dinner tonight. She looks so pretty. I'll bring it to the room in a few minutes."

Three of us? I wondered who was visiting Nan at dinnertime. "She always looks pretty, Lilah, and thank you for looking after her so well."

"It won't be long until she's out of here, she's improving every day."

"Oh, that's wonderful," I said. The truth was I had very mixed feelings about Nan returning to the cottage and being on her own during the day. What if she fell again? It was an old house with uneven floorboards and steps that could be a death trap if it happened a second time. I still needed to talk to Herman about the value of the cottage and get his opinion on an equity loan so she could hire someone to help her during the day when I was on the mainland. I knew he cared about her. When I'd asked Nan casually about him earlier in the week, the story she'd told me had made my heart tingly for days.

Nan and Herman had a romantic past I'd known nothing about.

It had been a long time ago. More than thirty years had passed since the time when Nan was a young widow with a small child, and Herman Blackstone had come courting. His parents didn't approve, so Herman broke ties with them and left the island for a long time. He ended up marrying someone else and started a family, but the marriage didn't last. And so he returned to Blackstone Island and stayed for good. Nan and Herman were still friends—

Whoa. Make that *very* good friends.

As I rounded the corner to her room, I saw something I'd never seen before. My nan kissing a man. Well, he was actually kissing her—I think. Herman was holding her face with his two hands so sweetly, as if she were the most precious treasure on earth. She had her hands at his waist as if she'd been practicing her walking and he'd been steadying her when they decided to go for a good snogging. The scene was straight out of *The Notebook* minus the rain.

I must have made a noise because they stopped and turned toward me in unison, their expressions mirroring the same peaceful happiness that only comes when the feeling is mutual.

We all blushed simultaneously I think.

Nan reached out a hand to me. "Brooke, my lovely girl, I have—that is—*we* have something to share with you."

I walked forward to take her hand in mine. "I already know what it is, Nan, because anyone can see the two of you are hopelessly in love with each other."

$$$

"SO, you won't be returning to the cottage when you come out of here, will you?" I asked.

"That won't be possible, Brooke, because she'll be living with me in my house," Herman said quietly before pulling Nan's hand up to his lips for a kiss. Mr. Romance was making the moves on my nan, and it was so damn sweet to witness.

Okaaaay. That would stir up the island gossips fairly quickly. I glanced at Nan to see what she thought of Herman's suggestion. "The gossips will have a field day with that news," I said cautiously.

She glowed with a love that shone so brightly I had to blink. "As husband and wife, Brooke darling. Herman has asked me to marry him and I've accepted."

Deep breath in. Deep breath out. "Oh. My. God. Nan! I'm so happy for you both. It's really the most lovely news I could ever hear. Congratulations, you two."

I hugged them both in turn, first Nan and then Herman, feeling the tears rise up violently in a surge I couldn't tamp down. This loss of control happened to me in emotional situations, so it wasn't a surprise to me at all. And it was totally unwelcome at a happy time such as the announcement of a marriage. Mortifying.

I was in good hands, though. Herman and Nan both seemed to understand my weakness when each of them opened an arm to me.

I fell in between them and wept until the overwhelming urge passed almost as quickly as it had come.

I'd never had this problem before my fatal mistake. I hadn't cried at the drop of a hat or in situations where happiness ruled *before* the accident that changed my life. Changed it for the better . . . and also for the worse. Duality. A situation where the line between good and bad could not exist because it was both.

And I had to live with it for the rest of my life.

I pulled myself together and gave them a huge smile that I truly felt all the way down to the depths of my heart, and said, "I suppose this means there is a wedding to plan."

"Can you pull one together in a few weeks?" Herman had quite the twinkle in his deep-blue eyes. He appeared to be one eager bridegroom, and I had to suppress a giggle at the thought. Nope. Not going there. Thoughts of my grandmother and her fiancé *together* could just go right on out of my head. Oh, my God. My nan had a fiancé!

"I'll need some help, but I know just the person to make it happen," I told him.

"Eduardo?" Nan asked.

I nodded. "He would be so honored and will make it magical for you, Nan, I know it."

"Sounds wonderful, my darling. Now, please, let's talk about you." She reached for my hand and rubbed her thumb over the top slowly. "How does this all sit with you? I know you came back to help me when I needed it, but I want you to be honest with me now when I ask you if you're comfortable living alone at the cottage?"

"Yes, Nan, of course. I've been alone in the cottage for the last five mon—"

"Let me finish, please, my lovely girl." She gave me that stern look of scolding I'd known for years. "I've discussed it with Herman and he would love to welcome you to live with us in his home if you want to."

She was worried about me living alone in the cottage, afraid I wasn't ready to handle the isolation. Yet. But she didn't need to be. I craved it actually. It was exactly what I needed.

"You two are so adorable, and I thank you for the kind and generous offer, though I wouldn't dream of intruding on newlyweds who've waited a lifetime to be together. I will be perfect in the cottage by myself. It is perfect for me."

"Then it is yours, darling. Herman will see to it the deed of trust is transferred into your name."

"Already in the works, my dear." Herman winked. "You own a piece of the island now, Brooke."

"I do?" I felt tears welling again.

"Free and clear," he said. "The property value has increased quite a bit from when your grandfather bought it forty years ago, obviously. The house is small, but the view is what counts and you have a beauty up there on the hill above the Fairchild Light."

"I love the view so much," I whispered, suddenly at a loss, and completely overwhelmed.

"It appraised at just over two million, but with some renovations that would increase nicely, depending what you want to do with it, of course." Herman nodded his head, happy to be the bringer of good news.

"Two—two million dollars?"

Herman laughed and patted my hand. "Two point two five to be precise."

"You've both shocked the hell out of me—in a good way mind you—but I had no idea about any of this. I've been so worried about the money I was going to ask you, Herman, about taking out a loan on the equity to pay medical bills." I was light-headed with relief.

"That's not your worry anymore, my dear. Everything is paid in full, and my Ellen is going to marry me," he said, before giving Nan another kiss to her hand, and making her blush beautifully. "It's only about thirty-five years too late but I will take it gratefully."

What a wise man Herman Blackstone was. Take your happiness when it comes. It was good advice I mustn't forget. When . . . If happiness graced my life again. Possibly not of the romance variety for quite some time, but that was okay. Time on my own was exactly what my heart needed. *Joy instead of sadness.*

I'd been so worried about Nan being alone. But I didn't need to worry about her anymore. I could focus on getting my life back. It felt like a huge weight was lifted from me, and I barely knew what to do with such a light heart.

"Dinner is served," Lilah announced as she rolled a cart into the room, breaking the spell of disbelief that had me wondering if I would wake up from this dream any moment and be thrust back into the cold harshness of reality.

Apparently not, because Lilah told us what we were having for dinner, and it struck me as absolutely hilarious. Spaghetti and . . . meatballs.

Of course I immediately thought of Caleb and the flowers he'd sent to me. But more so my very rude rant when he'd called me to flirt. He had been flirting with me. I knew it, and I shut him down anyway. I'd been rather a bitch to him, and Caleb had been nothing *but* nice to me.

I pulled my phone out of my purse and took some pictures of Nan and Herman first, because they were adorable and so happy together it was a must. Then I arranged my plate of spaghetti and meatballs for a photo op and snapped some foodie pics.

"What on earth are you doing, Brooke?" Nan asked me.

"I'm taking pictures of your engagement dinner, Nan. Every woman should be so lucky to have spaghetti and meatballs when she gets engaged."

$$$

I left Nan and Herman after dinner and took myself home to the cottage. Home to *my* cottage. Now, that little idea was going to take some getting used to, but I felt confident I could manage it. How did I go from paranoia about money to owning a two-million-dollar cottage on Blackstone Island in the space of an evening? How was that even possible? My nan was marrying her long-lost love, Herman, who just happened to be the mayor. They were getting married in exactly one month and I was planning it with Eduardo, who didn't even know he'd been commandeered into service.

God.

I wanted to do a bit of research tonight, and make some notes on ideas for the wedding, so I could be ready to begin full speed ahead with the actual plans in the morning. Only a month's time to prepare. I knew it would be a challenge, but I'd make sure it was special for Nan and Herman if it killed me.

The first thing I did whenever I got home was change out of my work clothes. By the end of the day, I was beyond ready to ditch leather leggings and boots after nearly twelve hours of wearing them. The bra, too. Nothing felt better than to exchange the pretty stuff for cozy flannel pajamas and warm socks that maybe weren't quite so pretty.

I made some tea and drafted a long email to Eduardo with the details and invited him to come over to the island tomorrow—if he was free—so we could search venues. I assumed they would want it at Stone Church, the old stone chapel perched against the rocky shoreline. Very stark, but reminiscent of the chapel on Cumberland Island where JFK Jr. and Carolyn Bessette married. It was going to be gorgeous.

It was just past ten when I picked up my phone to look at the pictures I'd taken of Herman and Nan. I saw the spaghetti and meatballs pictures, too. I don't know why I decided to message Caleb. It was stupid really, but I wanted to reach out to him and apologize again. I felt badly with how our conversation had gone about west-side vs. south-end. Ouch. So bitchy on my part. My comments had been cringeworthy, despite the fact I couldn't remember them exactly. Thank. God.

I did remember, however, that Caleb had said for me to think of him whenever I saw a meatball.

It was the least I could do to be accommodating, I told myself as I tapped out my text.

Thought of you tonight at dinner. –Brooke

I attached a picture of my plate of meatballs and pressed Send.

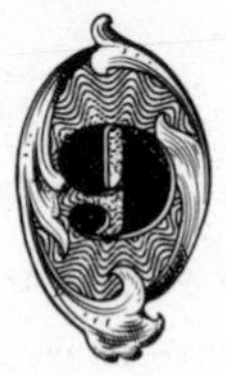

Caleb

Fuck!” Fuck, shit, cocksucker, motherfucker. What were the odds she would contact me now? I stared at Brooke’s text and wanted to call her so badly. I wanted to talk to her, mostly to hear her say my name in that beautiful, oh-so-proper voice of hers. “Is this Caleb calling?” I could hear her saying it. Knew exactly how she would sound when she did.

But I couldn’t call her right now no matter how badly I wanted to.

It would screw up my plans for Monday. She didn’t yet know I’d retained her services for my penthouse, and of course, had no knowledge my family employed her grandmother at Blackwater from the time before I was born, either. I had to set my plan for Blackwater in motion first, and then I’d tell Brooke who I really was, when we were at a point where the mistakes that’d been made were being set right. She’d never give me a chance otherwise. Brooke would tell me to fuck on off to my west-side mansion with the rest of the filthy-rich bastards who didn’t understand how things really worked.

I could hear her voice saying those words, too.

I wasn't really concerned about my name because there were a lot of Blackstones in this area, probably distant relations, but it was still a common enough name to pull off anonymity when we met on Monday. I didn't want her to know I was on the island this weekend, either, and if I called her back now, I knew I would cave and ask to meet her somewhere. She was too tantalizing to me and the temptation too immense for me to trust myself.

Her message made me fucking happy, though. Brooke thought about me at dinner tonight. She remembered the idiot with the black eye and the inability to be coherent—and she hadn't ditched my number, either.

I stared at the picture she'd sent and wondered what time she'd been eating her dinner, and where she ate it, and with whom. I wanted to know every detail.

I suspected it was right about the same time I'd been jerking off in the shower to thoughts of her. Pretty pathetic. What would she think of me if she knew?

Lucas strolled back into his game room with a bottle of Lagavulin in one hand and two Cohiba Espléndidos in the other. "What was the f-bomb for?"

"I'm gonna need some of that Lag before I can go there, bro."

"Brooke is why you came here. I figured out that much already."

I looked pointedly at the bottle of Scotch in his hand as a reply.

"Okay, I got you," he said, before plopping his ass down beside me, and started to pour.

I didn't answer until I was on my second glass of Lag, and the Cohiba had been cut, toasted, and was burning properly. I didn't indulge often but I enjoyed the hell out of it when I did. Smoking a cigar was a lot like tasting a fine wine, because you never inhaled with a cigar. You sipped it. Sipped the smoke and then blew it back out, leaving nothing behind but the flavor of ultrapure tobacco.

Smoking this fine Cuban cigar was perfect for my mood right now. I watched the white smoke swirl in front of me and slowly fade out. Lucas had a beautiful view of Black Bay from his game room. In fact, the whole house was amazing, and I was glad I had come to see my brother, regardless of what I'd discover tomorrow at Blackwater.

"Did you ever want something so badly that you were afraid for your future if you couldn't have it?"

Lucas didn't answer for a long time. He sipped on his Cohiba, and seemed to be far away in his own thoughts. My brother was probably lost in the past to a time when he didn't have the scars that now marred much of the right side of his body, including his face. They looked mostly superficial to me, and always had, but I didn't have to live in his skin, so I didn't know how it was for him. Women didn't seem to mind his scars. If anything it made him more attractive, his personal wealth notwithstanding, because he was a mystery. Pussy was never his problem.

"Yes."

"What do you do about it?" I asked.

"You accept it for what it really is."

"And what is that, exactly?"

He turned toward me and read me like a book. "You love her, Caleb."

I shut up for a while and just let that idea roll around in my head for a bit. It seemed totally impossible for Lucas to be right, but no desperate urge to deny it as false came over me, either. And even weirder was the peaceful feeling of calm that settled in my chest. I felt relief for the first time in days.

How could I love someone I barely knew? Is that how it worked for people? They just met a person and fell for them that easily? I didn't know the answers because I was unable to compare what I was feeling about Brooke to anybody else I'd known. It was a totally different experience with her. I had no guidebook to spell it out for me, either. This was one I'd have to figure out as I went along.

Time kept marching forward no matter what. The grains of sand continued to fall until the last one slipped through and there were no more. I thought of our dad and some of the conversations we'd had together before he died. One really stuck.

The idea that right *now* was the most time you had left to live of your life. This day, this hour, this minute of your life—was the greatest amount of time you had remaining. The time you had left only grew shorter . . . and so, more precious.

Maybe the Cohiba was more potent than I thought, because my head was way out into the next galaxy tonight. I took another sip of the Lag and savored it across my tongue.

Tomorrow. Tomorrow, I would text Brooke and let her know I liked the picture she sent me—maybe ask her to dinner in the city. I'd go up to Blackwater in the morning with Lucas and evaluate the property. Then I would figure out what to do and have faith I was making the right decisions for the future.

"So are we going to play or what?" he asked with a nudge to my shoulder. "Because I wouldn't dream of denying you the pleasure of losing to me. I have to keep you in line, remind you who has the better skills—the bigger brain."

"Bigger brain, little brother?" I scoffed. "Bitch, please!" I grabbed a controller and started setting up the newest version of a game he'd created called iInVidiosa. I knew it inside out because I'd invested heavily in its development. Lucas was a brilliant designer, but he didn't need to hear it from me. The proof was in the half billion dollars we'd made on this one game alone. "Oh, before I forget—Victoria said to tell you hi."

I caught it. The flash of emotion lasted for only an instant and just appeared in his eyes before he masked it, but I knew what I saw. "Cool," he said after turning back toward the game. "Tell her congratulations from me."

So the poor bastard was interested in Victoria, which might have worked out well for the both of them, if not for the fact his friend Clay was planning on marrying her.

$$$

ONE shared bottle of Lagavulin, one fine Cuban cigar, and eight hours of sleep with the sound of the ocean against the rocks had worked wonders. I woke up feeling much better, like the cobwebs had been blown out and the dark mask lifted away, so I could see clearly.

I grabbed my phone off the nightstand and fell back onto the bed with a stretch. I opened her text from last night and read it again.

> I am honored, Brooke. You remembered our deal to think of me whenever you see a meatball. I hope it was a good thought.

I felt better after I texted her back. It was torture not to respond late last night when it came through. I didn't expect her to answer me right way, but at least she wouldn't think I'd blown her off like an arrogant prick. If only she knew what I really wanted to do. I'd drive Lucas's Escalade over to the cottages above the Fairchild Light, find the one that she lived in, and knock on her door. Then I'd—

Then I'd do what? Take her in my arms and tell her she was the woman I'd been searching for all my life and demand she marry me?

That sounded really fucking stupid and a whole lot like a movie a woman would love to see—but a guy would have to be dragged into the theater without the promise of anal afterward.

This was all seat-of-the-pants stuff for me, and probably not a good idea to be pondering when I was naked in bed and sporting morning wood. I had no idea what I was doing anymore. Scary as fuck, too. To realize my whole life had destabilized because I'd met a girl who'd transformed my idea of what love might be about. I still didn't know because, well . . . I didn't even really know her yet.

My phone vibrated and my heart dropped like a rock when I read what she'd texted.

May I call you right now, Caleb? Always so proper.

Of course. I tapped out with shaky fingers.

There went my heart again, pounding painfully with nervousness when my phone started going off. I gave it two rings before I picked up. "Brooke?"

"Good morning, Caleb." *Why was her voice so soothing? And what am I needing soothing from?*

"It is a good morning, I agree." *You called.* "How were the meatballs?"

She laughed softly, and I pictured her lips as she did it. "Remarkably good, considering where they came from."

"Oh, where did you eat last night?"

"Blackstone Therapy Center with my nan. That was hospital food if you can believe it."

"She's in the hospital now?" *Jesus . . .*

"It's a rehabilitation hospital and temporary, so not for much longer. She had a bad fall five months ago and needed to have a knee replacement."

"I'm glad to hear she will be leaving soon." I couldn't help wondering about the medical costs and how she was paying for it since there were no medical benefits forthcoming from her grandmother's employment at Blackwater. Ergo the need for a second job.

"Oh, I truly am, thank you, Caleb." Such proper manners my sweet Brooke used in conversation. I'd love to see her lose control, though—for example like when we were in the heat of fucking. My dick started throbbing.

"Caleb, I have a confession."

If you only knew, Brooke, if you only knew . . . "Oh? Please tell me then." Maybe teasing would help diffuse all of the blood that had suddenly decided to travel south to the region of my cock.

"Our conversation last time—about west-side verse south-end—it was horrible of me to say those things to you, and I just wanted to let you know I don't really feel that way. Nobody can change who their parents are or how much money their family has, only how they choose to use it. You were very kind to me the night we met and offered your help. I want you to know I did notice your random acts of kindness to a complete stranger, and I do thank you very much for being such a gentleman. And for the beautiful flowers as well. I'm very sorry for the things I said to you when we spoke last time."

Was I hearing this? She was reaching out to me for some reason.

"Are you still there, Caleb?"

"Yes. Yes I am."

"Can you find it in your heart to forgive me for being a tad cunty with you?" Only a Brit could say *cunty* and have it sound classy and funny as she just did.

"It's forgotten, Brooke, but only on one condition."

"And what's that?"

"You let me take you to dinner on Monday."

"Hmm . . . I don't even know your last name, and you don't know mine," she said cautiously. It didn't bother me, though. I liked that she was careful about who she went with. She was smart.

"Actually, I do know your last name is Casterley."

"So, you have been stalking me after all." Yep, she was smart.

"Only in the most honorable way, Brooke. I've thought about you a lot since that horrible cocktail party, and I felt really bad about what happened. I just want to be able to talk to you over some good food and get acquainted in a normal environment."

"Unfortunately the reception where I met you was a normal environment for that shit-show of a job. I'm so glad I quit. I hope your suit wasn't ruined. I'd be happy to pay for the cleaning bill if you drop it by Harris & Goode."

"The suit is taken care of, Brooke, and I am very glad you quit the shit-show of a job, too. Your boss was an ass."

"You are right about that, Caleb, but you still haven't told me your name."

"It's Blackstone like the island. It's a fairly common name around here."

"Yes, I remember Massachusetts state history in high school. The Reverend William Blackstone was the first European settler in the area and settled in what is now Boston Common in 1625. I've seen the statue."

"You were a good student, Brooke, but you still haven't told me your answer about dinner." It was fun to copy her choice of words.

"The last ferry to the island leaves at eight thirty on weeknights. Can we make it an early dinner, Caleb Blackstone?"

"We can do whatever you want, Brooke Casterley."

"Ah, you're a stalker, thanks for reminding me." She had a natural wit I really liked. A lot. When she teased it turned me on.

"A nice stalker, though, and before you ask, I found out your name when I stopped in at Harris & Goode for a consult late yesterday afternoon."

"Oh? Are you in need of a designer, Caleb?"

More than you will ever know . . . and only one designer in particular. "I think you'll get all of the details on Monday morning from Mr. Harris."

"So a stalker and a master manipulator both?"

"Nice, Brooke, only in the *nicest* possible way."

She laughed again. The sound of her laughing did something to me. Something very sensual and erotic—to the point I knew I'd be back with the soap and my hand in the shower as soon as we hung up. *When in the hell have I ever had to do that with one woman in mind? Ever?*

$$$

ISLAND air smelled different. Clean and sharp with scents of the sea and the earth.

I shouldn't have stayed away for so long. Eight years was a long time.

But Brooke was here, and I certainly planned on getting to be very good friends with her, so maybe I'd be coming here a lot more often.

Blackwater had been built in 1890 by my great-grandfather, Nathaniel Blackstone, who was a direct descendent of the man who'd founded the city of Boston in 1625 as Brooke reminded me on the phone earlier.

My great-grandfather made his fortune in the continental railroad, and in early oil-well development in Texas. He built Blackwater after he'd made his fortune and wanted to return to where he'd been raised as a child—Blackstone Island. I guess so he could reminisce about simpler, more innocent times.

I had my own memories of simpler times during holidays on the island as a kid with my brothers and sisters. I recalled those times as happy and innocent. Dad taught us all to sail and went with us boys on Boy Scout campouts. He taught the girls how to shoot a bow and arrow and to swim. He was a hands-on father. Mom was not as enthusiastic about the island, but she was always there with us that I remember—organizing clam bakes and beach picnics with my aunt Cynthia who was also her cousin. Yeah, we're an incestuous mess of a family. Money likes to keep with money. The law of averages is in your favor that way.

So, as I stood staring at the historic stone mansion that had been in our family for more than a hundred years, I couldn't understand why my mother would sell it off. Especially without having a family meeting first, to ask her children if they had any interest in it for themselves.

Something was off with this situation—I just hadn't found out what.

Yet.

I took a photo of the realty sign and texted it to my attorney who handled property acquisitions. I could always buy it outright, but that didn't seem like the correct move when I had four other siblings to consider, and also what our dad would want for all of us.

The house was still solid, with a strong foundation laid high on the cliffside overlooking Massachusetts Bay. It had been created by my family for my family. The value had to be in excess of thirty million dollars, but that part didn't concern me at all. The legacy was much more valuable.

My mother was dreaming if she thought I would ever let Blackwater go to strangers.

Brooke

The black clouds screamed their intent to release angry rain at some point in my near future as the ferry pulled into its berth in Boston Harbor.

Monday morning.

It felt as if the weekend had passed in a complete blur after Nan and Herman's big announcement. Eduardo had shown up on Saturday and stayed with me until Sunday afternoon to help plan the wedding. We'd gone to the hospital and consulted with Nan, talked through all of the major points, and managed to decide on the venue, the flowers, and even a dress. She found exactly what she wanted, so I placed the order online with a bridal shop in Boston. Her friend Sylvie would do the alterations if any were needed after I picked it up later in the week. My grandmother would be a beautiful bride when she said her vows in Stone Church with Herman. The wedding might be small with an intimate guest list but that would only make it more romantic in my opinion.

So, after only one little weekend of planning, I felt accomplished as I left Starbucks with a latte warming my cold hands before the start of my workweek. I stepped through the tiny alley that separated Starbucks from my building and saw the alcove where Caleb had paused to take a call out of the way of the streaming street traffic. He'd seen me that morning, he'd said.

I was having dinner with him tonight.

That fact alone surprised me. Because I had absolutely no intention of dating anybody right now. It was a date, right? Handsome man who flirts mercilessly asks girl to dinner who accepts his invitation. That qualified as a date in my book. I didn't know Caleb at all, but in some unbelievably weird way, it very much felt like I did. He didn't push me the way ninety percent of the men I might meet would, but he didn't give up easily, either. I really hadn't expected him to ask me out after I'd been so obnoxious about the division of wealth on the island. So, Caleb goes one further by accepting my apology point-blank—on the condition I go to dinner with him. How could I say no to him? And if I was honest, I wanted to go. He was really charming and very polite—a true gentleman. I didn't have a lot of experience with men, but I recognized something trustworthy in him. I recalled how he'd been almost tongue-tied with me at the cocktail party, which was ridiculous really, especially given the sophisticated world he came from. But he'd stood up for me gallantly and offered his help. And then he sent *me* flowers. So very thoughtful. Could I trust him? I felt I could.

Don't measure every man to him. Caleb was nothing like that.

For the first time since I'd left LA, I wasn't fearful to be alone with a heterosexual male who clearly appeared to be showing the usual signs of pursuing me.

I'd just have to see how it went with him at dinner tonight. After he'd asked me the customary questions tested out on a first date and heard my story, I was certain his curiosity would be swiftly, but politely, satisfied. My past was so very untidy in so many ways, the recent past a literal slag heap of a mess that had nearly ended me.

When Caleb Blackstone heard that bit?—and I would answer truthfully so that nothing was left out.

I couldn't imagine he, or any man, would want to be involved with me. *No. Happiness with a man is not in the cards for you at the moment. Someday, but not right now.*

$$$

EDUARDO showed up after me, which hardly ever happened. "*Ay Dios mío*, my head hurts, *condesa*."

"Too much partying to get in and not enough weekend, huh?" I *had* taken up the majority of his "lifestyle" time. "Sorry you don't feel well, but that pumpkin button-down you're wearing this morning is very autumn-festive. Do you want me to go next door and get you a pumpkin latte to go with it?"

He groaned dramatically and waved me off. He would go lie down on the sofa in the back for a bit and then reappear later as a new man. Eduardo cracked me up continually.

"Brooke, good morning. Do you have a minute?" Jon asked from my doorway.

"For you, Jon? At least two or three, and good morning to you as well." I usually didn't see him first thing because Jon was not a morning person. He needed to be plied with coffee and a pastry before he came 'round to the land of the coherent any time before 10:00 a.m. I think he suffered from the same condition Eduardo did—a very busy social life after hours, which I suppose applied to most single people. The only person at work who wasn't single was Carlisle. He was married to a heart surgeon at Massachusetts General named Colin. Colin and Carlisle were shortened to CC whenever they were discussed as a couple. Absolutely adorably in love with each other.

Jon eased himself into my pink velvet slipper chair, causing it to give out a small squeak of protest, which I politely ignored. "What's up, Jon?"

"We have a new client with a 1920s Back Bay penthouse undergoing a complete renovation. It's quite a job, Brooke, because of the scope and also the impressive budget. In excess of five million to be exact." He smiled hugely. "It's three floors, six thousand square feet with four bedrooms and four and a half baths. There are five fireplaces, a media room, home gym, two home offices—the owner's an international businessman—five deeded parking spaces, and a landscaped roof deck with unobstructed views across the Charles River to the Boston skyline."

"Wow. It sounds incredible. And you're here to give me the good news that I get to do one of the rooms," I said. "I hope . . ." I added, a bit more humbly.

"Not exactly, my dear." He tilted his head meaningfully before dropping the bomb on me. "You are in charge of the whole project. He asked for a woman designer—and only a woman will do for him apparently. He made sure of it when he paid the retainer fee directly to you." Jon pulled what looked like a check out of the folder he'd brought in with him. He laid both on my desk, the check facing up. "Five percent of the total budget is our retainer fee. Your client paid ten percent—a fifty-fifty split between you, the lead designer, and the shop. Congratulations, Brooke. Please come to me for anything you need help with, or Carlisle obviously. You have a magnificent budget, and the opportunity to *make* your design career right here." He poked his finger onto the file folder. "Clients like him bring in more business if they are happy with the experience because they talk to their friends."

I swallowed deeply and said nothing. The city of Boston, and everything and everyone in it, had certainly just been sucked into a swirling vortex of space and time. I think.

I stared down at the amount written on the check. *Unbelievable fucking hell?*

My name was written clearly on the line. *That is your name, idiot.*

Last Friday's date at the top. *He said he'd come here and had a consultation with Jon.*

And along the bottom right, the signature of one Caleb J. W. Blackstone, written in the same bold handwriting I had on the card that accompanied my flowers, sitting not more than two feet from me at this very moment. *The same Caleb who is taking me to dinner tonight.* Surreal.

"Make Mr. Blackstone happy with his design experience, Brooke."

"Yes, Jon. I will make sure of it," I managed to croak out, despite the fact I was fighting for my sanity in the swirling vortex of time and space which had swallowed up the city of Boston about ten minutes ago.

$$$

MARTIN was the last person I expected to see walking through the door, his pleasant demeanor even more of a surprise. He handed me an envelope, which I accepted stiffly.

"Is this my final pay, Martin? Why didn't you just send it here instead of coming in person? I won't be returning to work for you in any case."

"Yes, I know that. I wanted to come and thank you in person, Brooke."

"Thank me?" Poor Martin was seriously deficient in the brains department. "Whatever for?"

"For having your boyfriend pay for the damages of the eight ruined designer suits. The cocktail sauce . . ." He trailed off.

"I don't have a boyfriend. Who paid for it?" I couldn't imagine who—

"Your friend, Caleb, then. He gave me his card after you quit and said he'd take care of any damages. He paid close to fifty grand for all those suits. Designer threads are expensive." He shrugged. "Anyway, thanks for your help with everything. Good luck, Brooke."

He waved once as he went out the door, to which I lifted my hand in response.

I think.

For the second time today, I'd been rendered completely speechless by the covert activities of Caleb Blackstone in regards to me.

What in the hell was he doing? And more importantly, *why*?

$$$

"MR. BLACKSTONE is here." Eduardo wore a telling smirk on his face as he leaned into my doorway, an extra sparkle in his dark eyes. It was easy to see he was clearly enjoying the spectacle caused by Caleb's visit today, along with everyone else. The man was definitely worthy of a head turn from what I remembered, and the pictures on the Internet were helpful in jogging my memory as well. His good looks had a bit of a harsh edge to them, but my God, it only made him more attractive. Google had his personal net worth between one and two billion dollars, mostly in oil and sustainable energy. Caleb Blackstone was a legitimate billionaire. What he wanted with me was much more of a mystery. I'd have Eduardo breathing down my neck for that very information as soon as the solemnly hot Mr. Blackstone put me in the know.

"I still don't understand why he's asked for me specifically. Why didn't he request Jon or Carlisle? His budget is bloody huge and I am a junior designer."

Eduardo cocked his head to the right and his hip to the left in artful unison and rolled his eyes at me. His flair for the dramatic was as expected as it was ridiculously funny. "I can safely say it's because Jon and Carlisle don't have a rack as nice as yours, *condesa*." He crinkled his nose in distaste. "Although Jon is catching up—he must be a solid B cup by now. All of those midmorning runs for French pastry aren't helping," he whispered loudly.

I cut him off before he could lapse into a tirade that I didn't want to hear right now. "Yes, thank you, Eduardo, for that scintillating assessment of Jon's developing breasts. What does Mr. Blackstone want from me?" Panic was starting to settle in.

"I think he wants to play hide the sausage with you, but that's just me."

"You are so unhelpful right now it's scary. I know why Jon and Carlisle offered me a part-time assistant. They had absolutely no idea what else to do with you."

"But I am always honest and that's a valuable trait to have in an employee," he told me with a sassy grin.

"Right." I sighed heavily and realized there was no point making Caleb wait on me. He owned five million dollars of the company's design services—from me personally—and so I suppose that made him my new boss. I couldn't put him off for another second. "Eduardo, please show Mr. Blackstone in."

I listened for Eduardo's flamboyant announcement and cringed. "Miss Casterley is ready for you, Mr. Blackstone."

I stood and held out my hand in greeting as he walked inside my office, his tall frame filling the small space immediately with a presence that made my heart take a sharp dive. "Caleb . . ."

He took my hand but not to shake, rather to pull me in toward him so he could kiss me on the cheek. "Brooke," he whispered below my ear. The brush of his beard stubble and soft lips to my skin brought an instant heat that threatened to burn me. He held me just an instant too long before he released me. I stumbled slightly as I stepped back, utterly rattled. His arm came out to steady me, and his eyes locked on to mine. I could see the color of them as they blazed at me—dark blue with a thick golden ring around the pupil.

Unusual but beautiful eyes held me overlong for what they should have.

It dawned on me that I was not in control of the situation, and that helped to snap me out of my hypnotic episode.

Bloody hell . . . Caleb Blackstone. Those pictures I'd looked at earlier on Google Images didn't even come close to the actual man in the flesh. I hadn't really taken a serious look at him that night we'd met. Yes, I'd thought him handsome, but there had been so many men hitting on me I'd been too distracted to focus on the details. Wow.

I separated my arm from his touch and moved toward my own chair, praying my legs wouldn't fail me. "P-please have a seat." I indicated the chair for him before I remembered to ask, "Shall I take your c-coat?"

"No, thank you, I'll keep it." He flicked open the buttons before lowering his big masculine body to sit in my pink velvet slipper chair. It was quite the contradiction of image, and I had the freakish urge to take a picture of him sitting in it. I wanted to kiss the damn chair when it didn't creak as Caleb leaned back and relaxed into the seat as if he owned it. He did own it now actually, I reminded myself. His long legs encased in dark-gray silk trousers, showing the cut definition of his thigh muscles, seemed to take up all the space between the chair and my table desk. I didn't know where to push myself in without being practically on top of him. Now that was an image . . .

Stop it. Stop looking him over like a piece of meat, tit-head.

I managed to get my arse into my own chair and give him my attention. Just barely.

"I've surprised you, haven't I?" He gave me a half grin turned up on only one side, both charming and wicked at the same time. I was in very deep trouble here. As in Marianas Trench depth level of trouble.

"Caleb—please help me understand why you requested me as lead designer on your renovation. Surely you want a designer with more experience—"

"Brooke, I want you," he said, cutting me off neatly. "That is all you need to know about my reasons."

In what way do you want me? Because I'm getting all kinds of mixed messages here, Caleb Blackstone, with the beautiful and unusual eyes. "Well, it would help me to feel more comfortable with the situation if you might share a bit more with me. I'm—I am a junior designer and I've not the years of experience Mr. Harris or Mr. Goode could give to your project."

"I told Mr. Harris I wanted a woman's touch in the elements of the overarching theme for the penthouse. Didn't he tell you?"

"No. He only said to make you happy in your design experience." He smirked at that comment, and weirdly it didn't appear cocky or arrogant—just rather mischievous.

"Well, you can start making me happy by accepting the project, Brooke." His thumb tapped his knee where he'd rested his hand. It felt like he was waiting me out, playing his hand at a game of cards, all while keeping that cheeky smirk on his face.

I would never get a chance like this again. Renovating a billionaire's Back Bay penthouse would be the making of my whole career. Jon agreed. If I turned it down, I would be a moron who didn't deserve to be an interior designer and might as well go back to working for arseholes like Martin.

"Right. I accept the very generous offer of your job, Caleb."

His smirk turned into a smile that made his blue-and-golden eyes twinkle. "This makes me very happy, Brooke."

Caleb had a way of making a suggestive comment come off innocent and sweet. I could sense the double entendre in his answers, but they didn't cross the lines of propriety, or make me uncomfortable to be around him.

He checked his watch, which probably cost the amount written on my retainer fee check, and rose from the chair. "It's after five, and I promised you an early dinner. Shall we get going?"

Just like that he took charge. It was done smoothly and effortlessly on his part. The next thing I knew was the weight of his hands on my shoulders as he helped me into my coat. A minute later he was guiding me out the door with his strong fingers pressing solidly to my back. There was a strange mix of dominance and deference emanating from everything he did, whether I liked it or not.

"I'm afraid it's raining pretty hard at the moment, but Isaac will take care of you," he said as we stepped outside.

A distinguished gentleman with graying hair ushered me under a huge umbrella and into a black stretch Mercedes without one drop of water catching me.

Caleb slid into the seat beside me.

The door was shut behind him, instantly silencing the noise of the pounding rain drenching the city. We both turned our heads and studied each other. No words were exchanged, just looking.

Physical space had been used up by our bodies sitting very close on the seat together, so there was nothing left to do but experience it. I felt his body heat and smelled whatever scent he'd used. Spicy and masculine—drugging my senses from his closeness.

As his driver eased into traffic, Caleb took my hand in his and held it.

I didn't pull away. I didn't want to pull my hand from his because I liked very much how it felt, so warm and protective.

He sighed just slightly, but I caught it. It reminded me of an expression of relief from him.

I didn't understand why or what his interest could be in choosing me for his five-million-dollar penthouse renovation, but now I was well past caring.

Because I very much liked that feeling as well. *Peaceful. Excited.* Distinctly different, yet equally describing what it felt like to have my hand claimed by Caleb's hand. It maybe should have felt presumptuous of him, a tad rude even. Yet strangely it only felt right.

Caleb

She smelled so good and looked so pretty it took some restraint not to crowd her. I wanted to. I wanted to do a lot of things with Brooke.

Once I had her beside me in the backseat of the car, I felt myself relax—immense relief, which was fucking unbelievable, but exactly how I felt. It made no sense because the whole experience was unfamiliar to me. I had to process everything from scratch. Brooke was a step-by-step exploration of territory I'd never ventured into before. I wanted to stake my claim on her—to her—with her. I wanted more than I could have of her right now. I instinctively knew I'd have to take it slow in order to have any chance at all with the girl who had worked her way so deeply under my skin I barely recognized myself anymore. *Was this love like Lucas said?*

I didn't want to let go of her hand when Isaac delivered us at the curb in front of the restaurant. It was just the touch of hands—hers and mine intertwined. Just a touch. But not enough. The Smashing Pumpkins understood my pain.

So, as soon as we were under the awning and out of the rain, I took her hand again and didn't let go until we were inside and seated across from each other. The freedom to rove my eyes over Brooke to my heart's content was amazing. She was beautiful, of course, and I loved looking, but having her complete attention directed at me was unlike anything I'd ever experienced. She hadn't pulled away when I'd held her hand. She hadn't clung for more, either. Brooke was not desperate for my attentions. She just accepted it.

"I hope this is okay," I said, looking over my menu. Boscono's on the Hill was a new Italian place in Beacon Hill. "I've never been here before. My PA suggested it actually, after I told her I wanted somewhere quiet with great food and a decent wine list. I figured you liked Italian because of your picture the other night."

"It's perfect, and I already know what I'm ordering."

"Even I *know* what you're ordering, Brooke." Some variation of something with meatballs, no doubt. I loved her humor. "What kind of wine do you like?" I asked.

"Something on the sweeter end of the scale. I hope that's okay," she said quickly.

"I like it sweet," I said softly, and then watched her blush again. *Fucking hot.*

As the waiter came to take our orders and deliver the most expensive Lambrusco that existed at twenty-eight dollars a bottle—and that was probably including a thirty percent markup for the restaurant—I had to appreciate her lack of interest in my wealth. It was refreshing.

I remembered how I'd pressed my lips against the softly scented skin of Brooke's cheek in greeting her at the design studio. I'd wanted to lick my way down her neck instead, pull her in against me, and suck on the place where her neck drifted into her shoulder. I wanted to feel and experience her response to me. What would she look like when I had my lips on her body? How would she sound? What was she like during sex? Did she taste sweet like this wine we'd been served?

This dinner was going to test my control, but I had to remember to keep things low-key. Coming on too strong would not be the right move with Brooke.

She studied me for a moment before saying, "Just right now you reminded me of someone I know on the island."

"Oh?"

"Yes, my nan's fiancé." She shook her head and smiled. "Gosh, that sounds so strange but I have to get used to it because the wedding is in a month, and I'm planning it."

"Congratulations to the happy couple." I couldn't help wondering who Mrs. Casterley was marrying in her golden years. I'd bet she was still as lovely as I remembered—pretty, kind, and very British, ruling over the house at Blackwater, making sure everything was as perfect as it could be for our imperfect family. I remembered a great deal of patience on her part, especially when we got into trouble and made huge messes as children do.

"I just thought of this, but Herman will be my grandfather once he marries Nan."

Herman? The back of my neck tingled. Herman was not a common name. I could safely predict that the only Herman living on the island was my uncle. "Herman Blackstone?"

"Are you related to Herman?"

"He's my uncle. So, Uncle Herman is getting married. Wow. That is awesome." I'd have to come clean to Brooke about Blackwater. There was no way to keep that secret going. "Have you seen the guest list for the wedding?"

She shook her head in disbelief. "No, they're still working on it."

"Well, I imagine my name will be on there when you do." I was thrilled for him. Herman deserved some happiness after the shit deal he'd been saddled with the first time around. Aunt Cynthia had not been a nice woman. In fact, she was remembered fondly as a fucking hydra. My mother would be beside herself when she heard the news. *Imagine a former servant marrying into all that money.* I could hear her moaning the words over her chardonnay. I'd be lying if the thought of my mom's distress over Herman's news didn't amuse the goddamn hell out of me.

"So your father and Herman are brothers?" She frowned. "I thought he just had one brother—"

"He did. My father, John William, or JW as he was known, was his only brother and ten years younger than Herman."

Her expression grew compassionate and I figured she had now finally made the full connection. Such a smart girl.

"Oh, Caleb, I am so sorry for your loss. It happened right before I came back to Boston to help Nan. She thought the world of your father and was heartbroken to hear that he'd passed away."

"Thank you. I miss him every day." I took some comfort in knowing his passing had been relatively peaceful with all of us right beside him when he died.

She studied me thoughtfully for a moment, focusing on my eyes mostly. "Caleb, I assume you've figured out my nan was housekeeper at Blackwater. Why—why then did you hire me for your renovation after those terrible things I said to you and the hideously disrespectful way I spoke about your family?"

She blinked several times as if she was trying to hold back tears. So tenderhearted.

"Brooke, please let it go."

"But I don't understand. I don't know what you're doing here, Caleb. With me. The flowers, the job offer, the fifty thousand dollars of damages you paid on my behalf for destroyed suits." She turned toward the window and stared out at the rain. "My old boss stopped in to deliver my final pay and to thank me in person for having my *boyfriend* pay for the extensive damages."

She turned back from the window to hit me with her blazing amber eyes. Sensuous eyes I fantasized about at night when I was alone in my bed—how it would be, having them locked on me while I was buried balls-deep inside her. And I had no doubt it would be fucking spectacular.

"You didn't even *know* me that night, Caleb, so why did you do all that for a stranger?"

I reached across the table and took both of her hands in mine. I caressed the back of each one with my thumbs, admiring the delicate bone structure. *You're a banquet for my starving soul. My brother believes I love you. You've completely owned me since I first laid eyes on you.* "I don't know why. That is the honest-to-God truth, Brooke. I do not know why I offered to pay the damages, or why I followed you outside to see if you were okay, or why I listened in on where you told your cab driver to go, or why I sent you flowers the next day, and then purposefully gave you my number. I don't know why I did any of it, except for the fact I wanted to help you . . . when you so obviously needed some kindness from another person. I couldn't stop thinking about you and needed to know you were all right the following day. You intrigue me, Brooke. I feel like it was fate meeting you, especially now with Herman and your grandmother getting married. We will be connected by their marriage from now on anyway. What are the odds of that happening? I don't want to think too hard about it; I just want to give fate a fighting chance here."

"But after I was so horrible to you on the phone?"

"You know what? You were right about everything you said to me. It took me a bit of time to find out the truth. I had no idea Blackwater had been shut down and all employees terminated. No one told me, and possibly even went out of their way to keep me ignorant of that fact." I didn't want to say it was my own mother who'd done it, but once Brooke met Mom, she'd understand much better. "But please know I am working on fixing it. Your grandmother and everyone else will be compensated for absent wages and benefits since they lost their jobs. That is a promise."

"Oh . . ." She trailed off uncertainly. "But you don't have to do that because of me. Ah, I get it now. You must've thought I had figured out who you were when I called to apologize, hmm?"

"Actually I didn't. Brooke, you surprised me with your phone call, yes, but don't forget I had already retained you for my renovation *before* you reached out to me, so I would have hired you for the job anyway. I only found out last Friday who you really were and how our families are linked. I haven't visited the island in nearly a decade, until just this past weekend. My brother Lucas filled me in on a lot of what's been going on. I wanted to keep Blackwater out of . . . us," I waved my fingers back and forth between our bodies, "until I could assess how best to move forward, reclaiming the property and fixing the giant mess made by *my* own family."

"I did *not* know who you were, Caleb." She brought her hands up to curl beneath her chin. "I never dreamed it was your family who owned Blackwater. I am so horrified right now, just so you know."

"Well, you look beautiful even when you're horrified, Brooke. You keep surprising me at every turn. I didn't want to tell you that it was my family who owned Blackwater until I'd had a chance to right the wrongs." I really hoped she believed me.

"I want you to remember what I said to you about how it's not how much money you have, but how you choose to use it. I meant it. You are trying to fix something you had no knowledge of, and I admire your integrity for doing so, but I really hope you aren't doing it for me, or for the promise of something you might want from me."

Like having you in bed with me every night? We were speaking the same language at least.

"I'm doing it for me, Brooke." *But I do want you in my bed.*

She blushed. I saw her color darken as the blood traveled up her neck and face. I wanted to see that happen when she was naked and in my arms.

"It would have been one big surprise if you showed up at the wedding with neither of us knowing all of this," she said.

"Like I said before, it feels more like a twist of fate to me."

"My nan has known you since you were born, Caleb. I just can't believe it."

Seeing Brooke so animated in conversation, I wanted to kiss her breathless. "Ask her if she remembers the tomato launchers I made at Boy Scouts when I was twelve. I'm betting it will be a yes."

She laughed. "I am envisioning an epic tale of squashed tomatoes and the terrifying scolding from my nan that came along with it."

$$$

EVEN watching her eat was entertainment. She'd ordered pasta with a giant goddamn meatball that she then proceeded to cut into tiny pieces and savor one by one. I liked the fact she seemed to enjoy normal food and didn't care if a lettuce wedge with half a cherry tomato for garnish and a slice of lemon for taste was only thirty calories. Christ, or how filling that crap was to eat. It was all bullshit, and I'd had enough of those types of dinner dates to last me a lifetime.

"Can I ask you a question, Caleb?"

"You just did, but yes."

"Do you even *need* your Back Bay penthouse renovated?"

Yes indeed, she was a smart one. Made me hard every time she reminded me of that fact, too. "I'll let you be the judge once you see it."

"What if you don't like my interpretation of your vision for your home?"

"This is why I've hired you, Brooke. I need your ideas because I don't really have an opinion on décor or a particular vision for the place other than transforming it into something more family centered than it is now."

That got me an eyebrow raise. "Are you planning on starting a family soon?"

I went there in my mind. Yes, I fucking did. I could not stop myself from doing it, either. The image just appeared in my head as if its place was predestined, completely natural and what I envisioned for my future—Brooke holding a baby in her arms, and knowing both of them were mine. *Holy. Hell.* My heart started throbbing again. In march step with my dick. I was falling in too deep with her to pull myself back out again. And I knew it. There was nothing I could do differently with any of this evolving situation with her. The emotions and feelings of attachment to Brooke just kept piling up bit by bit, growing stronger by the day.

"Ah . . . eventually I will." *Not a lie.* Truth.

She cracked a grin that only curled up on one side, making her look sassy and sexy. "And you feel you should be prepared in advance for this future family?"

"Yes, Brooke, I am always prepared. Did I forget to mention that I am an Eagle Scout?" I winked and watched her blush for me again.

$$$

"YOU said you only came back to Boston five months ago when your grandmother had her accident. Where were you living before?"

I saw her eyes flick down and sensed discomfort. I was willing to drop the topic—anything to make her smile at me again—but she blew me out of the water with her answer.

"I was living in LA with my husband." *What the fuck?*

Not what I was expecting her to say. I looked at her left hand. No ring. And I would have known if she'd worn one the first time I laid eyes on her. I always check for wedding rings.

"You were married?" So very young . . .

A flash of pain filled her eyes, and then a sort of resignation before she answered me. "Yes, for a short time. He died in a car accident nearly a year ago, and our baby—I was in the car, too—was born too early to survive after the trauma from the accident put me into labor."

Holy. Fucking. Shit.

No wonder I'd recognized such sadness in her. And here I'd just joked about filling my penthouse with a family. I felt like an asshole.

"I am so sorry, Brooke." I picked up her hand and stroked over the top of it. "Fuck. Devastating. I can't imagine your pain. Your . . . sadness."

"Ah, yes my relationship with my friend Sadness is quite solid." She toyed with her wineglass as she spoke, and then after a long moment she looked up again.

I tilted my head in question, not getting the joke. I was probably in shock at what she'd just told me. *She's been married. Lost her husband and baby in a car accident.* I was reminded that when we meet people as we go through our daily lives, we really have zero understanding of what painful shit those poor souls have had to endure. No fucking idea at all. Thoughts of how Aldrich treated her that night made me want to kill the bastard now. I should pay that cocksucker a visit very fucking soon to enlighten the piece of dog shit on the matter of just who he had assaulted at a business reception.

"The movie, *Inside Out*? It's a wonderfully insightful animated Disney film about our individual inner emotions and how we need all of them working together in order to function properly. Sadness is my go-to girlfriend."

"I've never heard of that movie."

"I'm sure it's not your cup of tea, but perhaps you might watch it one day. You'd get it then."

"Will you watch it with me?" I asked.

"Maybe," she said shyly.

"You are very brave." I pulled her hand up to my lips and kissed the back of it. "That is all."

"I don't always feel brave, but I do try to be," she said, looking down at her wine again.

$$$

DINNER evolved into a nearly three-hour affair. Dessert, coffee, conversation that was interesting to the point I was really goddamn disappointed when we had to leave so she could make the 8:30 ferry. I actually hated the thought of her riding that ferry at night. *Fucking* hated it. But I held my tongue because I was certain she would tell me to mind my own goddamn business.

I had nothing to do with the worse-than-usual traffic. Monday Night Football at Gillette Stadium could take credit for that one.

And the steady rain.

And the four-car pileup that closed the main road down to the harbor.

I could sense Brooke getting more and more anxious as Isaac did his best to get her there in time.

But I am a filthy bastard, and as the minutes remaining until she missed the last boat to Blackstone Island ticked away, I fucking rejoiced silently in my seat beside her.

"No, no, no, Will, you left without me," she cursed against the window, looking very frustrated and utterly tantalizing sitting inside my car. We could all see the boat had pulled away from its berth and was already moving into open water. Nope. Brooke wouldn't be going home tonight. She would have to stay the night with me at the penthouse. I think my teeth were in danger of cracking from how hard I was grinding them together to hold back my victory yell.

I chose not to mention I owned a helicopter that could get her to the island in fifteen minutes. Nah, I wouldn't say anything about my helicopter to her, because I wanted her to stay.

I wanted her to stay with me more than I've ever wanted anything in my life.

Brooke

"You are welcome to stay at my place tonight. I have three guest rooms for you to choose from."

I knew Caleb would make the offer before he said the words. I could feel his eyes on me, burning at my back as I watched my ride home float away. A shiver rolled through my body as a feeling of impending change came over me—something big, and something over which I had absolutely no control. It was being set into motion right this very minute. And it scared me.

The partition drew closed with a quiet hum, giving us privacy from his driver. Another shiver shook me.

"Are you cold?" Caleb put his hand on my shoulder and gently pulled me closer.

"No." I turned away from the window and toward him. "I just—this was the very last thing I expected to happen."

He smelled so good. I had to fight the urge to fall into his arms just so I could breathe in more of the delicious sexy-man-scent thing he had going on. I was well aware my hormones were screaming, "Yes, bitch, do it now, please!" as they slapped me across the face.

It had been so long since I'd been held with any kind of tenderness. I was tempted to accept his invitation. His presence was commanding up against me on the seat, but he pulled it off without being the slightest bit threatening. Something I'd had ample experience with to know exactly how that felt . . . unfortunately.

He waited patiently for me to say something.

I didn't know why, but it felt as if Caleb was protecting me. It felt nice, but I needed a bit of clarification from him. He'd hired me for a massive job and had paid an enormous sum of money in the form of a retainer fee. I needed to believe he wasn't using his position over me to get sex. Was I supposed to just dance my way into his bed whenever he asked me to? Was he asking me to do that tonight? I didn't think Jon or Carlisle would throw me into a situation like that with a client, but Caleb was infusing a great deal of money into Harris & Goode. I imagined they didn't want to risk losing him by imposing restrictions—either moral or contractual.

"I don't think I should stay, Caleb. I—I really don't know what you want from me—what you are expecting . . ." Well, that sounded awkward. Did I just ask him that question? God. "But maybe I should get a hotel room—"

"I'm not expecting anything from you, Brooke. It's just an invitation from me to you because it's the right thing to do. I feel responsible for not delivering you in time to make your ferry. Now you're stuck in Boston for the night." He grinned at me in his cheeky way—the one he'd somehow perfected to look utterly devilish without the obnoxious and lewd. "I do have a big house and I'd like you to stay. And really, if you think about it this way, you *should* get a feel for the space you're going to be renovating. It can be preliminary research for the project."

I took a deep breath and considered his logic. He had a good point on getting to know the penthouse I'd been hired to design. I decided to be blunt and ask him the question I really wanted answered. I'd know better what to do after I'd heard from him. "But what is going on here with you and me?" I asked, flicking my fingers back and forth between us. "Is this you trying to get me into bed?"

"Literal answer or figurative?" he asked easily, as he reached for my hands and enfolded them in his to rest on his chest. "I won't lie and deny wanting to be with you. You've totally captivated me from the moment I first spoke to you. You're beautiful and funny and smart, Brooke. And I am a human male. Everything's in working order just as it should be." He tilted his head down toward his crotch and smirked. "Trust me."

I couldn't help cracking a smile at his announcement, but there was no way in hell I was going to get caught having a go at his cock, so I just focused on his blue-and-gold eyes instead. Why was this beautiful man so persistent with me? He could have any woman he wanted, and from the pictures on the Internet, he'd had many. Models, celebrities, heiresses: they were the women from his world, not someone like me. Caleb really didn't have a clear picture of my past. He might think he wanted me right now, and surely wasn't the first guy to think with the brain that lived in his trousers. But if he knew everything—he probably wouldn't want me then. I didn't know that answer yet.

I liked the feel of his hands around mine, but realized he'd conveniently trapped me by holding them together against his chest. He had me right where he wanted me. I stared at his lips and remembered how they'd felt against my cheek when he'd kissed me there: soft, determined, erotic even. I would wager Caleb Blackstone was spectacular in bed.

He drew even closer and whispered, "Let's just say I won't turn you away if you find yourself considering it."

I tugged my hands out of his grip. "Well, thank you for the honesty, but I won't fall into bed with you, Caleb. I don't do that with men I've just met—"

He put two fingers gently on my mouth and stopped me. "That was my literal answer, Brooke. The figurative one goes something like this: Of course I don't *expect* you to sleep with me. I'm not trying to take advantage of you, and this is not some orchestrated seduction on my part. I'm just letting you know I'm very interested. Nothing has to happen that you don't want to happen. And nothing will happen unless you want it to. I will always respect your choices."

Well, he said all the right things. I'd give him props on that. I supposed it was stupid to pretend I wasn't feeling attracted to him. I totally was. I could tell he was attracted to me. Again, not a surprise, but I knew it was just biology at work.

"Better answer?" he asked, with a smile.

I nodded again. "Thank you again for being such a gentleman. It's a very different experience for me."

"Why does that bother me and please me at the same time?" he asked wryly.

"I said it was a different experience for me, not that I didn't like it."

"I know. I can work with it, beautiful Brooke Casterley with the sexy voice."

Deep trouble. Did I mention I was in very deep trouble with this man? "All right, Caleb Blackstone with the beautiful eyes, I accept your invitation to stay over at your penthouse, but on one condition."

"Name it," he fired back confidently.

"You're taking me to Target first so I can get a few things for this slumber party you've invited me to."

He clearly did not expect me to demand a shopping trip to a discount store like Target—whose doors he'd probably never darkened—but maybe Caleb liked surprises, because he threw his head back and laughed.

Then he lowered the partition and said, "Isaac, Miss Casterley would like to go to Tar-zhay."

$$$

CALEB appeared amused as he followed me around Target, gathering up the things I wanted. He pushed the cart for me but didn't say a lot. Mostly he observed, and I had the strangest feeling he was taking notes in his head as if he was . . . learning. Had he never been inside a Target before? Did billionaires even shop for themselves, or did other people do it for them? I would never allow someone to shop for me. I loved shopping, and lucky for me it was a huge part of my job to search out the unique and artful accent pieces that *made* the room and showcased the individuality of the client. Flea markets were some of my favorite places to find treasures. I wondered if Caleb had ever been to anything like a flea market.

Nothing was more uncomfortable than being stranded without necessities in a strange place. If this was indeed going to be my first experience with the space I'd be transforming, then I wanted to enter into the process on my terms and feeling at ease. Which meant having my own toothbrush, some clean knickers, and something to wear to work tomorrow morning at the very minimum. I always carried a bit of makeup around in my bag, so I was covered on that end. I didn't like going faceless, either. I loved my makeup and that was just my preference. Maybe it gave me some sort of perceived shield from the world, but I totally needed it.

I found a really soft sweaterdress in black that hit just above the knees. It would do nicely for work tomorrow and would pair well with my boots. A large-checked, fringed scarf in cream and black pulled it all together. In the lingerie section I grabbed a three-pack of lace boy-shorts knickers in pink, baby blue, and black polka dots. I watched for Caleb's reaction when I tossed the package into the cart.

He was paying attention all right.

Because he picked up my new knickers and gave them a thorough inspection before bestowing another one of his signature cheeky grins.

All men were such teenage boys at heart—apparently even a sophisticated billionaire couldn't keep back the giggles when holding a pack of ladies' panties in his hand.

"Are you enjoying yourself, Caleb?" I couldn't help asking the question.

"Very much, Brooke," he answered quickly. "Thank you for bringing us to Target. It's quite a different experience for me."

It was very close to what I'd said to him earlier about him being a gentleman. "I'm almost finished. I just need to find something warm for sleeping and a weekender bag." I plucked the pack of knickers away from him and tossed it back into the cart.

Again with the cheeky smile.

I had the insane urge to bury my fingers in his purposely mussed hair just so I could feel it for myself. He smiled lazily at me and proceeded to make my hormones put on their slut show inside my head. Very. Deep. Trouble.

"No rush at all, Brooke. I said it was a different experience for me, not that I didn't like it."

And my same words used back on me a second time. Or was it the third? The man was a dedicated tease, but I had to admit he was also very adorable whilst doing it. An idea hit me that Caleb was paying attention to everything in Target as I shopped—for a reason. He was committing his new knowledge to memory and filing it away.

A flannel pajama set in black and very pale pink, and some soft thick gray socks took care of sleepwear for me. I also spied a black felt bolero and couldn't resist taking it after trying it on in front of a mirror. It would look perfect with my new sweaterdress, I rationalized. "I have a slight hat fetish . . . er . . . problem," I admitted.

"Good to know, Brooke. Please, feel free to keep on sharing your secrets. I'm taking notes."

I was right. Caleb *was* taking notes in his head. He remembered everything. It was probably the secret to his success in business . . .

which just reminded me, yet again, of my curiosity as to why he was interested in me. Why, when we came from such polar opposite worlds?

He left me to do some shopping in another part of the store when I went to the travel section to find a weekender bag. I just wanted something inexpensive, but capable of holding all my purchases. An orange-and-gray woven bag in an Aztec print fit the bill perfectly. I knew I would put the thing to good future use as well. In my line of work, I *always* needed bags to carry around the plethora of crap I discovered for decorating.

Lastly, I cruised through the trial sizes of toiletries and selected the necessities: toothbrush, toothpaste, shampoo and conditioner, a hairbrush, deodorant, body lotion, and some moisturizer for my face. A waterproof cosmetic bag to house everything and I was done.

My rather-filled shopping trolley was now ready for the checkout line. I texted Caleb from line as the attendant rang me up. I'm finished. Checking out now.

I headed for the Starbucks located inside the store as I looked over my receipt. All of my awesome loot had come to a grand total of 167 dollars. Not bad at all, I thought. I knew I'd get good use out of everything I'd bought, even if I hadn't planned on shopping for any of it tonight. I stuffed the receipt into one of the bags and felt my phone vibrate with Caleb's reply: Wait for me, please. In Electronics . . . almost done.

Ok. I've already paid. I'll be in the Starbucks --> front of the store. What would you like me to get for you?

He didn't answer so I assumed he didn't want anything.

"So I have a grande pumpkin-spice latte decaf for Brooke. That'll be five twenty-five."

I handed over my debit card to the barista, but he didn't take it from me. His attention was focused on someone else behind me because he nodded and mouthed, "okay."

Then I felt Caleb's hand on my hip as he put an arm around me. "I've got this, and I'll have a venti flat white," he said, and handed over a solid black American Express card. I did a double take because I'd never seen one before. I don't think the barista had, either, because he gave it a good stare as well. It dawned on me it must suck to have people speculating on how rich you were whenever you paid for something normal at a place like Starbucks with a black AmEx card. The problems of the rich . . .

I looked up at Caleb and smiled but he wouldn't look at me. In fact, he'd lost the easygoing expression altogether and looked rather annoyed.

"Did you find what you went searching for?" I asked as we waited for our coffees.

"Yes," he answered as he tapped out something on his phone. He put it in his pocket and then gave me his attention. "Why did you check out and pay without me?"

Huh? "I beg your pardon?" I wasn't letting him pay for my knickers and toothpaste for Christ's sake.

"It's a simple question." He didn't look annoyed anymore but rather surprised if I had to put a name to it.

"Because I'd finished my shopping and it was time to pay for my things and leave the store. I didn't think I needed permission to go through the checkout line, Caleb. In fact, I *know* I don't." His concern was confusing. "I texted so you would know where I was. You brought me here. I wasn't planning on ditching you if you were worried." I shook my head at him. "Why should you care that I've paid for *my* things?"

He laughed and smiled for me again, his earlier mood restored. "Forget it, beautiful. Let's just say this is all a new experience for me and leave it at that, okay?"

"Shopping at Target not to your liking?" I asked, hoping he would tell me how he really felt.

He pulled me in closer and pressed his lips to my forehead. I felt his lips move across my skin and heard him whisper softly, "Everything about tonight has been to my liking."

Thank God he was holding me up because I rather melted into a puddle of goo after that.

Deep. Fucking. Trouble.

Caleb

Isaac texted his reply in the form of a photo scan of her Target receipt because I'd told him to find it when he put our bags in the car. Only $167.44 for all of that shit she just bought? Unbelievable. In fact, just about everything about her was unbelievable. She was completely indifferent about what I could buy *for* her—she only seemed interested in me, the person. I made a screenshot of her text asking if she could get me something from Starbucks. It rarely happened that anyone offered to buy me anything, and the women I sometimes dated *never* offered. Not that I ever expected them to, but it was nice to be asked once every six months.

Brooke was so different, so guileless in everything she did. She'd weighed her decision on whether she could stay over with me and then named her condition to make it possible. Understandably she wanted to feel comfortable and have the things she needed with her. Target just got 167 dollars of her money, and she got some peace of mind in return. A good exchange. And the fact the goddamn place was open until midnight on a Monday night was a fucking bonus. I'd seen a sign in the store that said you could shop online and pick up in the store. I could send someone to go get it after I'd shopped from my phone. The place carried just about everything anyone could possibly want. I'd been suitably impressed with the electronics in particular. Lucas's iInVidiosa was there on an end-cap display, front and center. Being impressed was something that rarely happened for me.

I'd make sure she was reimbursed the amount of the receipt as an out-of-pocket expense on the renovation, but I wasn't telling her tonight. She would protest the reimbursement no doubt, ergo the reason to shelve the issue for a later time.

I didn't want to hear protests from her right now.

Because right now I had Brooke close to me in the back of the car as we sipped our coffees and watched the rain still steadily pouring down over the city in a kind of cleansing baptism.

Kind of like how I felt, too.

She's coming home with me.

$$$

"YOUR view is stunning, Caleb. City lights at night are my favorite." When I brought Brooke into this room, she headed straight for the wall of windows and looked out at the city with the Charles River stretched out in a wide arc.

"I agree; it is stunning." She was talking about the view. Brooke had no idea my stunning view was her looking out at the city lights reflecting over the river on a rainy night. Those long legs encased in tall sexy boots topped with a short green skirt, her wavy blonde hair spilling down the back of her black velvet jacket, the contrast of colors she chose against her skin and hair—all of it perfection. I needed to feel her hair in my hands. I *needed* my hands on her.

The moment she'd come into my house, I knew she belonged here. The whole experience was crazy and impulsive for me. Things were moving quickly with her—far too fast in fact, but there was no slow-down in progress on my end that I could tell. I just kept pushing and seeing where it would lead. I knew it was too soon for me to be feeling this way about Brooke, but that didn't make my feelings go away. If anything, I wanted her even more. I would let her tell me when she was ready, and then the second that happened, I knew there would be no possibility for me to turn back.

I just knew.

My father was right on the money when he'd said I would know when the right girl came along. I was looking at her right now. I had found her.

"Caleb, I think I know just how to redesign this room to make the view stand out even more."

Just stay here forever and that'll do it. "That's great you're already getting some good concepts for designs. See, wasn't this a great idea I had for you to get acquainted with the space?"

She turned her head back to smile at me. "Yes," she said shyly. "I can't believe I'll be working with all of this." She lifted both hands up. "The interior has marvelous bones, Caleb. I can't wait to see the rest of it, especially the garden on the rooftop."

Marvelous bones—marvelous everything. "Hopefully it won't be raining tomorrow and you can stroll around up there." I moved behind her where she stood at the window and breathed her in. She smelled like oranges to me. It was an intoxicating scent that drew me in like a moth to a flame, careless of the heat that would eventually incinerate its wings.

Is that what would happen to me? Would the heat of my desire for her incinerate me?

"Oh, I hope so," she agreed. "I want to explore everything in the daylight."

Me too. "Are you tired?" I asked.

"You know, not very. Must be the multiple cups of coffee I drank far too late in the day."

"Well, would you like to watch a movie with me?"

"Which movie?"

"This girl I know recommended it. She is very passionate about certain things and this movie is one of them. I picked it up just tonight on her recommendation. Something to do with emotions and giving them each their rightful place."

"Caleb? You bought *Inside Out*?" She spun around to face me, and I realized I couldn't resist her anymore. Not one more second of time was going to pass before I got the chance to know what it felt like to kiss her.

"Mmm-hmm." I took her face in my hands and went for it. Slowly at first, with just lips touching . . . but it wasn't enough.

I doubted I would ever find *enough* with her. The instant I had her mouth against mine I only wanted to experience more of her. I pushed in tentatively with my tongue and paused for her reaction, praying she would let me in. If I didn't find a way inside her somehow, I would probably fucking die. It sure felt that way.

Soft. She was soft when she opened her mouth against my invasion. I tasted her pumpkin latte from earlier and groaned into her mouth. Spicy. Sweet. And so fucking soft as she responded to me. I played with her lips, sucking and pulling on them with just a scrape of teeth, over and over again. She liked it. I could tell. Beautiful Brooke kissed me back, her tongue tangling with mine as she explored me at her own pace—and allowed me to do the same. Her hands found their way into my hair where she buried them in and tugged me closer. *Oh, that felt fucking good to have her hands in my hair.*

I held her in my hands and enjoyed the very best kiss of my lifetime. Kissing Brooke held no comparison to anything that came along before—

She pulled away abruptly, and that did *not* feel so nice. As I fought off the unpleasant feeling of the loss of her lips against mine, it took me a second to register we weren't alone—that someone was speaking in the room. Shock was more like it. I'd been so into kissing her I hadn't even heard Isaac come in. Brooke had heard him, though.

"Sir, where would you like Miss Casterley's purchases to be delivered?" Isaac asked from behind me.

"The room across the hall from mine." I answered him without turning around. I stared down at Brooke's soft pink lips instead and liked seeing them puffy from what I'd just been doing to her. Then I got a good look at her eyes and saw how they revealed the evidence of passion in their fiery golden depths as she gazed up at me.

I fucking *loved* that.

I reached for her again, but she stopped me with her palm against my chest. I could feel a slight tremble in her touch as she held me back. "I think we should watch *Inside Out* now."

"Okay," I said, remembering my vow to let her set the pace. It had to be that way or this wasn't going to work. I did understand clearly now after her revelation at dinner. Brooke was a woman who needed some level of control over her situation because the terrible loss of her husband and baby had afforded her none. I got it.

"I just—I'd like to be comfortable while we watch it." She gestured down to her boots.

"Of course. You should change and get comfortable. I'll show you to your room and then just come back out here when you're ready. I'll change, too. We want to enjoy this together."

She nodded and did that thing where she rolled her lips together as if she was suppressing a smile. I knew it because her golden eyes still smiled at me.

At the door to her bedroom, she turned back toward me, looking a little hesitant but still determined. "We're just going to watch the movie, Caleb."

Ahh . . . the rules for the night were being set. I could live with her rules as long as she kept letting me in a little bit at a time. I could be patient.

I couldn't resist brushing her blushing cheek with my thumb, though. "We're just going to watch the movie, Brooke."

She smiled at me, and I fell a little bit more in love with her.

$$$

THIS evening had to be one of the most interesting I'd ever experienced. For one thing, I'd never done anything like it before. My agenda with women after we'd retired behind closed doors was all about getting naked and fucking. End of. Once it was over, I went on my way. I never stayed the night with any of them. Janice had "slept" here a total of two nights in six months, and she was the only one who had ever received an invitation.

I'd never worn sweats and a T-shirt while cuddling on the sofa to watch an animated film. I don't think I'd watched anything animated since *Toy Story* when I was eleven, to be honest.

Brooke was still gorgeous, even with her hair in a long braid and thick gray socks on her feet. The pink flannel pants she'd picked out at Target swallowed up the shape of her killer legs but I liked knowing she was comfortable and warm after a long, cold, rainy day.

Inside Out was a total surprise. More so the enjoyment I got from watching Brooke watch the movie. She knew it by heart, but she didn't do anything spoilerish to ruin it for me. She let me hold her close against me with my arm around her so I could get my fingers woven into her thick braid. I already had a fascination with her hair and ached to have it spread out with my hands buried in it. We played the dancing fingers game with my other hand. I'd never done that with anyone before, either.

But I would have happily danced fingers with her all night long.

It was close to midnight when the credits started rolling, and I knew it was time to end the party. Bedtime. She was falling asleep and I was almost there myself. I wasn't disappointed, though. *Was this what normal couples did? The boyfriend-girlfriend thing?* The whole evening with her had been better than anything I'd ever done, and I'd happily accept any more evenings like this one that she might generously throw my way. I knew I'd get to see her in the morning, too, and I couldn't fucking wait to experience the whole breakfast-before-work thing with her.

So I helped her up from the couch and delivered her to the guest room with only one sleepy kiss goodnight. "Thank you, Caleb, for inviting me to stay here," she said while stifling a yawn, "and for being patient . . . with me." She held the side of my face with her hand and studied me with her beautiful amber eyes. "I love that you are always such a gentleman."

Again, something I'd not been before—not with any woman I'd ever wanted sexually at least. Even as I had the thought, I understood it was far more than sex with Brooke. It was just a driving *want* to be with her.

"Thank you, Brooke, for accepting my invitation to stay here tonight," I whispered against her lips because I liked to mimic her words. "And for giving me the chance to deserve you whenever you're ready," I added before stealing another kiss.

The conversation we had before saying goodnight was pretty damn surreal when I stopped to think about the topic—to fuck or not to fuck. The contrast between how strange, and how normal it felt to discuss it with her, was starting to mess with my head.

No. Not true. My head was messed up from the minute she first spoke to me.

$$$

HER crying woke me sometime later. Once I figured out what I was hearing, I listened in like a voyeur, imagining the reasons she was plagued by terrible grief.

A shout of anguish, so great it gave me pain just hearing it, cut a path straight into my heart. Then softer sounds of crying followed, burrowing underneath my skin until I couldn't take it another second.

I bolted out of bed and threw on the sweats I'd worn earlier. And then I went into her room and scooped her up into my arms. She didn't even protest when I carried her across the hall and put her into my bed. Or when I crawled in next to her and pulled her against my body.

She just cried. And let me hold her and run my fingers over her hair.

It was the most natural thing in the world, and so I just went with it, figuring she would start talking if she wanted to.

"I dreamed of the accident. I never have before . . . that I can remember," she said eventually.

"Tell me about your husband."

"It's not a nice story. I don't think you'll want to hear it because you won't feel good afterward."

"But I want to comfort you. Help you feel better. Will talking about it help, Brooke?" I breathed in the flowery scent of her hair and focused on the sensation of having her against me.

"It will probably help me to feel better, but not you," she said.

"How can you know that?"

"I know, Caleb. What you said at dinner about my aura of sadness is correct. It's there with me. I've learned that being honest and open about the reasons for it is what works for me. I don't keep it a secret. People know what happened to me, and I am sure they feel very sorry for my pain. It's a totally normal response for them to feel that way. But it doesn't help me to *deal* with my sadness. It's just something that's with me now and I've learned to embrace it, and I've also learned how hearing the story of my *loss* is uncomfortable for most people. I don't want to do that to you."

"You won't be doing anything to me, Brooke. Why don't you want to tell me?"

"Because I like you very much."

"I like you very much, too, and I'm here to listen if you feel like talking about it." I kissed her forehead and just held her, grateful she allowed me.

In time she started to tell me her story . . .

"The last words I remember saying to him were, 'Marcus, you're drunk—let me drive.' A punishing grip to my chin and throat came immediately after my comment. 'Don't,' was all he said to me. *Don't* was the last word Marcus ever spoke to me. It was all he needed to say. The rest of his cruel message was written in his pale-blue eyes that had always looked gray to me. My punishment would come once we were out of sight from the prying eyes of his family, and the few compassionate souls who knew of his perverse mind fucking, but were powerless to do anything to help me."

A chill settled on me as I grappled with what she might say next.

"It would be more of an emotional punishment than a physical one, because that was just how Marcus was. He never beat me outright, but he loved to scare me, and make me frightened of what he might do. When I went to put on my seat belt, he blocked my hand, forcing me to leave it off. He did it to make me afraid, because he knew I didn't trust his driving, and because it was putting the baby at risk. My first punishment for the night. But it turned out to be a gift instead. The last good thing he ever gave me. It ended up being my ticket to freedom."

No . . .

"I didn't even see what caused the crash because I'd closed my eyes as soon as he drove away. I never knew whatever it was that caused him to veer off the road, nor did I hear anything other than the excruciatingly loud music he put on. I'd closed my eyes and willed it all away because that was how I conquered my fear."

I held her a bit tighter.

"That's all I remember before I woke up in hospital three weeks later. My injuries had nearly healed completely by the time I woke from my coma—a badly lacerated right knee and calf, and also cuts to the right side of my head at the hairline as I was ejected from the car upon impact. Marcus was wearing his seat belt, so he remained in the car as it exploded and burned."

Just like the vile fucker deserved.

"When the doctor told me my husband had died in the accident, I wept deeply as one would expect. When that same doctor held my hand comfortingly and told me the severe blow I'd suffered as I was ejected from the car had brought on preterm labor they were unable to stop—making it impossible to prevent the birth of my baby daughter at only twenty-three weeks gestation. Not enough development time to survive outside of my womb, he said. Her little life was over before it ever began. I cried even harder and longer for her loss, but inside I felt the most intense relief. I rejoiced that she had escaped what would have been a hellish nightmare, being born into that evil family. I wouldn't have been able to protect her, and that would have killed me slowly bit by bit. The fact I'd lost Marcus's baby was the only reason his family let me go. If I'd managed to stay pregnant, then I would have been bound forever—inescapably owned by a family of criminals to whom blood meant everything. I owed my baby thanks for her gift to me even more so than her father. She made it possible for me to start over."

She's been through so much. Too much.

"So I stayed in California for another six months, recovering. Physically I was fine, but I needed some time before I was ready to come back. I didn't want to face the many expressions of sorrow and the heartfelt condolences for my loss when it had really been my only way of escaping the hell I'd been in for a year. I couldn't tell them that I'd hated my sociopathic husband who'd impregnated me against my wishes when I was barely twenty-two years old." She burrowed her face into the crook of my neck and shoulder, and sighed deeply as if she was breathing me in. "That—that's all I can talk about tonight," she said. "It takes me back there and I don't want to go back. I want to go forward now, Caleb."

So do I. I had been holding my breath listening to her story, and now needed air. For breathing—so I didn't asphyxiate.

Holy fucking shit was about the extent of my immediate reaction to what she'd just shared. "I am so sorry, Brooke. I hardly know what to say." And I didn't. Christ, what a harrowing journey she'd been on in her short life. I could barely process all she'd just told me, let alone imagine how she managed to hold herself together most days. Brooke had certainly been dealt a shit hand of cards in losing her parents at fifteen, and then this—this—ordeal she'd endured, and for which there were no motherfucking words.

"There isn't much to say, Caleb, and anyway, I feel your sympathy and that's enough," she said softly.

"Was your grandmother's surgery the reason you came back to Boston?" I doubted there was much to have brought her back here otherwise.

"Yes. Actually, I think it was Nan's terrible worry for me that led to her fall down the cellar steps in the first place. She wasn't even notified I'd been in a coma. Nan didn't know anything until after it was over. After the fall she needed me, and so it was time to come home to the island. Having a purpose has helped me so very much. Coming back here five months ago was the very best thing I could have ever done. It is healing me back into my former self. I'm not a sad person, Caleb, I've just had some very sad things happen to me. I love my job, and I love my cottage on the island, and I love my . . . friends."

"Brooke?"

"Yes?"

"I am so fucking glad you came back home."

"Me too, Caleb."

We stayed close in the bed for a while. Quiet and just breathing in and out. Peaceful.

"Caleb, I want to ask you something," she whispered.

"Okay."

"My story—now that you've heard it, do you still want to be with me?"

I held her a little closer and kissed the top of her head. "Yes, Brooke, I want to be with you more than you can imagine." *I want to be the one to make you forget him. I want to be the one who loves you how you should have been loved in the first place. To make you feel safe, adored, cherished.* "The harrowing story you've just told me changes nothing about what I think or feel. If anything, I am in awe of you. You are brave. Very, very brave, Brooke Casterley."

"You are a wonderful man with a generous heart, Caleb Blackstone, and don't let anyone ever make you feel otherwise." Then she sighed deeply and detached herself from me with a small, sexy moan.

Fuck! She was going to leave my room and go back to her bed now. I didn't want her to go because I wanted to sleep with her in my arms for the rest of the night. Hell, I needed it after the terrifying tale she'd just told me.

Her second question surprised me. "Would you mind if I used your shower? I just need to clear my head and I think the hot water will help."

"Please do whatever will make you feel better," I said, mentally castrating myself in advance for all of the filthy dirty thoughts I was going to have about her once she was wet and naked in my shower. My cock would suffer, but it would survive being denied.

"Thank you," she said softly as she left my bed and padded toward the bathroom.

The light came on and then a few seconds later, the water. It took a moment for me to realize she'd left the door wide open. I could see everything as she stood in front of the bathroom mirror, completely still and staring back out at me using the mirror's reflection.

Holy. Fucking. Hell. She *wanted* me to see her. Me. Her. No one had *ever* so gently and yet confidently offered themselves to me. She wasn't using me. She wanted me. She wanted me to want her. I would never forget this for as long as I lived. It was all for me. *For me.*

I knew why she did it, too.

Brooke did it to let me know she wanted me the same way I wanted her. Fuck. Me.

If I am so lucky to live a long life, I will always remember how absolutely fucking beautiful she was when she stripped in my doorway—backlit in soft white light—just so I could watch every graceful movement . . . as her clothes fell away to reveal the most perfect vision in the world. Her. Naked. *Mine.*

Brooke

Caleb could help me forget. Even if just for this one night, it would be a gift I would treasure forever because he was the first to make it possible for me after Marcus. I might never have had sex again in my life if I hadn't met Caleb.

So, when I made my decision to be with him, it was for the hope of healing that last part of me still broken.

Caleb was unique and I realized it right away. He had the magic combination I needed in order to take this step with someone. There was the desire for me that I recognized, and my attraction for him, of course—but, it was the way in which he was so patient and careful in showing me he wanted me which allowed me to trust him. I'd never felt as cherished as when he pulled me into his arms and brought me to his bedroom.

Somehow, I knew I could trust Caleb with my body. He would make me forget the horrible nightmare of Marcus. He would give me pleasure. He could make me whole again, and he'd do it all without trying to trap me, or control me, or hurt me. I didn't want to think about anything more than just this night—my first with a man who made me feel like a desirable woman instead of a whore to fuck.

And I wanted him.

As he'd held me close in his huge bed, stroking over my hair and touching me with tenderness I'd never really known from anyone before, I knew what I wanted to do.

I waited until I was sure he was watching me in the doorway of his bathroom before I started getting naked.

Socks were the first to go. I peeled them off and dropped them to the marble floor, first one and then the other.

I put my hands on the hem of the soft black shirt and drew it up and over my head. My breasts were dragged upward from the friction of the fabric pulling on them before their weight brought them back down with a bounce. I imagined Caleb seeing my naked breasts and shivered. I felt my nipples harden into tight, aching knots at the thought of him watching me from his bed in the darkness.

My fingers shook as I dug them into the waistband of my flannel pajama bottoms and shimmied out of them. I kicked them aside with my foot and took a deep breath. I could feel his eyes on me, but the darkness beyond the light kept me blinded to him as I finished the final act of my strip show.

My new baby-blue knickers were the last to go. I turned away from him and faced the shower now pumping out clouds of hot steam, and slipped them off.

I tried to slow my thumping heart as I stepped carefully into the travertine-tiled grotto. Hot water poured over me from above out of three huge rain showerheads in a delicious soaking of body and spirit. Since there was no door for the shower, I didn't hear him when he stepped in to join me.

I only felt his presence, sensing the change in the water spray as his body came into its path.

His hand a gentle weight on my shoulder, his lips a soft brush on the other side where my shoulder met the base of my neck. I fell back against him and let him support my weight as he kissed up my neck and found his way to a breast with his hand. He cupped it, taking the weight and pushing the flesh up before squeezing down on the center. My nipple tightened even more when he tugged on it with two fingers. I felt myself letting go of all inhibitions as he worked on me. Caleb knew just how to touch me and make me forget everything except for him, and what he could make me feel.

His hands and lips wandered everywhere, his touch gentle—but determined, his kisses reverent—but demanding. Perfection . . . as he awakened feelings in me I didn't even know existed.

I was turned to face him with strong hands that held me back a distance. "I want to see you—every beautiful inch of you," he said, his words thick with desire. Then he backed me into the wall until I was flat against it, exposed with nothing between us but hot water falling from above in a simulation of rain. The only sound was the rush of the streaming jets of water pounding down to the floor.

His eyes flared as they roamed over my body, giving me the thrill of knowing he was affected by what he saw. But I was more interested in what he had on display. Caleb was a magnificent specimen of the male form in every way. Cut muscles shaped his arms and wide shoulders, which tapered down to washboard abs that melted into a carved V of masculine beauty that took my breath away. One spectacularly beautiful man.

One spectacularly beautiful man, with a really impressive cock at the end of his sexy happy trail, hard with wanting. Wanting me and straining to get to me.

On a low breath that started and ended with my name, he knelt before me and put his hands down on the tops of my feet. He found my scars immediately and ran his lips along the lines in slow, worshipful, healing kisses that inched upward bit by bit. I shuddered at the image of him drawing his tongue up the inside of my thigh as he masterfully positioned my right leg over his shoulder. But then, I put up no resistance, because the obsessive need to have him keep going ruled every other possible thought.

The first draw of his tongue over my sex pulled a raw cry out of me. I gripped the shower wall with the flat of my hands to keep myself from slipping down to the floor. Caleb licked and sucked me to the brink of an orgasm with his magical tongue, swirling over my clit and then sucking it deep between his soft lips framed with the prickly stubble of his beard. The contrast of soft and sharp sent me over all in an instant, on one glorious rush.

"Caleb . . . I—I'm c-coming n-n-now—" I lost the ability to vocalize. Didn't care about anything anymore . . . except feeling what he was giving me.

"Mmm-hmm, beautiful, you are," I heard him say against my pussy as I blew apart into a million pieces, drowning in pleasure, fighting to breathe.

I became aware of being carried out of the shower and set down upon a hard surface. The counter? "You are so fucking gorgeous when you come."

I moaned at the reminder of something so perfect I was sure I would never forget. "It felt fucking gorgeous," I replied.

"I—I need you now, Brooke." He held my face in his hands as if he was asking for permission, his dark-blue eyes piercing into me.

I nearly wept from the gesture. "Yes."

He pulled a warm towel down from the rack and dried me off in between desperate kisses that stole my breath away. "You looked beautiful—so fucking sexy stripping for me. I almost came from watching you," he said as he circled my breasts with the towel. "I want to make you come like that for me—all night long." Then he tossed the towel away. The words he spoke meant everything to me. I could almost believe none of the bad had ever happened, because of how Caleb was with me right now.

I reached for him and raked my hands over the planes and valleys of his chest, traveling south with my hands until I gripped the hard length of his rigid cock. He bit down on his lip and threw his head back as I stroked up and down, learning the feel of the satin skin surrounding his flesh as hard as bone. I wanted—no, I *needed* Caleb inside me.

He fumbled around in a cupboard to my left and produced a handful of condoms, with several packets scattering all around as they fell to a soft landing. The crazy thought danced through my head of his comment about an Eagle Scout always being prepared, apparently even while having sex on the bathroom counter. But it went right on out of my mind just as quickly when I watched him tear one open and sheath himself. His penis was beautiful, and I wanted it in me. Like right now would be a lovely time for it.

Caleb kissed me decadently with his tongue probing deep in an almost frantic plea as he hooked a hand behind each of my knees and spread me open. He took his cock in hand and aligned it right where it *needed* to be . . . and buried it all the way inside me on a deep slide.

"Fuuuck!"

"Ahhhh!"

We both shouted in perfect synchronization.

We both watched our bodies joining in the most primitive of ways as he worked his cock in and out in piercing thrusts. I had to close my eyes after a moment because the image of us fucking was really too much intimacy for me to take in all at once. I just wanted to experience the sensation and pleasure of him right now. Just feel.

Caleb must have sensed where I was in my head because he found my mouth again and kissed away any doubts that tried to creep in. He linked his hands under my bum and carried me, still impaled on him, to his soft bed. "This is where I want to fuck for the first time. In my bed, beautiful, where you belong," he told me as I was laid out upon ultrasoft sheets that smelled of him.

Where I belong?

Do I belong in Caleb's bed? The idea was crazy, but I couldn't deny I loved hearing it from him. His care for me was something priceless and ironically put me in danger of falling for him. Danger . . . I couldn't risk. I knew I couldn't fall in love with Caleb Blackstone. Sex. Recreational fucking. Taking pleasure in the act was all we would be able to have together. It would have to be enough for the both of us.

"But I have to see you while we do it." He fumbled with something and the lights came on in the room that'd been darkened for sleep.

"Yes me, too," I said, drawing my hands down to frame the perfect V between his hips, and admiring the godlike body connected with mine.

I got my wish.

I got to see everything in the light as we fought to find that beautiful, terrifying, exquisite end . . . together.

Caleb took my hands and dragged them over my head, trapping my wrists together with one hand, and gripped my hip with the other. Pinned in place beneath him, I got a bold taste of dominant Caleb, and it pushed me even closer toward a second orgasm I knew was barreling toward me.

Then he started to really fuck—hard, deep plunges that bottomed out inside the heart of me, filling me to the brink with his thick male flesh, giving me a jolt of pleasure with each slide. I despaired whenever he would pull his cock away, just to rejoice when he drove it back in.

I felt all the magical goodness to be had in sexual intimacy—for the first time in my life.

And I caught glimpses of him straining beautifully above me, his lean muscles tight with tension, golden skin glistening with water and sweat as he took me. I gave myself up, but Caleb took me . . . just as

I'd wanted him to. He was making me forget . . . just as I'd hoped he would.

Deep down inside me I felt his cock swell and harden even more, and knew the end was near. His hand pinning me down at my hip was removed as I felt his fingers slide over to stroke my sensitive clit. He was making sure I found my end. Bless him.

"Come with me. Come with me, Brooke. I—want—to—come—with—you," he growled harshly, sounding almost savage in his need.

"I aaaaaaam." The pulse started within me as I said it. I let myself fall over the razor's edge into the glorious river of pleasure as Caleb throbbed out his own release in pounding pulls to draw out every last bit of perfect heavenly goodness.

Bless Caleb Blackstone for giving me something I'd never been given before by another man. Adoration.

I might just fall in love with him after all, I thought, as I drifted away into nirvana with him still inside me.

Caleb

My world grew exponentially smaller in the space of one day. My world was named Brooke Casterley, and she was the most beautiful creature I'd ever seen as we came together in an explosive melding of our bodies. As my heart pounded down from the orgasm, and I struggled to comprehend what'd just happened, I realized it had been much more than a melding of bodies for me. It had been the melding of my heart with hers. I could tell myself it wasn't possible to feel any different after a session of really good sex, but I would be dead wrong. Because everything was different. Nothing was familiar when it came to Brooke. Each new thing we shared together felt to me as if I'd never done it before, and more importantly, as if I never wanted to do it again with anyone *other than her*—ever.

What could that possibly mean . . . unless I really was in love with her?

I pulled out of her carefully so we wouldn't have a condom accident, and was rewarded with the sound of her muffled protest at me leaving. Another first. Wanting to reassure her that I would be right back was also something I'd never had the urge to do—before now. "Be right back, beautiful. Do you need anything?" I couldn't resist tracing her lips with my finger.

She put her lips around the tip of my finger and sucked lightly. "Just you to come back and keep your promise," she said, shyly looking up at me all soft and pleasured from her climax. And beautifully naked.

Hell yes, I knew exactly what promise that would be. My caveman brain still remembered the vow I'd made just after we left the shower. The one about me making her come all night long.

Yes, I was in total-without-a-fucking-doubt love with this girl, right here.

"I will. And I will."

Only a moron would waste a lot of time in the bathroom cleaning the cum off his cock if his beautiful woman was waiting naked for him in the bed. So, no, I did not waste time. But I did pick her clothes up from the floor and fold them so she would see them when she came in here later. I collected up all of the spilled condom packets and put them back in the box, too. Then I took three out again and checked myself in the mirror. *Yeah, that's you wearing the shit-eating grin.*

A shit-eating grin because Brooke wanted me keeping my promises, and like the Eagle Scout I am, I had every intention of keeping the very first oath on the list: a scout is trustworthy. *Yes, why yes, I am trustworthy.*

I fixed the lighting in the room before I got back into bed with her because I couldn't bear not being able to at least see a little bit. I opened the blinds on the wall of windows so the city lights would illuminate my bedroom. I never did that because it was too much light for me to sleep comfortably, but sleep wasn't really on my agenda at the moment. I needed *some* light so I could see Brooke as I made her come for me . . . all—night—long.

$$$

SHE really did have the most beautiful tits in the world. The most stunning pair I'd ever met, hands down. Their shape was like a peach, perfectly round with just the slightest upward tilt at the nipples. I'm talking Victoria's Secret lingerie–model perfection, but all-natural just the way God had made her.

The show she was giving me right now was probably doing permanent damage to my corneas, but I didn't care. If the last sight my eyes ever saw on this earth was her gorgeous tits bouncing in my face while she rode my cock, then I'd be the happiest goddamn blind man on the planet with that beautiful image to comfort me.

I held one soft breast in each hand and pinched the tips at the same time just to hear the sexy gasp of pleasure I knew she would make. She squeezed her inner muscles around my cock in response, and I knew I was going to fucking go over the edge again. But not until I took her along with me.

I got my fingers between us and worked her slippery nub until I felt another squeeze gripping tight around my cock. "Say my name when you come, baby, I want to hear it."

Her eyes looked like liquid golden drops in the darkened room—so beautiful—wanton, wildly free as she reached the start of her climax.

"Caaaaa-leb." It was a shouted whisper, if there can be such a thing. Not loud—because it was softly formed—but something I would have heard her say clearly from across a noisy room. Because she was saying it to *me* . . . in a moment of total intimacy and complete trust, as we reached the peak together. I pumped everything I had left in me into her, our eyes locked on to one another as we rode it out. There weren't words to describe it.

She collapsed down on top of me, and I could feel her heart pounding against my chest. Mine was pounding, too. Our hearts just pounded into each other until things settled down and I could think. Thinking was hard, and my brain was exhausted. I wanted not to think, actually. But like the old saying goes, "don't think of a pink elephant"—and then that's exactly what your brain delivers up to you on a steaming plate. For me the pink elephant was the question of what she meant to me, and what I wanted from her. I don't think I consciously knew, as only my subconscious was in the know there.

I rolled us to the side and worked on dealing with the condom. The fuckin' things were a pain, and I suddenly had an intense distaste for using them with Brooke. Another first for me. I wondered if I should be keeping a tally of my new philosophy on life where she was concerned. We could talk about it later I decided. Right now I wanted her breathing against me as I held her.

She'd already fallen asleep, her head on my pillow, my heart in her hands. I kissed her forehead and stilled as I thought about how right this actually felt. Hadn't known I was missing anything. Hadn't known it was possible for someone to steal your heart without even knowing they'd done it. Hadn't known *I needed her*. I whispered the words I'd never said before to a woman who wasn't related to me.

"I love you."

$$$

THE daylight streaming through the windows woke me when I reached for her, but she'd gone. I hoped she was still in the house, though, or I was going to go full-on panic attack mode. I inhaled deeply. Something smelled very good. Bacon? Was that frying bacon coming from the kitchen? Impossible—but maybe not? I made a quick stop to take a piss and brush my teeth. And drank a glass of water because I was insanely thirsty. I pulled on the sweats from last night and didn't waste another second fucking around before searching out my Brooke and the delicious smells.

She was cooking breakfast.

In my kitchen.

For us to share.

I just watched her silently, hoping she wouldn't see me for a moment or two, so I could enjoy the vision of the woman I loved cooking for me the morning after giving me the most amazing night I'd ever experienced in my life.

The flannel pajamas and the socks were back. She'd braided her hair again, too. Brooke was a busy girl as she divided her attention between scrambling eggs, turning bacon, and toasting bread. I could have watched her for an hour and been content.

The curves of her perfect ass were shaped by the fabric of her pajamas as she moved side to side, working between the food prep. I remembered how it felt to have that sweet ass cradled in my hands as we fucked in the bathroom last night. I really hadn't intended to start us there, so that's why I moved us to the bed as soon as I physically could. I'd lost control is all. Just desperately, fucking crazy-out-of-my-mind to have her, to know what I was doing.

She hadn't complained or seemed to mind. She had been one hundred percent on board with everything.

She'd also shared a lot of information about her past last night, from which my head was still reeling.

I would have James find out the details on her husband. She'd mentioned his criminal family and I needed to know the story there. Marcus—the insane sociopath who'd hurt her—was hopefully roasting nicely in hell right about now. It was good he was dead—that way I didn't have to kill him and spend the rest of my life in prison.

I switched out that thought to something much better—and that was the number four.

Four times last night. My personal record for an eight-hour span of time. I was goddamn proud of myself, too. I was probably on the verge of severe dehydration, though. I should drink some more water.

"Good morning, Caleb." *Oh, that fucking gorgeous voice.* It was as if it sang to me every time she spoke.

"Good morning, beautiful." I came up behind her and carefully wrapped an arm around her shoulders and the other around her waist. "How did you know I was here?"

"I could feel your presence. It's quite powerful, you know."

"Hmm . . . is that a good thing?" I asked with my lips at the shell of her ear.

"Yes indeed, with you it is," she said as she reached a hand up to my face. "I hope it's okay I'm cooking in your kitchen. I figured it was a good idea to familiarize myself since I have to design a new one."

I frowned at the thought, realizing I didn't like her reference to the job. I didn't want her in here just because I'd hired her to do a job; I wanted her cooking because she sought it out—after a smoking hot night with her man. I had changed roles on her without ever asking, though. I now wanted to be her man, not her boss. For the first time, it dawned on me I might have made a mistake in hiring her.

"It's more than okay, Brooke. You can cook breakfast any time you get the urge. I fucking love it," I told her, taking in a deep inhale of the scent of her hair. "How can I help you?"

"You can transfer these plates to the table while I pour coffee," she said slowly.

"On one condition," I said.

"And that is?"

"I give you a proper kiss good morning first."

She froze beneath my hands as if she was trying to hold back. Then I heard it—the softest sob, and then another. She was crying.

"No." I turned her and got a look: eyes closed, tear streaked, shoulders shaking. "What is it, baby? What did I do?"

She curled into me and sobbed a few more times before pulling herself together. I waited because I sensed it was the right thing to do. I do not know how I knew that, but something told me to just wait her out. I rubbed her back and held her while standing in front of a Viking range I rarely used, in my similarly unused kitchen, and waited for her to say something.

"It's not you," she managed to say on the breath of a sob. "I—I do this now. It happens quite a bit, a-actually. I think my accident has something to do with it because I never had this problem before . . ." She took some deep breaths and seemed to be coming out of it, and my heart started beating again.

Fuck. Me. Sideways.

I did not like her crying. It freaked me the fuck out.

I'd thought for a minute she was going to tell me last night had been a terrible mistake.

"Was it—was it me asking to kiss you good morning that brought it on?"

She nodded against my chest, almost as if she were afraid to look at me.

"I need to understand, Brooke. Can you talk to me?"

"I get emotional at the drop of a hat . . . and it's led to a lot of embarrassing moments just like this one we're having right now."

"But, don't be—please don't feel embarrassed with me. I don't mind, I just want to know why."

"Whenever I talk about my problems to someone, my voice will crack and I'll start crying. Even wonderful moments choke me up, like when Nan and Herman told me they were getting married, or just now when you said you wanted to give me a good-morning kiss."

"Me asking to kiss you good morning was a wonderful moment?"

"Yes, it was, Caleb. For me it was, because it teaches me that you want me here." She sighed heavily against my bare chest, and I could feel the heat of her breath move over my skin. It started things up down south again. All she had to do was speak and I wanted her again. Didn't she realize that yet? "Rehearsing what I want to say to people doesn't really help, either, because I end up sobbing and thus can't get the words out of my mouth, or control that feeling at the back of my throat," she added with another heavy sigh.

Jesus. Not what I was expecting her to say. Again, I reminded myself that Brooke was someone I barely knew. My feelings for her remained unchanged, but as she revealed more about herself, I understood there were many layers of complexity in her life. Complexities she struggled to work around so she could function as a person. We all had them. Same, but different complexities, pushing in at odd moments, making us dance to their tune. The bastard fuckers.

"Well, let me say this then: having you here to say good morning to, after the night we just shared together, is a wonderful moment for me." It was more than wonderful actually, but I didn't want to scare her with how I really felt. *Insanely fantastic* was closer to the mark. I tugged on her chin with a finger because I needed to see her eyes and I needed her to see mine. "If I cry, too, will that help you feel better?"

My teasing worked because she laughed and her eyes smiled—and my world tilted a little bit more. I got my good-morning kiss, which was spectacular all on its own, but there was more to look forward to. So much more.

I was going to sit down with her and eat the delicious breakfast she'd cooked for me.

And then I was going to carry her back to bed and *make love* to her again, and reassure her just how much I wanted her here with me.

After that, I was going to carry her into the shower and make her come against my lips one last time before we both got ready for work.

Then I would have the pleasure of dropping her off and kissing her good-bye before she walked inside her building. I would watch her as she went in and know I was seeing my girl. Mine.

Brooke Casterley was mine now.

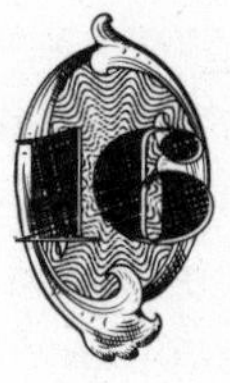

16

Caleb

James R. Blakney & Associates, PC was the only firm I'd consider with something like this—since it was me with the request and James doing the investigating—because I didn't trust anybody else when it came to my private business more than I trusted my best friend.

We met at boarding school when we were ten. Both of us dumped at a private institution where rich mothers and fathers sent their sons when only the most exclusive prep school would do. I remember standing in line for the phone we all had to share, so I could call my parents and beg them to let me come home.

When it was my turn, I made the call and got my mother on the line. I wanted to talk to my dad but she told me he couldn't come to the phone right then. I let her know how much I hated living at school, and how badly I missed my brothers and my baby sisters. I begged and pleaded to be allowed to go to a day school and live at home, but she just told me to stop crying and that I was embarrassing her. I often wondered if I'd been able to catch my dad on the phone that day, if things might have turned out differently. Dad was reasonable. Mom was not. She let me know in no uncertain terms that I was staying put, and wouldn't be coming back home until Isaac showed up at the end of November to bring me there for Thanksgiving. Then she told me it was for my own good and hung up on me.

Some of the other boys witnessed me crying and taunted me. They called me a baby and pushed me around before I ran off and hid behind one of the school buildings and cried some more. When I lifted my head up later, I discovered I wasn't alone. The boy who was right below me alphabetically in the class was sitting a few feet away. James Blakney. I asked him why he was there. He told me he'd called his parents the day before for the very same reason as me. James had gotten his father on the line. The same cold, hard message was delivered to him, only it came from his dad instead of his mom. We bonded that day and found out that boarding school didn't suck so badly when you had a friend to share it with.

That was twenty-one years ago, and boarding school had been exchanged for Harvard eight years later. Then it was grad school—Harvard Law for James and Harvard Business for me. Now our companies took the place that school had filled when we were kids. Not much was different between us today than it'd been back then, I thought as I walked through the doors of his law firm.

"He's free now if you want to go on in, Caleb." His legal secretary had known me since I was a kid, from back when she'd worked for Judge Blakney, James's father.

"Thank you, Mrs. Kennedy." I gave her a wink.

"Aren't you ever going to call me Marguerite?" she teased back.

"No, ma'am. It wouldn't be courteous for me to address you as anything other than 'Mrs. Kennedy' on account of my oath. A scout is always courteous."

"Still with the Boy Scout thing, Caleb, after all these years?" This was our little game.

"That's right, Mrs. Kennedy. I try to always remember to conduct myself like the Eagle Scout I am."

James looked at me weirdly when I entered his office and sat in the buttery-soft leather chair reserved for clients. Right now I was a client.

"What has this girl done to you, my friend?" he said, after a minute of staring.

"How much time do you have?" I answered.

"That good, huh?" He didn't look convinced.

I removed a piece of lint from my pant leg before replying. "The word *good* is insufficient and lacking in details to help you understand what she has *done* to me."

He gave me another thoroughly weird look before opening the file on his desk. It contained the information he'd found since I'd called him from the car, after I'd dropped Brooke at Harris & Goode this morning.

"Three hours isn't enough time to get a whole lot, but I've got some baseline stuff for you and it's a start. Brooke Ellen Casterley, twenty-three years old. Birthday, seventeenth May, when she will turn twenty-four. Born at King George Hospital, Essex, England to Susanna Casterley and Michael Harvey. Here's her birth certificate."

James slid it to me across the desk. "And the husband?"

"He was a bit more of a challenge, but I found his name on the public marriage record filed when he married Brooke. Marcus Kyle Patten, age twenty-nine at the time of the marriage, thirty years old at the time of his death. Born in Salem, Mass., died in Chatsworth, an affluent LA suburb, just seven months into the marriage. Here's his birth certificate."

He slid that one over as well. "How did she meet this guy do you think?"

"I think I can make a good guess there. They met at Suffolk University where she was an undergrad, and he was probably just finishing up law school. Patten passed the Massachusetts state bar exam two years ago in February. He married Brooke a little over a month later in April."

"But they lived in California and Marcus died there. Why take the Massachusetts bar exam and not California's?"

"I'm still working on that, but Brooke probably knows what she's talking about if she said the family operated in criminal activity. I'm thinking they needed an inside man versed in the law. Like the mob always sends their brightest bulb in the box to law school. Best way to keep all that money out of the hands of the IRS."

"The family is organized crime?" I asked.

"Looking that way. They own storage unit rentals. Hundreds of them all over the state. Could be a nice cover for smuggling: drugs, guns, anything that's controlled, plus a legit business helps to hide the money laundering activities they need to do. Oh, and this Marcus Patten had some anger management issues while in law school, and sounds like maybe a drinking problem, too. An aggravated assault charge was filed for a bar fight that turned vicious, before it was then quietly dropped. The family probably paid off the victim—that and maybe he was fearful of losing the other eye. Marcus ripped into the guy's face with a broken beer bottle and left him blind on the left side. He reads like one crazy motherfucker."

"Jesus, this guy and his family sound like *Sleeping with the Enemy* meets *Sons of Anarchy*."

"I know. It's a miracle your girl made it out in one piece."

She nearly didn't. "While we're on the topic of crazy people, how is Janice?"

"I wouldn't know, and I'd like to keep it that way, thank you very much. Besides I told you a few days later at lunch that I didn't fuck her, I just let her into my apartment. Which was the worst, most terrible idea ever. Why didn't you come down there and save me from her, bro?"

"Hey, I warned you to the best of my ability. I even let you know about the picture she sent me."

His face fell at my mention of the picture. "That picture of her sucking cock? It wasn't a picture of *my* cock. I don't know what she sent you, but it wasn't a picture of her and me. I did not let her anywhere near my dick even though she offered. Several times." He grimaced. "I really wish you hadn't deleted it so I could take a look."

When we'd met for lunch a few weeks ago James had been adamant about no sex with Janice that night. I'd deleted the picture mere minutes after Janice sent it, so there was no way to verify whatever twisted plotting she was up to. "I'm sorry. I guess I didn't think it through in the heat of the moment. I just wanted to cut ties with her, and then warn you before I got rid of the evidence. Maybe it wasn't you in the picture. Maybe I just assumed it was because I knew she was with you when she sent it to me. I didn't analyze the fucking thing."

"You know what they say about *assuming* things, Caleb?"

"Yeah. I made an ass out of you and me. Sorry about that. My heart was in the right place though—I thought of your dad and didn't want it to blow up on you . . ." I let that ominous cloud of paternal doom descend for a moment before deflecting. "How wasted were you?"

His eyes narrowed at the mention of his father. The judge. James's relationship with his dad was about as warm and cozy as mine was with my mother. "On my fucking ass, apparently, because I don't remember much about the preliminary activities that led to her showing up at my place," he said bitterly.

"I broke up with her after we came back from the American Cancer Society benefit and she went ballistic. By the time she left the penthouse, she'd given me the black eye and trashed my bathroom like something out of fucking *Fatal Attraction*."

James dropped his head and shook it back and forth. "She told me about that, I remember now. She went to town on the bathroom, thinking of things to do to mess with your head. Like toothpaste on the walls, and towels in the toilet, and destroying a whole box of condoms. Which sucks, because the good ones are expensive."

Destroyed condoms? "Janice didn't mess with the condoms. I checked the cupboard where I keep them and the box hadn't been touched."

"Well, that's good then . . ." He trailed off and tilted his head as if he was trying to remember. James had a really good memory, too, even while under the influence, so I tended to believe him when he said something important. And this was fucking important.

"James, what did Janice say?"

"She said she hated you, and that you would be sorry you ever fucked her over. Then she told me about trashing your bathroom and all the shit she did in there, and how much fun she had doing it. She said she wished she could see your face when you found out what she did to ruin your life."

"She said that? Janice said she was ruining my life?" Something wasn't right here with this story. "James, bro, you have to remember for me. A minute ago—why did you say she destroyed a box of condoms?"

James rubbed his head with the tips of his fingers. "Because—she said she did, Caleb. She told me about using a pin or a brooch from her dress and how she poked holes in them—"

Oh, my God. That is exactly the kind of psycho shit Janice would do, too. The bitch put them back in the box all neat and tidy so I wouldn't suspect.

I jumped up from the chair in his office and grabbed the copies. "Bro, I'm glad I stopped in here today, but I gotta go. Thanks for the intel on Patten so far. Keep digging." I nodded to the file on his desk and left him sitting there still rubbing his head looking disturbed.

As I waved good-bye to Mrs. Kennedy, I remembered the wisdom in keeping up to date with one's friends.

You never know what important news they might have to share with you.

Jesus. Christ.

$$$

I had Isaac drive me straight from my meeting with James back to the penthouse. Ann had already cleaned the bedroom, and the trash was long gone down into the bowels of the building's incinerator most likely, so I couldn't check the condoms I'd used last night. I went for the box and emptied it out onto the counter. The packages were black so it wasn't easily noticeable, but when held to the light, there were holes dead center in about three-quarters of them. Not every condom had been pierced, but a lot of them had.

I started opening condoms and filling them with water from the sink. Drip, drip, drip, right through the tips of the ones that had been poked. *Janice, you fiendish cunt.*

Well, fuck.

This was not good news.

I should probably tell Brooke, and I was fucking livid at my freak of an ex-girlfriend.

The more I thought about it, though, the more certain I was about *not* telling Brooke. It was a sordid tale of the twisted person I'd been with right before I met her, as well as the sleazy life I'd been living. I knew Brooke would be repulsed by all of it. But most of all, I was ashamed for Brooke to see me in such a horrible light. She always thanked me for being a gentleman, and I loved that she thought well of me. I was afraid to lose that earned respect in her eyes.

I rationalized the facts. I'd used five of the condoms from this box—four last night and one this morning. If I went with the seventy percent rule, three point five of them were damaged when I used them. But my selection had been totally random when they were spilled around the bathroom and later returned to the box, so it could have been more like two damaged condoms out of the five. Without the actual ones to inspect, I couldn't be sure. What were the odds Brooke was even in the fertile time of her cycle? She might already be on birth control for all I knew. We hadn't discussed it yet.

So, if there was some leakage, it still wasn't like I'd come inside her bare. A few drops max. I hadn't noticed any leaks when I removed them, but then I didn't pay too close attention, either, because sex is always messy, and you just want to get the damn thing off your cock as quickly as possible.

I hate this.

But I loved Brooke.

And I wanted her to love me back.

Telling her about Janice, and what she'd done, would poison the beauty of last night. I couldn't allow that to happen. Thank fuck the locks had been switched out. I didn't need Janice showing up and confronting Brooke, and something told me she might try it when she returned from Hong Kong. This proved just how unstable Janice was, and I needed to figure out how best to deal with her. Because I wasn't just going to let this one go. She'd crossed way over the line with this shit.

I made a decision. I gathered up all of the mess and trashed the whole lot of it.

I went into my home office and logged on to Target.com. I ordered new condoms and selected the option to pick up in the store. I forwarded the confirmation to Victoria and told her to pick them up and bring them to the penthouse. I didn't obsess over the awkwardness of my request, either. She was my personal assistant, and I paid her very well to do a job. If I needed her to pick up condoms, then her job that day was to pick up condoms—what I was fucking paying her to do.

Jesus, I was tense. I needed Brooke to de-stress me with her own particular brand of magic. X-rated images danced through my mind at the thought of exactly how she could accomplish it, too.

Aaaaaand that just led to wondering about what was happening tonight. We hadn't discussed it, and I imagined she would want to go home to her own house. A fucking depressing thought. I didn't want her on the Blackstone Island Ferry anymore. The weather was unpredictable and could sink a boat in minutes under bad conditions. The risk to her safety made me mental.

We needed to have a serious talk about a long list of things, but mostly I just wanted to be with her again tonight. I wanted to be with Brooke—pretty simple.

Now that I'd found her I couldn't be without her.

Pussy. Pussy! PUSSY!

"And what is your point?" I said to my inner demons.

$$$

"I have a problem." There's something to be said for unburdening your true feelings to someone you care about, because the minute the words were out of my mouth, I felt instantly better. I knew Brooke's beautiful voice would soothe me even if the building were in flames and crumbling down around me.

"Oh? Tell me about it."

"Well, I met this beautiful girl, and she has completely captivated me in just a short time of knowing her. Last night . . . aaah, we shared the most amazing night together, and now I can't stop thinking about her, or wondering when I can see her again."

She laughed softly into the phone, and I pictured her lips as she did it. "You say this is a problem, but if you like her and she likes you, then why do you call it a problem?"

"Well, that is a very good question. Have I told you yet, how smart you are? If I haven't, then I've been remiss, because I think you are very, very smart."

"So do you have a problem or not?"

"Oh yes, I have an additional problem."

"Will you share it with me, Caleb?" she asked with a hint of teasing.

"All right then. You won't laugh at me?"

"Ahhh, I might possibly laugh, but not at you—only with you—because you are funny."

"Back to my problem, Brooke."

"Right, the elusive problem you can't seem to spit out for the life of you."

It was my turn to laugh. She could string the simplest of words together in a statement, but coming out of her mouth, it transformed into pure poetic prose. "I'm going out of the country on a business trip the day after tomorrow on a red-eye. And I want another night with her before I have to leave for a week, because I know I will miss her every day that I'm away."

Silence. And then the soft sob I'd heard this morning when her emotions blasted her. *Shit. I made her cry, again?!*

"Brooke . . . baby . . . it's okay." I waited and tried to remember what she'd told me this morning, about how this—whatever the fuck they were: *sudden emotional episodes*—never happened to her before the accident.

"I'm fine," she breathed back at me after what felt like an eon of time. "You just surprised me with another wonderful moment, Caleb. You should maybe slow that down a bit."

I laughed again, and I felt so fucking relieved to know that if I was making her cry, at least it was the wonderful-moment kind and not the other. "I will try, but it's probably impossible to limit my wonderful moments with you, Brooke." Straight-up truth.

"I think I have a solution to your problem, Caleb. Would you like to hear it?"

"Yes, I'd love to hear it." It sounded like she might take pity on me and stay over again. I mentally crossed my fingers.

"Well, I am going home tonight. I need to be in my normal environment and go about my usual routines. I visit Nan at physical therapy, and there is the wedding coming up, too, which I work on planning at night, and also getting her things packed up to move into Herman's house in a very short time. She's being released from the hospital this Thursday, and I'll be taking the rest of this week off work so I can be home to prepare, and to help her get settled."

"You are very busy," I said, trying not to let her hear my disappointment at knowing she wouldn't be sleeping in my bed tonight. She wouldn't even be back to Boston at all before I left on my trip.

"Yes but busy doing things I love. It sounds as if you'll be booked up as well, considering you have an international trip in a few days. Where are you going?"

"Abu Dhabi. It's the World Sustainability Summit. I go every year." I suddenly hated the idea of going this year.

"Well, I don't know what commitments you have at work before you leave for Abu Dhabi on Wednesday night, but if you are free to take some time off, you could come and stay with me at the cottage . . . and experience south-end island life for a few days." She paused in the silence. "If the idea is to *your* liking, of course." *God, I fucking love you.*

"Yes, the idea is to my liking. Yes, I'm free to take the time." No wasted words there. My heart was about to explode out of my chest, but I was answering her in coherent sentences at least.

"Will you come on the five-thirty ferry with me, or are you getting there on your own at a later time?" she asked softly.

"Oh . . . most definitely on the five-thirty ferry with you, beautiful," I answered.

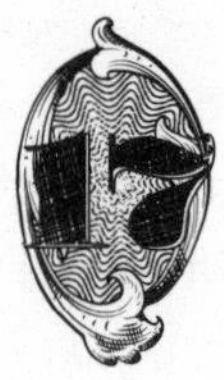

Brooke

Caleb emerged from the backseat of the Mercedes with a leather bag in his left hand and an autumn bouquet of flowers in his right. A supremely hot man boarding the ferry whilst carrying flowers got more than a few heads turning—and even some smirks, as he walked right over and greeted me with a kiss that stole my breath. Lucky me.

"Have you ever taken this ferry before?" I asked, after he ended the kiss.

"When I was a kid with the Boy Scouts I did," he said, looking over the side with a frown. "Why do you ask?"

"Oh, no reason other than you don't really have the vibe of a BIF annual pass holder going on, is all." I shaped my hands around the outline of his body for emphasis. Caleb still wore the navy blue suit he'd put on this morning, but he'd replaced the shirt and tie for a jumper in a mustard color that popped against the blue. It would be hard to miss him in a crowd. Even when dressing down, he still looked expensive. "But hot. Incredibly hot."

I forced myself to tamp down the images of us together last night still playing in my head and making me ache for more of the same. I had to suppress them, or I might do something utterly indecent in front of our audience on this very public ferry boat.

Caleb Blackstone had infected me with the desire to belong to him, to be more than just sexual partners in some really superb shagging. He made me feel like I mattered, like I was important to him and he needed me. It was the most wonderful feeling, experiencing that with him last night.

And absolutely fucking terrifying at the same time.

I could tell he liked my comment about being *incredibly hot* because his eyes flared. "No? And here I thought I was doing a good job of fitting right in." He handed me the mixed bouquet of flowers. "For you."

"They're gorgeous. Thank you for being so thoughtful, Caleb, as always."

"You are gorgeous. Thank you for inviting me, Brooke. I—I really wanted more time with you before I leave. There's so much I want to know about you . . . and experience with you," he said.

I loved how Caleb's eyes looked right now. The blue of them was intensified by his choice of clothing, and even the gold ringing the blue iris matched the color of the sweater he'd chosen. Beautiful eyes that penetrated right into my heart. Somehow Caleb had gotten inside my heart.

And that meant my heart was now in very grave danger of being hurt—which was the fucking terrifying part.

I led him inside to a bench seat where I was pulled in to rest my back against his chest as soon as we sat down and settled our things. He placed his chin on top of my head and took one of my hands in his. All of his gestures very sweet as he went about the business of touching me. Caleb seemed to need the touching as much as I did.

I felt warm and could smell the delicious scent unique to him enveloping me. I was being held by someone whose arms I *wanted* around me. All new experiences.

The hour-long commute would make me happy tonight.

Because Caleb would be holding me.

$$$

WATCHFUL is how I would describe Caleb as we left the boat. He carried both bags as I led him to where the car was parked. It reminded me of shopping at Target with him actually. He didn't use public transportation, and I'd only seen Isaac driving him around the city, so I imagined he was "learning" his way through this experience, too.

When I stopped at Woody and stuck my key in the lock to open up the back hatch, he paused—surprised—I was sure of it, before catching himself and stowing our bags inside. I doubted Caleb had ever been driven around in a car older than him before, but he didn't say anything. He merely followed me to the driver's side and opened the door for me after I'd unlocked it. Even though he was the passenger, Caleb did not forget his lovely manners. I had to pinch myself in the brief space of time it took for him to walk around to the other side and get in with me. Caleb was coming home with me. *Caleb. Was. Coming. Home. With. Me.*

Once we were both in, he turned toward me and said, "I need to do something first."

"What's that?"

He leaned over the console and took my face in his hands—a gesture I adored from him—and whispered, "This."

Caleb kissed me senseless, deeply and thoroughly until I probably couldn't remember my own name, let alone drive. His scratchy beard caressed around my lips as he pulled on the bottom one with his teeth, teasing me until I was a wet mess—ready to straddle him in a public car park. Seriously, the man was sexually dangerous, and all he'd done was put me in the car and kiss me.

"Careful, or I'll never be able to drive us," I murmured against his mouth.

"Sorry." He backed off, but he kept one hand under my chin and rubbed his thumb along my bottom lip. "I've wanted to do that all day." More with the beautiful, blue-with-gold-rings-around-them eyes studying me for a serious moment. "I'm okay now," he said with his little-boy smirk. "We can go." A beat or two of silence passed. "Where are we going?"

I couldn't help but laugh. It was so nice to not care about the awkwardness that much. We were going to have to figure it out somehow, but if Caleb kept up with being so adorable, it wouldn't be a problem for me. "We are going to stop in for a quick visit to Nan at therapy, and then I'm taking you to the cottage where I'll make us some dinner. After that, we can do whatever you want."

"*Whatever* I want?"

"As long as it involves warm socks on my feet, I am game," I answered wickedly.

"Uhmmmm . . ." he groaned lowly as he shifted in the seat. So he was feeling it, too . . .

Good.

Payback was fair play.

$$$

"NAN, I've brought a friend with me—someone who knows you well. Do you remember—"

"Caleb Blackstone, you may have grown taller, but I'd recognize your face anywhere. You look so much like your father when he was your age." Nan's face lit up, and she reached out her hand to him—which he took in both of his and held warmly.

"Mrs. Casterley, you haven't aged a day. It's so wonderful to see you again. Brooke tells me you are about to be released from here." I watched him greet my nan after nearly a decade and marveled at how lovely he was with people. Especially people he clearly adored. Caleb possessed social skills in conversation that, sadly, were lacking in many people of our generation, so I was content to sit back and watch them get reacquainted. I knew Nan would pin me to the wall later and want to know what I was doing with a man like Caleb Blackstone, and I'd have to tell her *something*.

And what would that be? *He treats me with respect, says he wants me, and makes me feel like the person I was before I made my terrible mistake.* It was the truth, even if it scared me to believe it. She would be skeptical of his intentions toward me and probably ask him outright. She didn't work for his family anymore, so she wouldn't be censored by any sense of obligation to hold back her opinions from a respected employer, plus Nan was very protective of me now, especially after Marcus . . .

My inner reflections were interrupted when Herman strolled in with his own bouquet of autumn flowers in his hand. The Blackstone men were certainly blessed with romantic inclinations—something that probably served them *very* well when it came time for their women to show appreciation, like I was going to do as soon as I had Caleb alone in my cottage.

"Is that my nephew I see flirting with my girl?" Herman bellowed.

"Uncle Herman, I think some congratulations are due if I'm not mistaken."

As I watched the two of them reconnect, I was struck by the similarity in body shape and bone structure. I knew why I'd told Caleb he reminded me of someone I knew living on the island. Blood didn't lie and it was clearly evident they were related. If I didn't know better, I would think they were father and son.

I overheard Caleb mention the Blackwater estate to Herman and watched the two of them go deep into conversation about it. He'd said he wanted to *fix* the situation of it being closed and the employees dismissed, so maybe he wanted Herman's advice on the matter. It would be lovely to see Blackwater restored for some useful purpose if the family didn't want it for holidays anymore. I hoped whoever bought the property had to consider its historic value beyond just an appraisal of house and land. I still thought it odd that he hadn't known about it being shuttered and on the market. Didn't his family communicate about something as important as a home that had been in the family for generations? Again, I had to shake my head at the problems of the rich . . .

$$$

"HERMAN and Nan certainly enjoyed your visit this evening," I said to him as I drove to the cottage over the twisty lanes I could navigate by the feel of the bumps and the turns.

"I enjoyed it, too. I'm really glad you brought me there tonight. Thank you." He reached over and gave my thigh a squeeze as if just his words weren't sufficient to express his thanks.

"Why so grateful, Caleb?"

He sighed before answering. "Well, I guess it has something to do with being ashamed of losing interest in things that should hold a higher place of importance to me. After I finished up at Harvard, I went off and immersed myself in work and business to the point I excluded pretty much everything else, even my family. I regret that now, because I know now I missed out on a lot of time with the people I care about."

"It's never too late to let them know how you feel." I hesitated before telling him the rest of my thoughts. "When I saw you standing beside Herman tonight, I could clearly see the family resemblance between you. Very handsome men in the Blackstone gene pool I must say."

"Thank you. It makes me happy you think so. I could say the same about you and your grandmother, though. You two look very much alike, and your voices sound similar. I can hear you talking in my head when she speaks." He leaned over the console again and spoke against my neck. "And beauty is something you have in abundance in case I've failed to mention it before."

He licked my neck, producing a shiver that shot straight down between my legs.

"Driving here, Caleb," I scolded him. "Behave or the *we can do whatever you want* offer goes out the window."

He just laughed softly into my ear before easing back into his seat. "I'll behave then."

When I pulled into the single garage, I could sense he was taking everything in again, back into learning mode. He quickly came around and opened my door for me. It was going to take some getting used to his mannerly gestures. I opened the back, and he carried in the bags to the front porch.

"This is it," I said. "The cottage I will never sell as long as I live." I busied myself with unlocking the door.

"It's very charming. I imagine the view is spectacular out the back."

"Oh, it is," I said. "We can sit out there after we've eaten dinner. It's lovely to see the lighthouse shining over the water even if it's a bit chilly. We can bring a blanket."

"Let's do that then." He spoke right up against my neck, pressing into me from behind. I could feel the hard length of his whole body. His impressive erection solidly against my arse, too. This attraction with Caleb was crazy.

Insanely. Wickedly. Crazy.

But, care—I did not. Not anymore. *How could I have ignored the man? He had wooed me.* I didn't believe he had wooed me for sex, either. My experience was limited, but it didn't feel like I was a conquest to him. Caleb was different in that way.

The key in the lock to my front door finally gave in to my attentions and turned. As it fell open, Caleb pressed us both forward. I heard bags dropping onto the floor along with my keys and the flowers—and then I was swallowed up by Caleb. I was lifted by strong arms that knew how to hold my body with care as he propped me up against the wall, and pushed in between my legs.

"Aaahhh," I moaned when I felt the press of his cock against my clit. I was already moving my hips against him, desperately needing him inside. "Please, Caleb . . . I—I want you."

"Sweet music to my ears, baby." He slipped two fingers inside my knickers and started swirling them over my sensitive flesh. "Oh, fuck, you're ready," he said harshly before setting me down to stand on my own. "I have to put this on first." He brought a condom packet out from his trouser pocket and shook it lightly back and forth.

I snatched it out of his hand and ripped it open. "Give me your cock." I was all business in my request. Which was: *give it to me now, Caleb.*

He got the message. Thank. God.

Caleb had his zipper open and his cock presented to me in under two seconds. I could feel him watching me as I sheathed the part of him that would be deep inside me in another moment and gathered he was enjoying the show. I was all about efficiency, hurrying to finish my task. His hands were up my dress while I toiled with the condom, already tugging down my knickers and working them out over one boot, lest we waste time. I didn't want to know why he was so skilled at the mechanics of sex, just grateful for his forward thinking.

I was lifted a second time, my back stationed flat to the wall, my legs split wide by his hips. I felt his hard shaft at my belly and nearly sobbed at the awareness of him so close. He was so big, consuming, and perfectly lovely. "Oh, God," I groaned as he positioned the tip at my entrance and impaled me deep.

"Fuck, it's good. You feel—" He lost the rest of his words as he dropped his mouth to mine and kissed me with the same zealous abandon he was giving me down below with his thrusting cock. It went on and on, both of us frantic and wild. Lost in the movements—seeking the blissful end of release. He pulled his mouth away and stared into my eyes as we fucked. *It's never been like this.* It was beautiful and savage—it was filthy and precious. I willed my climax to take me because it all became too much, too close, too wonderful to process. "I want you to come all over my cock, baby. Go ahead." His fingers found their way to my clit again and started circling. "Say my name, Brooke," he said, his neck muscles straining from holding me up with only one arm.

I let go and felt myself fall over the edge into paradise . . . on the whisper of his name. "Caaleeeeb." A whisper was all I could manage, because he wasn't finished. He was watching me, and I was glad for it because I knew the look of ecstasy on my face had been formed by him. It was his handiwork.

I enjoyed watching the expression of pure pleasure appear when he came about a minute later.

He kissed me for a long time, our bodies merged up against the wall until it was time to surface back into reality.

Reality was an annoying bastard sometimes.

$$$

"BROOKE can cook," he said with his signature smirk, totally sweet and pleased with his little rhyming verse. He also seemed pleased with the French bread pizza I'd thrown together as we sat across from one another, the pretty flowers he'd brought me perking up in a vase of water between us.

"Yes, well it becomes a necessary skill when you live alone."

"I live alone and I can't cook," he said.

"Yes, but you have the luxury of employing someone to cook for you, or do you eat out all the time?"

"I eat out about half of the time and usually because I'm traveling. When I'm not traveling, I like to stay at home as much as possible, which is probably the case with most people who have to travel a lot for work. You crave what you don't have. Ann, my housekeeper slash cook, makes meals for me and freezes them with instructions, or if I tell her in advance, she'll have something ready for me when I get home. Isaac is her husband, and they live in the same building on the floor below mine."

The relationship was clear in my mind between Caleb and his staff. I saw it when he spoke to Nan. Respect. He didn't see himself above Ann and Isaac, and seemed to appreciate their involvement in his world. I couldn't help wonder if some of that had come from having Nan in his life. She was a strong woman, and although she would have *known her place*, she would have had a firm but loving hand with Caleb and his siblings. Of that I was certain. But I was curious now that I had access to this delectable man.

"What is your family like?"

He obliged me and seemed not to mind. I could tell Caleb loved his family with every word he spoke.

"My father was JW, John William, and he died of stomach cancer last year after a long battle." I could see the strain in his expression as he held back his grief. I understood that all too well. "I took over his business interests when he got sick. My mother is Madelaine, formerly Lafarge, an old Boston family, before she married my dad. I'm the oldest, and I have two brothers and two sisters. My brothers are twenty months younger than me and identical twins: Wyatt and Lucas. Lucas is the one who lives here on the island year-round. He's a game designer and created iInVidiosa, if that name rings a bell for you. He knew exactly who you were when I asked him who the girl named Brooke, living on the island with her grandmother, with an English accent, was." He winked at me.

"Why does that not surprise me a bit? Your stalking tendencies at work."

"His twin, Wyatt, lives in New York City and keeps pretty quiet about his activities. I think he doesn't want our mom to know how he makes his money."

"How does he make his money?" I asked.

"I suspect it might be in the video entertainment sector. Read that as *soft porn*, or the stuff they show in hotels. I can safely say he just owns the distribution companies, and is not involved in the production of films." He drew one hand through his hair as if he was fidgeting. "I think. I'm not sure I really want to know."

I laughed and agreed with him. "And your sisters?"

"Willow and Winter are also twins, but not identical. They don't even look that much alike to me. Willow is blonde, but Winter's hair is dark like the rest of us. They have the same eyes, though. Willow is a writer and she's built up quite a following for her books. She's even made the *New York Times* Best Seller list for her young-adult fantasy series, which is quite an achievement for someone at only twenty-four years old. She lives in Providence with her fiancé, Roger, who is a professor of history at Brown University."

"W. R. Blackstone is her? I know the books, and I've read them all. She wrote *The Empty Handed* series. That's so awesome, Caleb, you have a famous author in your family. I'd love to have her sign a book for me sometime."

He smiled widely and I could tell he was very proud of her. As he should be. "I'll tell her you're a fan, and I'm sure she'll send you some books. She interacts with her readers all the time."

"I would be very honored."

He took a sip of the wine I'd opened to go with my homemade pizza and seemed happy to be here with me. He should be happy, considering he'd been fucked and fed—and in that order. God, I was still tingly from the orgasm and wondered if he was thinking about it, too. He was so caring with me. I still couldn't quite fathom how or why he kept pursuing me, but I realized now, it was good for me to do this with him. I'd needed some sexual healing, and Caleb was a very fine healer. I'd also needed emotional healing. Still . . .

After another smoldering look at me across the table, he continued, "Winter is finishing up her master's in social work at Boston University, and I probably see her the most because she has an apartment in the same building as my penthouse. I'm sure the two of you will meet soon since you'll be going over there for the renovation . . . and I hope just for the purposes of seeing me."

Awww, the charm factor was back. "Of course I'd like to *visit* you there again, Caleb, and actually, I remember your sisters—Winter in particular."

"You've met them before?" He seemed surprised, but interested.

"Yes. It was shortly after I'd come here to live with Nan. Your sisters were turning sixteen, and there was a big birthday party for them at Blackwater to which I was invited. I met your father that day as well, but I don't remember if I met your mother or not. I wasn't very socially inclined then—I'd just lost my parents and been plunked down into a foreign world, or at least it felt like it to me, so that time period is sort of a blur. But I do recall the birthday party. It was a hot summer day, and everyone was in the pool cooling off. I didn't go in, though. I preferred to watch the kids playing chicken fight in the pool—everything felt so very different here in America, and I was taking it all in at first. I wasn't ready to make friends or play games. But Winter came over to sit by me and asked about living in England. We talked about the Jonas Brothers, who were wildly popular in the UK at the time, and other teenage girl stuff, but mostly she took the time to make me feel welcome at the party."

His expression changed and lost the animation he'd shown earlier. "I didn't make it to their birthday party. I remember I had to be in Dallas for an IPO. I tried to get back home, but the planes were grounded due to severe weather and nobody made it out."

"It really bothered you to miss their birthday, didn't it?"

"Yeah. I've missed out on too much, though, and it can't be undone. I've learned that the hard way, and it pretty much sucks." He looked me in the eyes. "But I don't need to tell you that, Brooke, as I'm sure you've learned through your loss."

And there it was again. The shit tears exploding at the most random of times. If this wonderful man didn't start heading for the hills to get away from me, I'd never understand why. I lowered my head and took in gulps of air between the sobs.

Caleb was quiet. Patient . . .

He didn't ask if I was okay this time. He did not offer a consoling comment. He just reached his hands across the table and picked up both of mine. His thumbs rubbed circles over my palms in the most gentle of ways . . . and the tightness in my throat passed after a minute.

"—I—I can tell you l-love your family v-very much, Caleb," I managed to stammer eventually.

"I do love them."

I slowly breathed in and out to help settle my emotions back down where they belonged, when he said more to me.

"Brooke, I know this is too soon, but I also know I don't care that it's too soon, because it's already happening for me, and it can't be undone any more than missing my sisters' sixteenth birthday."

My eyes lifted to find his and there they were—beautiful, blue ringed with gold piercing into my heart. "What are y-you s-saying?"

"That it's too late to change back to the time before I met you, Brooke, because I know what you make me feel, and it's different."

"And what is it I'm making you feel?" My heart was surely going to split apart any second and then I wouldn't have to worry about finishing this conversation with him. It could just be over.

"Love." It was softly spoken, but I heard him clearly.

Love.

Love?

No. He can't.

Not love.

"No, you can't love me, Caleb. You just can't."

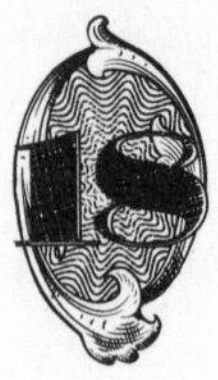

Caleb

Too late for that, beautiful.

An out-of-body experience. Yeah, that's what was happening to me right now in Brooke's cottage on the island above the Fairchild Light. I was out of my motherfucking body and floating somewhere around the ceiling, staring down and wondering who the fuckhead was, sitting across from her, looking like he couldn't remember his own name.

To be honest she didn't look much better. She was as lovely as always, but I'd shocked the hell out of her, without a doubt.

I'd shocked the hell out of myself. The minute the words were out of my mouth, I knew I'd made a mistake and said too goddamn much. I'd scared her. I was supposed to be going slow. I fucked up. Again. *Why are you such a dipshit moron? Why?!*

She pulled her hands away from mine and covered her mouth. She just stared across the table at me. Shocked. And beautifully perfect, even with her hair kind of messy from the desperate-but-oh-so-hot wall fuck we'd shared. But her eyes—they were truly stunning right now as she blinked like she was trying to hold back tears again. The eyes still had the look of a satisfied woman who'd been ridden hard and loved every minute of it, though.

And even after the crazed wall sex, Brooke had gone further by making dinner with her precious hands, putting it on a plate, and serving me at the table. What in the actual fuck? I'd been the one shocked then, because I'd had no experiences like it before. No woman had *ever* done that for me.

Brooke had such a generous soul, and she'd done it all with happiness in her heart just because she'd wanted to.

I wished I'd been inside her when I'd said it.

"Don't be scared of what I just said, okay? Just file it away somewhere and we can just keep doing . . . this." I tugged on her hands and pulled them back into mine. "Nothing has to change."

"Oh, Caleb . . . I—I don't think I can—I—I'm not ready," she said on a whisper, her eyes filling.

"It's okay, baby. I know you aren't ready, and I shouldn't have thrown that at you like I just did. I apologize. I'm not expecting you to feel the same way. I do have a small bit of intelligence, and from what you've shared about your past, I realize it's too soon for you. I get it. You don't have to say anything right now. Just know that I spoke the truth. Okay? Can you—can you do that for me?"

"You know—you've seen—Caleb, I am a complete mess emotionally. You don't even know me . . . how can it be the truth?"

"But what I just said—it wasn't about you, Brooke. It was about me. It's *my* truth, not yours. What *I* am feeling. And trust me, after thirty-one and a half years of knowing what love *doesn't* feel like, I think I'm a goddamn expert at recognizing when the real thing comes along to rip right into my heart."

She swallowed, making the skin at her throat flutter. "I've ripped right into your heart?"

"Uh-huh. Brutally. Savagely."

"But I didn't mean to," she said sadly.

"I know, baby. That was just fate doing its thing. Brooke, it's not about me expecting you to feel the same way. It's just the reality of you . . . for me. I knew it the night you first spoke to me. I didn't even know your name, but I'd already spotted you walking into your offices and knew of you. You are my fate personified. Your nan and my uncle are getting married, connecting you and me through their marriage whether we want it or not. That's fate at work—can't you see that? We were going to come together eventually, and I think my path to finding you was set in motion a long time ago."

"Fate . . . for me, has always been something bad, Caleb. I'm scared of fate. Fate terrifies me."

"Why, beautiful?"

"Because what we love can be snatched away in the blink of an eye. I can't have any more of that kind of fate, because if I do it will be the end of me."

"I know your heart has been horribly wounded, and you're afraid to be vulnerable again. I don't want to hurt you, Brooke. I just wanted you to know my feelings, and I've realized just now, that even if you never feel the same way about me, it still won't change anything. I will feel the same about you as I do right now."

"Caleb, I thought you just wanted to enjoy each other the way we have been . . . the sex . . . it's very wonderful. *You* are the most wonderful and lovely man. I have to pinch myself when I'm with you, because I think you're too good to be true . . . and I can't understand why you even want me. There's more you don't know about me, Caleb. I am not from your world and will never be accepted in it."

"I don't care, and I would happily come and be in your world with you, if that's what it takes."

"You cannot mean that." She was doing her best to push me away, but I sensed there was still some hope for me. I'd laid it out on the table for her, and hopefully she'd take it at face value when she was ready.

"Oh, I mean it, and I have the ability to make it happen. Watch me."

"I don't care for this arguing," she said stubbornly.

"I don't care to be told I cannot own my feelings." I finally snapped and asked the question. "Do you want me to go? I can stay with my brother tonight and get back to Boston in the morning." It would hurt like a bitch, but I would do it if she asked me to.

She eyeballed me.

I gave it right back to her.

I waited for her to say "Give me five minutes and I'll drive you to your brother's house myself," in the Jeep Cherokee that probably had a good five years on me.

She didn't, though. Instead she rose from her chair and came around the table to my side. She held out her hand to me.

I took it. *How could I not?* She was handing me a lifeline, and I'd fucking hold on to it.

"I don't want you to go, Caleb. I'd like you to stay and hear the rest of my story. I think you should know everything about me, and then you can evaluate if your feelings are still the same." She tugged me up from my chair. "You're right. It's not fair of me to tell you what you can feel for another person. I am sorry if I hurt you when I said you couldn't possibly feel more for me. I don't want to hurt you, Caleb. Never that."

I let her lead me up the stairs to her bedroom where I'd stowed my bag earlier when she gave me the grand tour of her cottage.

She peeled off her shirt first. Then her leggings. The bra came off next and my dick started throbbing. I was fully erect when the panties were dropped to the floor. I watched her reveal herself to me physically and wished she could do the same on an emotional level. Why is it we always crave what we don't have?

She came to me and I let her help me take off my clothes, piece by piece, until I was as naked as her.

"Do you know how easy it would be for me to fall in love with you, Caleb?"

"No." I shook my head.

"It would take no effort at all, but that doesn't mean it's a good idea—for me, or for you."

So that door wasn't completely closed. Good to know. "What do you want from me, Brooke?"

She smiled. "I want you to make love to me in my bed, and then I'll tell you the rest of my story. After that you can decide if you still want me."

Turnabout is fair play, baby. "I agree, but only if we switch it around. You tell me first, and then we make love. And for the record, I've already decided."

Her face fell and her eyes narrowed.

"I know what you're doing. You think that whatever you have to tell me will make me stop wanting to be with you; I'll leave, and you'll be vindicated of your fucking absurd notion that you are unworthy to be loved by me."

"It will," she said.

"Well, baby, you're just going to have to trust me then and see what happens." I smiled this time. "Let's get into the bed, shall we?"

$$$

SO into her bed we were going. Buck-ass naked, but not to fuck.

Both of us tense, unsure of how we fit into the other's life. I knew where I wanted her in mine, but she seemed pretty adamant about where I could be in hers. Sex was okay, but love wasn't, apparently. How was it possible to find the one woman on earth I *needed* to make life bearable, only to have her believing I shouldn't love her because she wasn't worthy?

My heart was being fucked from all directions.

I held out my arms to her and embraced her as she fell into them, loving how her soft skin melted into mine when our bodies aligned. I tugged her down into bed, tucked the sheets and blankets that smelled of her around us, and waited . . .

She talked and I listened. Her heart had been broken before, and mine was being broken now as she told me her story.

"I was truly born on the wrong side of the tracks as you say in America. The wrong side of the sheets is what it was called back home. My mother went to London for a semester abroad when she was in college. She met my father, Michael Harvey, and very quickly fell madly in love. She also fell pregnant with me. But my father was already married and had a family. My mother and I were his secret. He loved us and was a steady part of our lives, but we would always be the shameful secret that must be hidden away because that's just how it was. He was an MP, a Member of Parliament, and I never took his name. That is why my last name is Casterley like my nan. Dad had money, and he kept us well looked after, which was fine when he was alive—but there was no provision for us when he died. The one exception was my university education, because he'd set it up when I was born in my birth name. It was the one thing his sons couldn't take, because legally it was mine. I have two half brothers I've never met in person.

"My parents died while they were on holiday together, still very much in love as they had always been. It was fast and it was final, and before I could really process my shock, I was sent here to my nan, who is my only living family on my mum's side. It was hard at first, but I did settle in, and came to love living on the island. I finished high school here, and managed to find my place in a strange new world. When it was time for university, I went to Suffolk because it was close to home, and my nan. I excelled in my field of study, and my college years were happy. I couldn't have wanted or needed anything different in the time in my life before I met Marcus. I was close to finishing up university and hoping to work in one of the prestigious firms in the Boston designer loop after graduation.

"My friend Zoe, who was also my roommate at the time, went with me to a bar where we had far too many tequila shots and not enough common sense to fill a thimble between us. Marcus was there that night and he took a liking to me. I am sure he also put something in my drink because I don't remember going home with him. I was a virgin before I met Marcus. He was very attentive at first, and I don't even know why. He was a law student about to take the bar exam and eight years older than me. So, without much of an idea of how or why, I was suddenly with this man who'd become obsessed with me literally overnight. He just inserted himself into my life, and I couldn't escape him, because I was too young, and too naïve, to even be aware of the risk until it was too late.

"He got me pregnant and then demanded I marry him. I never should have agreed, but given my mum's history, I did it for the baby's sake. He moved us to California the minute classes ended. I didn't even get to go through graduation ceremonies. Los Angeles is where his family lived, and that's when my nightmare really began. Marcus had a mental illness I am certain, and his erratic behavior just grew worse as my pregnancy advanced. He would get angry at the most insignificant things and fly into a rage, terrorizing anyone within range.

"His family also ran some criminal enterprises of smuggling guns and other black-market items. They used their storage rental units as a front for the real business of smuggling I think. I tried to stay out of their way as much as possible, but it wasn't always easy for me to do that, because he used drugs to manipulate and control me. Prescription painkillers—I don't even know what drugs he gave me, just that they helped block out the nightmare that was my life. Which was living with a sociopathic criminal and expecting his child. I didn't want to have a baby. I was only twenty-two years old, just starting out, with so many hopes—only to find myself pregnant, in an abusive relationship, and addicted to drugs.

"Then the accident happened and he died. I was in a coma for three weeks before I woke up. Once my head was clear of the drugs, I knew I could get help and escape for good. I still worry that Marcus's dad will show up on my doorstep someday and try to make me go back to California, just to punish me for living instead of his son. Or to make sure I never talk to the police about them. I don't really know if they would try to hurt me or not, but I don't want to take the chance, either, so living on the island has its benefits, being so much more secluded.

"When I notified the hospital authorities I was in an abusive family situation, they quietly helped me into a women's shelter in San Diego. That shelter saved my life, because it was mostly a place of peace. I needed sanctuary after a year of mayhem and chaos. I lived there for six months, learning self-defense and how to be strong. It took my near-death to wake me up so I could have a second chance at living. In total I was away for eighteen months, but like I told you before, having a purpose has made all the difference in helping me to move forward. When Nan needed me, it was time for me to make my way home to Boston, and so here I am."

"And then you met me," I said.

"Yes, I met the most wonderful and patient man, who has never made me feel pitiful or weak. He tells me I am brave and smart and beautiful. He makes me laugh, and he makes me cry, too, but the crying is not his fault."

"It's not your fault, either, Brooke."

"He makes me happy, makes me feel so safe, and is such a gentleman always—all-w-w-ways—"

She broke down and couldn't say any more, so I just held her in my arms and drew my hand over her hair for a long time, imagining a world where there were no fucking lunatics like Marcus Patten, and no innocent young girls being terrorized without hope of escape, and nobody to help them.

How could she think that anything she'd just told me would alter my feelings? The things she'd just shared were all nonissues for me. Only the old New England society into which I'd been born kept track of any of that shit. It wasn't the 1890s anymore for fuck's sake. I'd lived in that superficial world for so long, it took Brooke bringing me into the real one to even realize it existed. I had some work to do, but there were good ideas rolling around in my head now. I would figure it out, but most of all I would be patient, because time was what Brooke needed.

I turned to the side to find her lips. She needed to be kissed for a very long time . . . and cherished, to help her remember she was once whole and could be so again.

When I kissed her, she came to life in my arms.

Like Sleeping Beauty in the fucking fairy tale, my beauty came to life in my arms.

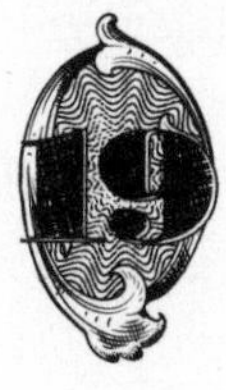

Brooke

His weekender bag open on the floor was the first thing I saw when I woke up alone in my bed the next morning. Caleb hadn't packed his bag and left me. He was still here, somewhere, as daylight blasted in through the slits in the shutters.

And I was still pinching myself.

Caleb was so unlike Marcus. He was also unlike any man I had ever known. He was patient and so very considerate, and he listened. Caleb was the most attentive listener. He never made me feel like he was sorry for me, either. He went out of his way to tell me I was brave or smart. He saw things in me I didn't see in myself, and now that I'd had a taste of his good opinion, I wanted more of it. So much more. Caleb would give me the world if I let him.

Could I possibly let him?

I pushed my face into the pillow he'd slept on and tried to catch his scent. It was definitely there, the notes of earthy spice I'd come to associate with him mixed with the unmistakable scent of sex. Lots of sex. I imagined how he must have looked while he'd been sleeping soundly in my bed: no doubt sporting some sexy bed head, the big body and long limbs that'd been all over me last night at rest and relaxed, his steady even breathing softly filling the silence.

I knew there had been a shift since last night, and it was a big one for me.

The picture of Caleb in my mind spoke of loyalty and strength.

I was now more afraid of losing him than I was of loving him.

$$$

I would be smiling when he first laid eyes on me this morning, I decided as I got out of bed and headed into the shower. He should have smiles coming from me, especially after the dreadful row and the things I'd said to him last night. Why had he made love to me so sweetly after hearing everything? *Why did he want to be in my world?* What man would sign up for the train wreck that was surely going to be life with me?

Unless . . . he'd meant it.

I'd never known that sort of love. Never known unconditional, fearless love. Apart from Nan. But from a man? Was it really possible?

There was something to be said for unburdening one's biggest fears, because I did feel so much lighter in my heart today. If he truly did love me, after what he now knew, then at least I could believe *for him* . . . it was real.

$$$

I went out through the back and headed for the high coastal plain. Maybe a little pixie was whispering into my ear that he was outside, looking over the land, and I might possibly find him there. Caleb didn't waste words. *I have the means to make it happen. Watch me.* He said exactly what he intended, so I wondered—I even dared to hope—if he really was going to come and be in my world with me.

I texted him.

B: Where are you?

C: I'm still here, baby. Do u miss me?

B: Always. <3

C: Where are u?

B: I'm at the grassy rise behind the cottage.

C: Take the south path and u will find me.

My Caleb could give proper directions.

B: Ok on my way.

After pocketing my phone, I went in search of my man. *My* man. Yes, I was claiming him as mine. I might not be able to keep him forever, but for right now, and in this place—he was mine.

I spied him about twenty minutes later. He wasn't difficult to spot. I could find him in a crowd easily now, because I was familiar with his body shape and build—which was all lean muscles and tall. He was in dark jeans and a black Henley with his coat unbuttoned. And he looked absolutely delicious to me as always. *He's said he feels love for you.*

But my Caleb wasn't alone. Another man was beside him, pointing across the field as if he was familiarizing Caleb with the island. My heart sped up as I went to him. He must have felt my presence, because he turned toward me. His face lit up with one of his gorgeous smiles as he held out his hand beckoning me to come forward.

How could I *not* fall in love with this man?

He drew me into his side with his arm snug around me, and put his lips to my cheek. I felt him inhale against my skin and instantly knew what he was doing. I did the same to him whenever I could. The scent of a lover was powerful in its ability to produce feelings of comfort. Caleb was breathing in my scent right now in front of a stranger. It was done discreetly, under the guise of a welcome kiss to the cheek, but it was oh-so-very intimate to me.

I gave him the smile I'd promised myself I would this morning when I'd wakened. I saw only happiness in his eyes, no demands and no hurt like I'd seen in them last night—just love. At least I could say it inside my head now and not fall apart. Baby steps.

He introduced me to Asher Woodrow, whom I'd never met in person but had heard mentioned by the locals. He was rather stoic, but polite in a broodingly handsome sort of way. Apparently Caleb and Asher went all the way back to their Boy Scout days on the island, but had lost touch over the years. He owned the Blackstone Island Airport and also the helicopter charter to and from the mainland. I was content to be an observer as they finished their conversation about helipad access at the airport in an exchange of sorts with Blackstone Global Enterprises' own helipad in the heart of the city. Caleb was just full of surprises with the news he owned not only a helicopter but a private helipad in the city of Boston.

And just like that my good feelings of *baby steps* took a dive. How very deep was the gulf between his world and mine.

It still didn't change my longing for him to choose to be in my world with me. How could it not? How would *any* woman not want Caleb to choose her? I still had trouble understanding why a man like him was still single in the first place. Why was that? What about the women in his past?

I feared I might *never* belong in Caleb's world with him.

After we said good-bye to Asher, we walked back up the path hand in hand, enjoying the stunning sight of an autumn sun over dark-blue water with the lighthouse standing watch along the rocks. I loved the beautiful views from the island.

"What were you up to so early this morning?" I was definitely curious now.

"I was eager to explore the south end of the island and orient myself to the land that is available." No wasted words from my Caleb. He said what he meant to do, and then he did it.

"I wondered . . . I hoped," I said as I turned toward him.

He stopped and pulled me against his chest and held me as we both watched the sea and the sky blending into continuous shades of blue. I breathed in his spicy male scent and tried to understand and accept all of the goodness I felt with Caleb. He was pure and simple *goodness* in every way . . . for me.

"So, when I build a house here, you won't be mad at me?"

I lost it. Fell apart again, for what felt like the hundredth time with him, and sobbed into his strong chest. "Nev-v-ver m-mad at y-you, Caaa-leb."

He held me and smoothed his hand over my head. Caleb understood I was happy crying and not sad crying, so at least there was that. And he wasn't running away from me at a fast clip, either. I'd given him many opportunities, and still he kept coming back for more emotional torture. It had to be utter torture for him. Men didn't like drama and emotional breakdowns. How could he bear it? I could barely stand myself when I did it. But Caleb just held me and showed his care and understanding in the most perfect way.

"I want to talk to you about a few things. Can we sit?" he asked me softly. "We can use my coat for a blanket on the grass. This is such a great view and we should enjoy it while the weather is good."

"Yes, I'd like that very much," I answered him with my cheek still pressed to his chest as I looked out at the sea, reluctant to separate my body from his.

He spread out his coat for us and sat down, situating me between his legs in front of him so I could lean back onto him. Surrounded by his touch and warmth, the panic of a few moments ago left me. It passed as if it had never happened.

"I got up early this morning and did some research."

"You were researching land for sale so you can build a house here?" I asked.

"Well, yes and no. The property search came later. This morning I wanted to know about the sudden onset of strong emotional responses, crying in particular."

"Oh?" My heart sped up. "Did you see my picture pop up when you typed it in the search bar on Google?"

He laughed. "Sorry, but that was very funny."

"I'm glad you think so. It's lovely to be able to laugh about this with you." I paused dramatically. "Otherwise I should start crying."

"Well, no, your beautiful image did not pop up, but something quite interesting did."

"Tell me." I dared not hope there might be some form of treatment.

"The site I found said it is one of the most hidden of all neurological disorders—a condition called pseudobulbar affect, PBA."

"It has a *name*?!" I was shocked.

"Here, let me read it to you from the site itself." He tapped into his phone and started reading. "People with PBA are subject to uncontrollable episodes of crying or laughing without an evident reason. While the exact causes of the disorder are not fully understood, it appears to be associated with injuries to neurological pathways in the brain that control emotional response. It is often seen in patients with diseases like ALS, MS, Alzheimer's, Parkinson's, and in those who've experienced *brain trauma*," he said with emphasis.

"Brain trauma . . ." I breathed.

"Let me finish the last bit," he scolded gently. "In some cases, a patient with PBA has an underlying brain injury he or she wasn't even aware of. One of the main things that distinguish PBA from depression is that the emotional episodes are unpredictable and very short, ranging from seconds to minutes, and they occur multiple times a day. They require a great deal of energy to hold back." He squeezed my shoulder. "You were right, Brooke, about not feeling depressed, because I don't see that in you, either. But you did have a serious injury," he said, while tracing the scar along my hairline with his finger.

"I was in a coma for three weeks . . . because that is what your brain does after a traumatic injury. The accident—I knew it did something to me. I felt that I was different, but I didn't delve further because I figured there was nothing to be done about it. Plus, I was so grateful to be alive, when I could've died so very easily, I just didn't dwell on the fact the episodes were happening more frequently."

"There is more."

I froze. "I am afraid to even hope there is a treatment that doesn't involve a brain surgeon and a scalpel."

He laughed again and kissed the top of my head. "You have a beautiful and brilliant brain, Brooke Casterley. You can think up the cleverest things to say to me at the oddest moments. It must be your British wit."

"Maybe so, but you have a beautiful and brilliant *heart*, Caleb Blackstone. You can do magic with it and in ways I never imagined. It must be your American optimism."

He leaned around to speak close against my lips. "There is a medication you can take that makes the episodes far less frequent."

"Amazing."

"When you're ready, I want you to see a specialist in the city. Will you do that for me?"

"Yes. After the wedding is over, I will." I could feel the warmth of his lips so very close to mine. "I want to do it for me, too."

"Thank you, baby."

Then he kissed me thoroughly and showed me yet again the range of just how far his beautiful and brilliant heart could go.

Caleb

Brooke on her knees with her lips wrapped around my dick was an out-of-this-fucking-world beautiful thing. So beautiful, in fact, I was having another one of those cornea-burning experiences. Yeah, I was gonna go blind soon, but it would feel so good as it happened and I would be smiling when the world went dark.

"Baby . . . ahhh . . . feels good. Jesus—it's good." I guided her head as she took me all the way to the base of my cock again and again. Being inside any part of her without a barrier was the fucking best feeling. She tugged on my nuts and rolled them around in her hand as I felt everything tighten up. "I'm going to come in your mouth. If you don't want that—stop now," I ground out, totally on the edge of losing my control. I removed my hands from her head and brought them up to mine, gripping handfuls of my own hair until my scalp stung. "Ahhh . . . fuuuck!" I threw my head back as it started.

But she did not stop.

She did not pull her lovely mouth off my cock.

No, she slid me to the back of her throat instead, and took every shot of my cum until there was no more, her eyes on mine as I emptied into her. It was a perfect moment of intimacy and generosity from her to me—almost. Because although I understood the need to show her patience, there was one thing I regretted.

She wasn't yet ready to hear me say *I love you.* I certainly would have said it in that moment as our eyes connected—because I certainly loved her.

I hauled her up from where she'd been kneeling and put her on my lap. Pressed us chest to chest and folded her legs alongside my hips. She nestled into me, and I inhaled the intoxicating scent of her. Hair that reminded me of a field of flowers reaching for the sun, and skin that held the essence of oranges for some reason. Maybe it was the perfume or lotion she used, but the scent of oranges would forever be something I associated with her.

Oranges mingled with the earthy scent of the seed I'd just pumped into her.

My caveman notions weren't lost on me, either. I was right there in the mental state of "woman mine—you come under my furs—my cave—we fuck now" with Brooke. She'd turned me into one horny fucking creature, that side of me wanting to get buck-ass naked and lick each other's privates for a day. The impulse was there; training just taught us to suppress it. But when we were alone with someone who felt the same way, the impulse was triggered, allowing us to act out our very dirty fantasies in a way that was totally liberating. Brooke triggered that impulse for me.

It was real and it was permanent, of this I was certain—I couldn't feel this way about anyone else but her, going forward.

I hadn't come back to the cottage with her expecting sex, either. We hadn't made it past her living room couch. It was just something that kept happening with us—our bodies needing the connection physically. There was no denying it was a primal drive with me. I wanted to fuck her every day for the rest of my life. An absolutely crazy idea to wrap my head around, but also brutally accurate for how I felt when we were alone and I could touch her. I craved to see her satisfied and marked with the telltale signs of being well used and pleasured by me. Especially after last night's soul baring. She'd been through a tremendous ordeal, and nearly lost her life in the process. I could not have the luxury of forgetting that fact or pressing her to move on from her past at a pace faster than she was able.

$$$

"HOW do you feel about birth control?" The time had come for me to ask the question.

"I am all for it," she said with witty sassiness plus a stealthily delivered dig into my side with her hand. She got me good, zinging me before I could tamp it down, revealing my weakness.

"Oh, you are so getting tickled for that little move, beautiful." I launched my attack, pinning her onto the couch with one hand and going to town on her ribs with the other. She shrieked and writhed, trying to escape my onslaught, but to no avail. Because my inner caveman impulses were being triggered by the sight of her perfect tits and flushed skin moving beneath me, ready to go another round of fucking.

"Noooo! Caaaleb, I'm sorry for starting it—really—I—I was going to bring it uuuuup to you."

"Oh, you were? Are you sure you don't just want me to stop tickling you, baby?"

"I want you to stop, aaaaaand we can talk about it," she begged.

I quickly moved my tickling hand down between her legs and found my way into her slippery folds with my fingers. "Oh yeah, you're wet for me." I stroked her in measured circles and watched her reaction to my touch. She came alive with movement, and her eyes flared in passion as she moved against my hand. "Because I want to be right in here with nothing between us. I want it, Brooke."

I lowered my lips to hers and plunged my tongue deep, claiming her mouth in suggestion of how I wanted to claim her with my cock where my fingers were buried in her slick, wet heat right now. I curled my fingers inward and found the place where the texture changed and worked her G-spot mercilessly. My tongue impaled her mouth and my fingers her cunt—mine completely in the moment. I was a motherfucking caveman with my woman beneath me.

The experience was incomparable.

She moaned into my mouth and gripped her inner walls around my fingers as she rode her way to climax. I felt her clench and spasm. I heard her gasps of pleasure as she came. I tasted her sweetness. Her breath gusted against my mouth as I used my teeth to nip at her lips while she descended from the high. I relished the way her whole body softened in my arms as I held her to me—a fusion of body and spirit.

I readjusted our bodies so she could lie on top of me, and drew the throw blanket from the back of the couch over us. I could have carried her up the stairs to her bed, but I didn't want to lose the moment we'd just shared. It was something too special to interrupt.

"Caleb?" she asked in a soft voice, after a few minutes had passed.

"Hmm?"

"I was only ever with Marcus . . . before you . . . and with him it was nothing like it is with you. I never knew sex could be so good until you showed me. I'd heard stories, of course, but it wasn't my experience. I just wanted you to know." She lifted her head to rest her chin on my sternum so we could see each other. She smiled. "And to thank you for healing that part of me, which was very much in need of it."

Her words gutted me in a way that was both wonderful and shameful. Wonderful that I'd been the one to show Brooke sexual pleasure for the first time—and shameful for being the guy who'd had his dick in countless women before her, women who were nothing more than a screw that ended in an orgasm. Nothing to be proud of there. Not something I wanted to discuss, either.

With my finger, I traced from the corner of her eye, down her cheek, and over her lips before I spoke. "Brooke, I feel like you are the one healing me." She shook her head in doubt. "No, I mean that. It's one hundred percent the truth. I've been with many, but none have made me feel the way I do with you."

"And how is that?" she asked wistfully.

"Like we have to be the *only* ones to work on healing each other from now on."

"Ahh . . . so *Sexual Healing* should be our song then?"

"Amusing. You say the wittiest things, baby."

"I only do it because you seem to like it so much."

"You're right, and I think you should keep right on being witty for me, too." I pulled her lips to mine and kissed her thoroughly, mentally preparing myself to tell her the part I wished I didn't have to bring up. "I want you to know I was with someone before I met you. She left me in doubt about what she was doing, and who she was doing it with when I wasn't around. Even though we always used protection, I still got tested immediately after we split. I'm clean. I never would've gone there with you just now if I wasn't, Brooke. You can trust me."

As much as it pained me to mention Janice, even in the past tense, I felt better telling her myself, because the Internet was loaded with a multitude of stories and photos about me. If Brooke wanted to know about Janice and others I'd been with, the pictures were there for her to find in living color right along with some gossip's take on where I'd been, with whom, and for what purpose. She'd probably seen some of it already. I hoped Brooke realized most of it was absolute bullshit, too. The kind of press I loathed because it was paparazzi reporting based only on my name and personal wealth. Nobody wanted pictures of men with barely two cents to rub together when out with a date. Just once I'd love for some press on the clean well water Blackstone Global was bringing to third-world farm villages to be plastered next to my picture. I wouldn't hold my breath, but it would sure be fucking nice for a change.

"I know I can trust you, Caleb Blackstone." She reached up and held my face. I wondered if she knew I was her captive when she did small things like touch her hand to my face. "So, about the birth control . . ." She rubbed her thumb over my lower lip, which I struggled to resist from claiming by pulling it into my mouth. "Before I left the shelter they offered testing and an exam, which I had done. The doctor gave me a prescription for pills. I never filled it because it felt like I would be putting myself out there for casual sex, and I wasn't ready. I wasn't ready emotionally for much of anything when I first returned to Boston. I needed those five months to work and take care of Nan and rediscover myself even. But that was before I met you, Caleb. I can't deny that after meeting you, it was different for me, too. I *wanted* to be with you. I knew that you would be good for me, and I could safely entrust my body and my heart to you. My point is, I can have my prescription filled now and start them. We should be protected by the time you return from Abu Dhabi."

She gave me a look when I didn't respond in an appropriate amount of time, and then a little squeeze to my cheek where her hand still rested.

I guess I was too busy falling more in love with her to notice.

$$$

THE Black Bay Club was situated right on the rocks, overlooking the bay from its miles of manicured green fairways that were prized by golfers the world over. Golf had been my father's game, but it wasn't mine. I'd kept the exorbitant dues at his private golf club current after he'd died, though. You never knew when it might be useful, and tonight being a member of Black Bay was *very* useful—affording me a private venue for taking Brooke to dinner and saying my dreaded good-bye before I took off for Abu Dhabi around midnight. She'd cooked for me and spoiled me rotten for two solid days, and now I insisted she have a break.

The thought of leaving her behind on the island was a bit easier to take than the idea of leaving her in Boston. I knew she was taking the rest of the week off from work to help her grandmother get settled after her release from physical therapy. I couldn't deny being pleased my girl would be tucked away safely on the island for most of my business trip. I didn't trust the media getting hold of Brooke and my relationship with her. I knew it would happen in time, and hopefully when it did, I could have her more under the shell of my protection to shield her from the worst of their scrutiny. The paparazzi were fuckers, pure and simple. They would dig up any dirt to be dug up and share it with the world just to sell a few papers. I didn't want her hurt by their certain insensitivity to her past or anything to do with her life before I'd met her.

"I haven't had a chance to hear about your work much. What inspired you to become an interior designer?"

"I was following in my mother's footsteps at first I suppose."

"How so?"

"Well, she attended Suffolk University when she was in college, and she studied design. I told you how she met my father while on a semester in London."

"Right, I remember." I'd seen a picture of her parents on display at the cottage. Her mother looked like a 1990s version of Brooke in the photo—the same beauty easily recognizable in their shared features. "You said 'at first.'"

"Yes, I think I liked the idea of learning the same material as what she had studied, and even going to the same school. It gave me a way to feel close to her by having something in common." She rubbed the back of the left side of her neck, which was a tell as clear as day from where I was sitting. I hadn't earned my billions without learning to read people over the years. "I love my job. I really enjoy the challenge of finding the perfect design for a client's vision," she said.

"Why do I hear a *but* at the end of that statement?"

She gave me a sweet smile. "You are observant, Caleb."

"With you, even more so than usual." It was the truth. I wanted to know everything about her. "So, if you could do anything at all, what would you choose to be?"

She answered quickly. "I would choose to be a Marni Cole."

I tilted my head and waited for her to explain, certain it would be an interesting story at the very least.

"When I was first at the women's shelter in San Diego, I was probably still in shock. And I know I was grieving the loss of my baby. I named her Sophia. I didn't even know she was a girl until after I woke up from my coma because I hadn't had the second-trimester sonogram yet—the one where the sex of the baby can be revealed if the technician can get a good enough view between little squirmy legs." Her eyes grew glassy, but I didn't interrupt. I was spellbound by her story and wanted to hear more. "Even though I hadn't wanted to be a mother at such a young age, I still bonded with my baby, and it was . . . hard . . . to let go emotionally once I didn't have her inside me anymore."

I reached across the table and took her hand in mine.

"I didn't want to socialize or do much of anything at first. Like I told you before, I just wanted to find some peace from the awful noise in my head. When you live in a state of constant turmoil, tranquility becomes a precious commodity."

I turned her hand so her palm was facing up.

"Shelters run on volunteers who come and do a variety of jobs that need to be done. Some work in the kitchen and help with meals, some offer counseling or legal assistance, others might balance the books, or work the phones—usually the volunteer offers their time, doing whatever their regular day job is or providing a skill they have. There was this woman named Marni and her skill was gardening. I found out she was a certified master gardener during the course of knowing her. She would come to the shelter and work her magic with the flowers. Being San Diego, the growing season is nearly the entire year, and the weather rarely prevents a person from being outside, so Marni came often. As soon as I arrived at the shelter, craving the peace I hadn't known for more than a year, I was immediately drawn to the gardens. I'd sit out there among the flowers and basically started to heal . . . in my coveted peaceful place. A beautiful garden surrounded with blooms, where nobody screamed in mindless rages, or toyed with my head, or got perverse pleasure from scaring me."

I traced the letter *I* on her palm with my finger.

"Marni didn't push me to talk about my past. In fact, she didn't talk very much at all. Marni was in need of her own peaceful place, and coming to the shelter to volunteer was helping her as much as it was helping the facility. One day she just handed me a garden trowel and pointed to some weeds that needed thinning and that was when I really started my healing journey. As I spent time in the garden with Marni, we got to know each other. I learned she had a husband who was a pediatric surgeon and lived in a lovely home in La Jolla with her dogs and a koi pond in the backyard. She told me about her son, Phillip. He had been an only child with his whole life ahead of him when he was killed in a car accident one week before Christmas at the age of twenty. It was the Friday school let out for winter break, so drivers were jittery when Phillip was exiting the freeway on his way to work. A delivery truck on a deadline jumped lanes without looking first, and just obliterated Marni's only son in the blink of an eye. He was gone."

I traced the shape of a heart three times.

"Marni told me how she lost herself for quite some time. She took drugs to silence the voices in her head and became addicted. She was found wandering the streets dressed in clothing that had been put on inside out and backward, high on pills with no memories of days and weeks that had passed. Her husband had her committed to a private clinic for recovery and rehab, and in time she improved and was able to come home. Marni was lucky in the sense that she had the monetary resources for the help she needed, and someone who loved her enough to make sure she received it."

I wrote out the letters *Y-O-U-R* slowly.

"After she came home, Marni started volunteering at the shelter in San Diego. She said that it helped *her* more than anything. Volunteering gave her a reason to get up and live the rest of her life one day at a time without Phillip, because making the world more beautiful was a good reason. I agreed with her. Because by then I'd shared with Marni how the only thing I wanted to find was a peaceful place and that her beautiful garden had been it." Brooke lifted her golden eyes to mine. "So, I realize that was just a very long answer to your question and I hope I didn't make you uncomfortable with my rambling. I've never shared that story with anyone before."

I traced another heart in the palm of her lovely hand and saw her smile.

She gets me.

I love her.

"I love your heart, too, Caleb."

Brooke

Lucas lived about one mile from the Black Bay Club where Caleb took me to dinner. Caleb had asked Lucas to fly him back to Boston in his helicopter so he could have one more evening with me. It was a very sweet gesture from my man, who also let me in on the secret about the mainland only being fifteen minutes away by *chopper*, as he called it. I shouldn't be surprised by now. The Blackstone brothers conducted their pissing contests over whose helicopter was better. Rich boys and their toys . . .

As I pulled up to the helipad and parked, I could make out the shape of a man waiting in the shadows. The similarities in build and size were apparent even in the dark so I knew it was Lucas. I'd heard of his scars from my nan's friend Sylvie, who cleaned his house. Sylvie spoke well of her employer, who remained somewhat of a mystery to the local residents due to his desire for privacy. Lucas Blackstone could afford to keep private on the island, which from what I'd heard, he mostly did.

When Caleb introduced me to Lucas, I wasn't really sure what I was expecting from him, but the confident and warm greeting he offered surprised me. Lucas shared the same height and lean musculature of his older brother, as well as the dark-brown hair and wide shoulders. He even had similar facial features and expressions to Caleb when he spoke, but his right cheek—from the corner of his eye, down and around the bottom of his ear, leading even farther down his neck and disappearing into his shirt collar—was marred with considerable scarring. His eyes were also unusual like Caleb's in their coloring, but not in the same way. Lucas's eyes were green but his right eye was partially brown. An anomaly of genetics but strangely beautiful. Similarly, his prominent scarring didn't detract from his handsomeness at all in my opinion. I imagined it probably made him even more attractive to women. I wondered what the story was there. Regardless, the younger Blackstone brother was no Quasimodo, living in seclusion on an island in desperate need of social skills. He was doing just fine.

"Lovely to meet you finally, Lucas. I hear nothing but good things from Sylvie. She adores you."

"Ahhh, well I am a lucky man because she spoils me rotten. It's nice to meet you officially, Brooke." He handed me a business card. "My cell is on the back. If you ever need anything please don't hesitate to reach out to me. I am here on the island ninety percent of the time."

I tilted my head at him. "Did Caleb tell you to look out for me while he is away, Lucas?"

"Ummm . . ." he stalled, darting his eyes between his brother and me.

"It's okay, Lucas. I won't take it out on you," I said, focusing my annoyed eyes on Caleb, who was doing his best at melting me with his signature cheeky charm.

"Well, in that case, yes he did, Brooke, but please know that I am nothing but honored." Lucas gave off his own version of the Blackstone charm in the form of a sincere smile. These men were good at charming women of all ages, I'd predict. Very, very good.

Must be a superb gene pool.

"Well then, I thank you, Lucas. That is very kind." I put his card into my pocket.

"I'll just start her up then, bro, give you a minute. Brooke, I'll see you soon." Lucas kissed my cheek before walking over to the huge machine and climbing inside it.

Caleb waited until Lucas was out of earshot before asking, "Did that make you mad I asked my brother to watch out for you?"

"Not really, but it will take some getting used to," I answered truthfully.

"You can trust Lucas with your life. If you need *anything* at all, you call him. Can you do that for me, baby?"

He pulled me against him, and I took in his scent in a deep inhale. "I will remember. It's nice that you are so protective and concerned."

"It's the only way I can leave you right now and not lose my mind."

"I'll be busy here for the rest of the week, and then on Monday I'll be back at work in the city. You don't have to worry about me. Just miss me." I lifted my lips for him to kiss.

He brought both hands up to my face to hold me to him. "The first request is impossible, and the second is definite," he said, before kissing me deeply enough that the taste of him would linger for a while.

"My PA, Victoria Blakney, will have the keys delivered for the penthouse so you can get in for whatever you need to start on the job. I'll be back a week from tonight, and I would love it if you'll plan to stay that night with me, because I will need to show you how much I missed you while I was gone."

"Oh? You plan to demonstrate this?" I couldn't resist winding him up.

"Most definitely. I will need to show you over and over again just how *much* I missed you. In fact, it will probably take me all night long.

I would plan on taking Thursday off from work if I were you, because I'm imagining a sick day for both of us."

"I see." I put my hand on his chest right over his beating heart and felt the pulsing rhythm. "I will remember to be well rested on Wednesday afternoon, then."

Teasing was the only way I could get through sending him away without crying. Of course, now was not one of those times I burst into unexpected tears or laughter. Thank God. I did feel like I was finding myself again, though. I'd lost my sense of fun with Marcus. It was as if he'd turned off the light within me, which I'd never allow anyone to do again. I was strong, able, and tough when I needed to be, and now I was finding joy again, too. And all because of the gentle, attentive, loving man who I would miss terribly during the next seven days.

Accept it, fool. You're already in love with him.

$$$

LUCAS gave it three days before he called.

I was delivering the last boxes of Nan's things to Herman's house and feeling more than a little emotional, so his timing was perfect. "Brooke, can I invite you to dinner tonight? We can talk about politics, religion, and money to make each other awkwardly uncomfortable before we bond over embarrassing childhood stories about Caleb."

I laughed at his teasing, knowing I'd say yes for a couple of reasons. I knew it would make Caleb happy, and I was curious about his family. "Well, Lucas, when you tempt me like that, I have no choice but to accept. I'll be over by six o'clock, and I like my wine on the sweet side."

$$$

LUCAS had a glass of sangria waiting for me and a collection of delivery takeout menus to choose from when I arrived at his house. I accepted the delicious, fruity wine and vetoed the takeout. Instead, I asked to be shown to his kitchen where I found two aprons—one for each of us—and announced we would be cooking something much better than anything we could order in. Making myself at home in his pantry, I rummaged through ingredients and fired off some questions about any possible dietary restrictions until we settled on a salad and chicken fettuccine Alfredo.

By the time our dinner was ready, we'd progressed to well past the getting-to-know-you stage and were down to being best buddies. When crying over chopped onions and minced garlic together, those walls go down quickly. The only reference he made to his scarring was to tell me his hearing was impaired in his right ear, so to speak to his left side if possible . . . and not to take it personally if he seemed to ignore something I said. I told him not to take it personally if I suddenly started weeping or laughing for no reason . . . and pointed to the scar at my hairline. He nodded in understanding, and I would bet Caleb had already filled him in on me, because he didn't question my bizarre statement in the slightest.

In that moment, I knew I'd made a true friend in Lucas Blackstone, because we had clicked. For whatever reason, we just sort of bonded in a way that was easy and very comfortable. I felt that our friendship would stand regardless of wherever Caleb and I ended up, and that was something meaningful. I didn't have a great many friends, but the ones I did have were very precious to me, and it was always welcome to make a new one.

Lucas spent the remainder of the evening teaching me to play iInVidiosa, the game he'd created. I sucked at video games, but he sucked at making dinner, so it all evened out in the end. I made him promise that our next dinner would be at my place before I left. Lucas made me promise to call him as soon as I made it home to let him know I'd arrived safely.

It just went on like that until we were both laughing as I backed Woody out of his driveway, him signaling me with the hand to the ear gesture for "Call me." The Blackstone men had a strong protective streak, and I felt very fortunate to be at the center of their care. My life had been rather bereft of male presence for a long time, and this felt good.

The time difference between Boston and Abu Dhabi was nine hours, which made calls with Caleb difficult, so we texted mostly. After I got back to the cottage, I dutifully called Lucas before getting ready for bed and bringing my phone with me. Once I was settled under my covers, I calculated the time in Abu Dhabi to be seven thirty in the morning, which was actually a good time to catch him if I was going to have any shot at all, because he would probably be up and starting his day.

B: I had dinner with Lucas tonight so you can stop worrying about me.

C: I already told you that would be impossible, baby. But do you miss me?

B: Always, Caleb. <3

C: I bought you something today I can't wait to give you.

B: I have something I cannot wait to give you, too. *blushing*

C: Is my Brooke sexting me? Please say yes, and send me a picture of your naked tits so I can make it thru this dreadful day.

I'd never done it before, but that didn't stop me. I stripped off my pajamas and selfied myself naked in the mirror for my man. It was a side shot, but I was *naked*, and Caleb would know it once he saw it. I held my breath and pressed Send.

> B: Here you go, but only one is showing. My first sext ever! And you are the lucky recipient! I have to go to sleep now but I will dream of you. Miss you tons. xoxo –Brooke <3

I tried to imagine him looking at the picture I'd just sent him, and even though we were separated by thousands of miles, I could feel him close to me in that moment. I waited for his response before I put my phone away.

It came instantly and made my heart flutter inside my chest.

> C: You are fucking beautiful and I miss you much more now . . . thank you for the picture. I will be right there in your dreams, Brooke . . . and I'm never leaving. You're stuck with me now, baby. –C xx

I am sure I fell asleep smiling, replaying his words over and over again in my head.

$$$

CALEB'S personal assistant was nothing like I'd imagined her to be. She was young and beautiful, with long dark hair and blue eyes, but with the no-nonsense personality of someone much older than what could only be early twenties. Kind of like my nan, if I had to put a person to it. She wasn't rude or obnoxious, but she was all business when she dropped off the keys and alarm codes to the penthouse at Harris & Goode on

Monday. I didn't miss the diamond engagement ring she was wearing on her left hand, either. I couldn't help that part, I suppose, when meeting my boyfriend's beautiful personal assistant for the first time. Knowing she was engaged to someone else did not hurt. She also gave me her personal cell number, insisting I call if I needed anything at all. Victoria told me she shared the twelfth floor with her brother, James, in the same building as Caleb's penthouse, so she was close if I ever needed her.

So weird—the PA thing—having someone to do the tasks that ninety-nine percent of the population did for themselves. Like pick up dry cleaning, drop off keys, and order flowers for the girl who trashed her boss's suit with shrimp cocktail. I thanked Victoria for her choice of the red peonies and showed her how well they were thriving in my office.

That earned me a smile and a sincere, "You're very welcome."

$$$

ON Wednesday, Eduardo and I worked at the penthouse, measuring everything and finishing up the initial programming. Before starting any project there needed to be an inventory of the existing furniture, and some analysis to identify the positive attributes of the space, as well as any potential problems. I could hardly concentrate on the job, though.

Because Caleb was coming back tonight, and I'd see him again in just a few hours.

"That's the last of the measurements for this room. I'm thinking we'll start in here before moving on to the kitchen," I said as Eduardo packed up the equipment. "It's really a huge job, and since he's given me absolutely no solid plans for what he wants, I'm flying a little blind here."

Eduardo looked up from his phone and smirked. "Because he's much more interested in giving you his *solid cock* until you go a little blind, *condesa*. Just warm up the color palette and buy some pieces that are fuck friendly and he will be very happy, trust me." He nodded enthusiastically.

"My God, Eduardo." I scowled at him, and even though I'd never admit to it, he was probably right.

"I can design this shit in my sleep, I tell you. All a man thinks about when it comes to designs and décor is if it can be used for sex. Make sure there are many places for him to play pound the *punani* with you in here and he will love it. As I said before, fuck *friendly* should be your theme for the whole—"

"Hello?" a feminine voice sounded behind me, and I cringed at what she might have just overheard.

I whipped around with a smile plastered to my face and met the voice. I was sure whoever it was had just gotten an earful. "Brooke Casterley, from Harris & Goode Designs for Mr. Black-s-stone," I stammered, "and this is my assistant, Eduardo Ramos."

"Winter Blackstone, Caleb's sister. I just wanted to meet the woman who has captivated my brother," she said with a grin, "and don't worry, because I absolutely didn't hear a single thing that was said just now."

Oh, I like you, Winter Blackstone. She was still just as lovely as I remembered—dark-brown hair and green eyes with the same gold rings around the iris as Caleb had around his blue ones. The Blackstone children had genetically unusual eyes it seemed. We shook hands and chatted easily, and after her comment about not overhearing Eduardo's outrageousness about fuck-friendly designing, I could have kissed her. Jesus, so embarrassing, but she put me completely at ease—as if it hadn't happened. So I had the privilege of meeting another Blackstone sibling. Well, meeting her for the second time, because technically we'd met eight years ago at her birthday party.

"I remember you at my sixteenth birthday," she said.

"Oh, I remember the party. You were very kind and sat with me."

"We talked about the Jonas Brothers and watched the others playing chicken fight in the pool."

"Yes. The party was at Blackwater, and I remember how pretty the grounds and garden were that day," I said honestly. From what I could recall, the grounds at Blackwater had been just beautiful. I wondered if they had fallen into disrepair along with the house when it was shuttered.

Winter looked thoughtful, as if she was reflecting on a memory. "It makes me sad the place will be gone out of our family soon. My mother is determined to sell since we don't stay there anymore. I've always thought it could be repurposed as a school or a retreat of some sort. The location is ideal, but sadly, I can't imagine anyone who can actually afford to buy Blackwater being very altruistic." She frowned. "Trust me, I know from experience."

"Caleb shared with me that you are finishing your master's in social work."

"Yes, I will finish in spring and then it's time to find something to do with it. I will. There are plenty of people who need help," she said optimistically.

"You are right about that," I agreed. "I am sure you will find just what you need."

"I'm going to go now, darling. I know you have to prepare for your all-nighter so I am off to find my own something to twerk." Eduardo flounced the end of his yellow scarf as he kissed me on both cheeks. "Nice to meet you, Winter Blackstone." He took her hand and brought it up to his lips in far too familiar a fashion for someone he'd just met, but this was Eduardo and he got away with shit like that all day long. I was so used to it by now I barely registered he'd just referred to my *all-nighter* reunion with Caleb in front of his little sister. God.

Winter giggled as he sailed out the door with his yellow scarf bouncing along behind him, as only my friend could manage. "Oh, you've got another one," he called to us as he disappeared out of sight.

Eduardo's final comment made sense a few seconds later when a tall, dark, and handsome man walked into the main room and introduced himself. "Hi there. James Blakney, two floors down. You must be Brooke." He held out his hand in greeting.

"Yes." I shook his hand. "Nice to meet you, James Blakney, two floors down. You must be the brother Victoria told me about. Are you also a friend of Caleb's perhaps?"

"Been wreaking havoc together since we were ten years old," he said, grinning wickedly.

"Somehow I don't doubt it." I noticed Winter had gone quiet beside me. "You must know Winter then," I suggested.

James Blakney's eyes changed as he directed them onto Winter Blackstone. They went from a green-brown to fiery dark as he raked them over her longingly. "Mmm-hmm. The twelfth floor is mine, and Winter is right . . . underneath me."

I caught the tension—or whatever was going on between them—and just smiled. I pretended ignorance at just how badly James Blakney had it for Caleb's very beautiful little sister.

Interesting. I wondered if Caleb was aware, and if so what his thoughts were.

"So, did Caleb tell you to stop by and check on me?" I directed my question to the both of them.

Winter nodded, smiling.

James said, "To meet you and take you to dinner actually. Caleb's instructions are to bring you and Winter to dinner at Callihan's, and he'll meet us there. He should be in Boston in under two hours—he just texted me and ordered it done. The bastard's a bit of a dictator sometimes."

"I see. Please don't tell him that I find his *dictator*-ing utterly adorable, okay?"

Yeah, you love him all right.

Caleb

What in the hell had I been thinking?

Reuniting with Brooke after so many days apart in a public restaurant was the worst idea ever. And I couldn't even begin to understand why James and Winter were here, too. James was supposed to deliver Brooke to Callihan's, not invite himself along on a double date—with my baby sister for fuck's sake! *Asshole.* The restaurant was situated on the level directly above the Blackstone Global offices, and just below the helipad. I'd thought it would be extra convenient for me to arrive via chopper, and then merely take the elevator down to meet Brooke for dinner. But things were not even remotely going to plan tonight.

Fail.

I'd wanted Brooke alone in a private dining corner of Callihan's where we could make out over a plate of food and not have to worry about being seen. After dinner we would've taken the elevator down to my executive offices where I'd give her the grand tour, and if she were game—we'd break in the bed in my attached en suite apartment. Then I would've taken her home to the penthouse and fucked the longing I'd lived with for the last seven days out of my system, until we were both too exhausted to move. Finally, I would have fallen asleep with my beautiful woman safe in my arms and in my bed.

That was how this motherfucking night was supposed to go.

But—no—I was being cock blocked by my best friend while trying to tamp down a raging hard-on.

Brooke *was* sitting beside me, though, and I had zero complaints about that. Inhaling the scent of oranges, I squeezed her hand under the table and turned to her ear. "I want to be alone with you so badly I might die before this dinner is over," I whispered.

She curled her neck into my lips and laughed quietly. "I'm not in the slightest bit hungry, Caleb . . . for dinner," she answered so softly only I heard.

Not one more second was wasted before I was standing up from my chair and helping Brooke from hers. As soon as I comprehended what she'd said to me, I knew I was done here with the public show. I needed privacy and her naked—and in that order. "We have to leave," I said.

"But you just got here," James said. "What about your dinners?"

"It's an emergency, so thank you for picking up the tab for this one. Next time is on me." I really hoped he heard the silent *you fucking idiot* attached to the end of my explanation. I think my sister did, because she looked away with her lips pressed together like she was trying to hold back from laughing. Christ, I hoped he could get Winter home safely without any problems. *What the fuck is wrong with you tonight, James?* If I wasn't so desperate to be with Brooke, I would probably be worried about him.

Nah.

As I got her the hell out of Callihan's, I knew my desperation for Brooke far outweighed any worry I could possibly ever have for James.

$$$

THE second the elevator doors shut, I had my tongue in her mouth and my hands up her top. I found breasts, and held one in each hand, remembering the weight and shape as I tried to get in close to her. I thumbed her nipples through the material of her bra and felt them tighten as she moaned sexily in my mouth. Doors opened. I prayed there was nobody standing behind me getting one hell of a show, because only a bullet to the head would've probably stopped me, I was so needy to touch her.

Not true.

Brooke had the magic, calming presence capable of settling me down.

She had equal powers really, because she could make me instantly wild and raging to take her, but then switch me down to a more mellow need—just by using her voice. Both worked in tandem, but only she held that power over me. Nobody else had ever possessed such powers, and never would in the future, either—only her.

Brooke put her hands to my face and pushed me back a bit out of her personal space, her lips sensuously red and puffy already. My whole body throbbed at how sexy she looked with her swollen lips. Lips I could imagine wrapped around my hard cock in a few, short minutes.

"Let's go." I pulled her by the hand out of the elevator.

"Where are you taking me, Caleb?"

"My office has a suite with a bed in it." Relevant information was all that was needed here. My Brooke was very smart, and I knew she would understand.

I think I was nearly at a run, and dragging Brooke along by the hand, when we made it inside the executive offices of Blackstone Global, and then the suite. I fumbled for lights and made sure to lock the door. The most critical tasks were behind me now.

Thank fuck.

"How has my beautiful girl been?" I asked against her neck.

"Dying to be with you again," she said as her hands buried in my hair.

Yeah, I might come before my dick ever made it inside her.

"Get naked for me, baby."

"Okay," she said breathily as she bent down to unzip her boots.

I lost my suit jacket and tossed it somewhere, conscious only of her personal strip show as I tried to get out of my own clothes.

She went to work at peeling away each layer as I watched in silent appreciation.

And my dick grew painfully harder.

When her perfect tits came into view as the black lace bra went away, I knew I had to have a taste of them on my tongue, or I wouldn't make it past five minutes. I would be dead from sexual torture.

"You are the most beautiful thing in the world, Brooke. Don't ever doubt my feelings about that."

As the vision of her came into view—an angel kneeling, naked on the bed with her soft womanly curves and long legs folded beneath her—I relished my lovely prize and came forward to meet her.

She reached out her hand and put it over my heart, drawing over my nipple and leaning in with her lips to kiss me there and suck it into her mouth. I hissed at the feel of her tongue abrading my sensitive flesh, knowing this would have to be a quick and dirty fuck in order to clear my head.

I pushed her backward onto the bed and spread her legs wide, admiring her feminine assets, because her pussy was just as perfect as her tits. Bare and pink with just a sculpted strip of pale hair for decoration . . . I. Fucking. Loved.

I braced myself over her, hesitating on what to do first. It was a hard decision, and the delay just made it a little sweeter. Brooke looked up at me with her amber eyes glowing like golden fire and licked her lips. I drew two fingers through her oh-so-fine pussy and separated the folds, found her clit, which was slippery and ready, and rubbed up and down. She arched and thrust against my hand, making the sexiest sounds imaginable, until I just couldn't wait anymore.

"I need to take you now."

"Yeees, please, I want—"

She never finished whatever she was going to say.

Because I'd already aligned my cock and slid home deep—all the way to my balls.

Tight, hot, and wet perfection gripped my bare cock—and it was a fucking joyful feeling, too. Skin on skin with Brooke for the first time. It stole my breath for a moment, in fact, because I'd never done it before.

My first time.

I'd never been in a relationship with anyone that'd made it to this point before. There had to be a certain level of trust, and before I met Brooke, that trust just hadn't been present for me with any of the women I'd ever known.

"Okay, baby?" I asked her through a haze of desire.

"Yes . . ." She squeezed the walls of her cunt and gripped around my cock blissfully tight.

"Oh holy fuck, you feel good. Do you know how much I've thought of this moment when I could put myself bare inside this tight little pussy, ready to take my cock?"

"Oh God, Caleb—please!"

"What, baby? What can I do for you? I think I need to hear the words come out of your pretty mouth."

"You can get busy with fucking me," she moaned with a thrust of her pelvis to bring me even deeper.

No more talking, my girl had spoken. I circled her wrists and dragged them over her head, pinning her, bound to the bed and captured by my driving cock. I fucked her like a madman, hard . . . deep . . . and wildly.

She loved it, and met me at every stroke, her legs folded and spread wide, quivering and shaking from the building climax I was going to give her. Along with a hot load of my cum to mark her as mine. I'd never done that, either.

I took her mouth in an almost punishing kiss, showing her how deeply I could possess her body, because she'd possessed mine from the moment I'd laid eyes on her. Moving down to lick at her nipples, I suckled on her tits, demanding each one in turn, leaving marks behind to show I'd been there. She made those sexy sounds of pleasure that made me say every dirty thing my pitiful brain could think up to say to her—half out of my mind with lust. How much I needed to have her spread out underneath me like this—how good she smelled with the scent of us fucking in the air—how beautiful she looked with my cock drilling in and out of her tight cunt. Crazy shit I would never say out loud to her when I was sane.

But like this—with her—sanity was fuckin' impossible.

I felt her spasms clench around my shaft as it started the tightening rush of blood that swelled my cock. "Come with me, Brooke. I need that with you right now. I need you to feel me loving you so you never forget what that feels like—coming from me."

She arched her back and froze, lifting off the bed as she cried out her release, along with some really fucking beautiful words. "I do feel you loving me, Caleb."

Her golden eyes filled with tears as I filled her with my seed, spilling every last drop I had to offer in some primitive gesture of claiming her as mine—screaming to the world she belonged to me and no one else.

Total bliss with my girl.

I moved my hands down to grip her hips and pumped the last few delicious slides into her body before I collapsed, my skin fevered with sweat and the heat of her surrounding me. I rolled us to the side, still joined, and stared into beautiful golden eyes. She continued to spasm and tighten around my cock as she settled down from her rush, drawing out our pleasure. I brushed the strands of hair off her face and kissed her gently, finally able to relax with her in my arms after a week of longing for her.

Also adding to my euphoria was the way in which Brooke allowed me to possess her. She accepted my crazed need to get lost in her body, only making me need the intimacy with her even more. Brooke was the whole perfect package for me, and I loved every glorious inch of her, even if I wasn't supposed to tell her with words yet.

But I could show her by letting her know how it could be like this . . . with us . . . forever.

"Thank you for that welcome home," I whispered against her lips.

"I missed you very much, Caleb, and I'm so glad you're back." She smiled before tucking a piece of hair behind my ear, her hands roaming over my body wherever she wanted to touch me. I loved when she touched me.

"I still have lots of *missing you* to fuck out of my system, but I want to do it properly in my bed at home where I can take my time. This was just a frantic detour to help tide me over, so I didn't lose it in front of a restaurant full of Boston's finest. I have no idea why James and my sister were there, either. The plan was to have you all to myself in a dark, private corner. He must have gotten his wires crossed."

"I didn't mind. James and Winter are lovely and both went out of their way to make me feel welcome in your life. So, thank you for sending them round to meet me." She cupped my cheek and traced over my lower lip with her thumb. "I'm just *really* grateful you have this convenient apartment." She winked sexily.

The urge was overwhelming to make certain she knew honest truth controlled what I said next. "I want you to know that I only use this suite to shower, change clothes, and for an occasional night's sleep when I've worked so late there is no point in going home. Before tonight, I've never done this here."

"Good to know," she said with a half smile. I wished I knew what she was thinking right now, because it would have helped me feel better. But how fucked-up was that concept? I needed reassurance from her about my whoring sexual past? I just needed her—period. Brooke made all of the emptiness of the days and nights I'd known before her fade away into nothingness.

I kissed her thoroughly and tried to memorize the feeling of being inside her as we were right now. I didn't want to leave her body. I wanted to stay connected like this for a long time, because I needed to feel her. She made me this way. Brooke had turned me into a fuckin' needy bastard. Just the facts—I'd realized during our time apart. Distance did indeed make the heart grow fonder, and I'd already accepted it without struggle long before tonight. Being with her now merely cemented the feelings even more deeply.

Before reluctantly pulling out of her warm depths, I thrust back into her slowly one last time. The sensation was different without a condom. One hell of an amazing sensation for me—but a lot messier for her. So, I wet a washcloth with warm water in the bathroom and brought it back to clean her up. Intimacy pretty much on its deepest level, and it made me happy she allowed me to do it for her.

Her eyes never left me as she watched. "You are amazing, Caleb Blackstone. The way you take care of me—right now after making love to me so well—and while you were away by having your family and friends check in on me—by showing me you couldn't wait through a tortuously long dinner to be with me again. I'm having such a wonderful moment with you, I think I'll start crying."

"Go ahead, baby, that's what I'm here for—to give you wonderful moments."

I plan to give them to you for the rest of my life.

Caleb

November

Herman Blackstone and Ellen Casterley were married in a small, elegant ceremony at Stone Church with the autumn sun shining in an arc over Blackstone Island where it merged with the sea. It appeared that Mother Nature had been clued in that the day was a celebration. As I held hands with Brooke and witnessed their vows, the irony wasn't lost on me that a Blackstone and a Casterley were being joined in holy matrimony.

And if I had to guess, I was pretty certain the same thought was crossing more than a few minds in this ancient stone chapel right along with me.

Only Wyatt was missing from my siblings, which wasn't a huge surprise given he kept his life a mystery and could be in another country at the moment for all I knew. Herman's children were there to support their dad, obviously. Reese, Jason, and Jordyn had been blessed with the temperament of their father rather than their mother—thank God—or I doubt we would have ended up so close to our cousins. Aunt Cynthia's death fifteen years ago had loosened her hold on her children, but her marriage to Herman had been long over when she'd died. My mother had pseudo filled the role of mother to Cynthia's children, even if in her own particularly detached method of parenting, for the intervening years.

My mother and Herman had an understanding over his three kids, and neither overstepped each other's roles. They both adhered to the cardinal rule that blood family took precedence over all else—even when you couldn't stand to be around said family member. Personal feelings were the last thing to matter in our world. Instead, wealth and status were next in line, right below blood connections.

Which was the very reason she had to grace us with her presence today. Madelaine Blackstone was showing support for her brother-in-law at his wedding. The key word was *show*. We all knew she'd rather chew glass. The whole thing was just another example of ignoring the pink elephant in the room. My family had a whole zoo full of elephants we ignored. Fucking experts—every last one of us.

My mother had managed to behave herself thus far, but I didn't trust her to continue with the celebratory charade for very much longer. She would grow weary of faking it after a while. It took exceptional energy to swallow the bitter pill of knowing her former housekeeper was now her sister-in-law. That part *was* legitimately weird, though. Brooke's grandmother was now my aunt. My uncle was now Brooke's step-grandfather. We were definitely connected by family, and as much as I tried to set the thoughts aside for the time being, it was impossible for me to deny my truth.

It was very simple really. I was going to marry Brooke. Someday, it would be the two of us in front of a priest. Another Blackstone and Casterley would be joined in holy matrimony. I knew she wasn't ready yet and probably wouldn't be for a long time, but I would wait until she was. We had plenty of time to get there.

The few weeks since I'd been back from Abu Dhabi had been the best of my adult life because of her. Every simple and mundane task was interesting and fun when doing it with Brooke. She liked cooking for me and said it was healthier than eating out all the time. In fact, she didn't want to go out very often because clubs and parties did not interest her. When I could convince her to stay overnight at the penthouse with me, we did simple things like shop for the ingredients to make dinner and watch cable TV. More likely we were making love in front of the fireplace while the TV was on because I don't remember much of anything about the shows we "watched."

Even right now in the middle of a wedding ceremony, I couldn't keep my eyes off her. She had on a pale-gold, lacy dress that only served to make her eyes . . . shine in contrast. My golden girl looked beautiful, of course, but today she didn't have one trace of the usual present sadness. Today she was joyful. Joyful for her grandmother—and it showed.

Seeing Brooke this way gave me a goal. My plan was something only I needed to know as I worked out a way to achieve it. But achieve it I would.

My goal was to give her more reasons to be joyful than opportunities for remembering the sadness of the past. I couldn't delete it or take it away. The fucker who nearly killed her was gone. But I could ensure happiness for her future.

When we filtered out of the chapel after the ceremony, Brooke and I were the last ones out because we'd been the first ones in after the bride and groom. She was quiet beside me as we waited for the people ahead of us to move aside so she could go to her grandmother and Herman. "It was perfect, Brooke. You did a wonderful job of planning and making everything come together."

"Thank you. I am so happy right now." She squeezed my hand and leaned into my chest.

Supporting her body against mine, I propped one shoulder in the doorway while we continued to wait. I kissed the top of her head and breathed in the flowery scent of her hair. "I know you are. I can see it as clear as day, and happiness is a very good look on you, baby."

"You're a big part of it, Caleb." She said it softly as we paused in the entryway of Stone Church.

I heard every word.

Yeah, I'm marrying this girl.

$$$

"SO, Brooke tells me Herman is taking you on a cruise around Europe. Are you looking forward to being on a boat for all of that time?"

Brooke's grandmother gave me a leveled look. "I am thrilled to be free again after so many weeks of therapy, quite honestly. I feel like I've been let out of prison, albeit my guards were very helpful during my incarceration," she joked with me as we took a moment to chat together during the reception. "Herman feels the confinement of the ship will keep me from overdoing it with the new knees. We can take a leisurely pace with touring at ports, or stay on the ship if it becomes overtaxing for me. I'm not too worried because I feel strong, and I'll be busy looking after Herman." She winked mischievously.

"Mrs. Caster—ah—I mean, Mrs. Blackstone, you reminded me so much of Brooke just now. I could hear her saying the same witty comebacks."

She smiled warmly. "Now, Caleb, I think calling me Mrs. Blackstone is a bit too formal, don't you?"

It was awkward, because I really didn't know what to call her. She was still just as approachable as I remembered her to be, but she'd married into my family now, and I sure as hell couldn't call her Mrs. Casterley anymore. "Well, probably yes," I answered honestly.

"I think Aunt Ellen would be appropriate if you feel comfortable with that. Technically, I am your aunt now that I've married your uncle."

"I will surely make the mistake of calling you Mrs. Casterley regularly. In fact, I know I will, but I'll be honored to call you Aunt Ellen as often as my poor brain can remember to say it."

She laughed and agreed to still answer to Mrs. Casterley for me. "Caleb, I'm so glad we are getting this chance to talk, because there is something I've been wanting to discuss with you. I feel as if I don't have a choice in the matter, because I am the only advocate she has."

"Brooke?"

"Yes, I mean Brooke."

"How can I put you at ease, Mrs. Caster—shit, I mean—sorry for the language . . . er . . . Aunt Ellen . . ." Not the best start, but I was curious about what she wanted to discuss.

She patted my hand in reassurance. "Don't worry, Caleb, I come in peace, truly I do. I am just a concerned grandmother looking out for my precious Brooke. You see, I just want to make sure you understand how her past has shaped her."

"She's told me about her husband and about losing her baby. I know her life with Marcus was terrorizing for her. Brooke has shared everything with me."

She nodded thoughtfully. "Yes, I know she has shared with you. She told me. And, Caleb, I feel, or rather—I can *see* you care for Brooke. I can see she cares for you. That part is for the two of you to figure out, although I don't imagine you'll have much of a problem with it." She winked at me again.

"Aunt Ellen, you are going to make a grown man blush."

"Well, good then. It only further supports my observations about you two, but this is not what I want you to take away from our conversation, Caleb." She patted the back of my hand two times with firm taps. "It is about Brooke and how her whole life has been impacted by a lack of choice."

"How do you mean?" I asked.

"Well, her illegitimate birth was out of her control—just something she had to accept. Limited time and access to her father, being his little *secret* was her reality, and something over which she had no control. The death of her parents was a horrifying shock, of course. Being ripped away from her home to come to live in a completely different country was suddenly mandatory. Having to live with me became her only option, regardless if we did end up making a wonderful life together. Just at the moment when her life seemed to finally be on track with the path she was choosing for herself, Marcus came along and ruined everything she'd worked toward. Becoming pregnant, marrying Marcus—neither are things she'd ever have chosen for herself at such a young age. He stalked and trapped her deliberately. Add in the terror she endured the whole time she was imprisoned in her marriage, and you can see how most of her life has been forced down her throat. The ability to choose has been taken from Brooke time and time again, and nearly ended her life in the process."

"I think I understand where you're going with this."

"Do you, Caleb, because you cannot assume she is healed from all of that pain. In fact, she isn't healed yet. I'm telling you, that in order for things to work out with you and Brooke in the long term, it will require you to let her take some control over her life. If you try to force her into a corner, she will run from you as far and as fast as she can, and she won't look back, either. This is my darling granddaughter I am speaking of. I know her. I know what she needs in order to keep the demons at bay."

"I do understand, and honestly, I've sensed the same need in her. I can be patient with her, and I plan to, Mrs. Casterley—goddamn it—I mean, Aunt Ellen!" Her lecture frustrated me because I heard her, I really did. "I hear you. Sorry for the language, again, too."

She laughed at my obvious distress, but it wasn't in a mean way. "You always were very respectful when addressing your elders, Caleb. I think your father raised some fine sons and daughters."

"Thank you for bringing him up. I know he would have been very happy for the two of you. He would have been thrilled to celebrate with everyone today." I noticed she only referred to my father and not my mother. I wondered how their relationship had gone down over the years. It couldn't have been sparkling because my mother didn't pal around with the staff—ever. Madelaine Blackstone liked to keep the lines of status well partitioned at *all* times. Which is what made this wedding celebration all the more uncomfortable for her, by forcing her to blur those lines while bearing a fake smile upon her face.

"I feel the same way about your father," she said with a nod, "but now, Caleb, I want to know how you *really feel* about my Brooke. Do you love her or is she just a distraction for you after the loss of your beloved father?"

Whoa. Talk about going straight for the jugular and digging in with a twist of the blade. Mrs. Casterley—fuck—*Aunt Ellen* . . . didn't beat around the bush; she jabbed a fuckin' spear into it instead. My hesitation to answer spurred her to say more.

"I do apologize for my direct approach, but you must understand I am her only family, Caleb, so think of the question I've just asked you as coming from a very concerned parent." She tilted her head with emphasis. "It is reasonable for me to ask, considering where Brooke has been and what she has endured. She *cannot* be hurt again." Ellen delivered her final statement with steeled intent to *hurt me* if she didn't like my answer.

I liked the fact she was bulldogging me, actually. She was entitled to be protective of her only granddaughter who she had raised for the most part. She'd taken on the role of a parent to Brooke. I put myself in her place and could guarantee I wouldn't be so accommodating to the guy "sleeping" with my daughter. I'd want his balls on a platter if he harmed a single hair on her head—if he ever got close enough to her in the first place, would be debatable.

"I love her. She's not a distraction." The truth was very easy for me.

"I thought so, but I just wanted to hear it from you, Caleb." She now gave me a true smile.

"I am going to marry her," I blurted. She raised an eyebrow at me. "I know she's not ready yet, and I will wait until she is totally ready," I assured her. "And then I'll come to you and ask properly."

Ellen's expression softened again, and then we went right back to generic conversation topics as if the one we'd just finished had never even happened. Strong, gentle, determined, kind. Four words that definitely suited both Casterley women. Well, soon to be two Blackstone women when I get my wish.

"What were you and Nan talking about? It looked fairly intense from across the room," Brooke asked a few minutes later when she made her way back to me after being dragged away by my sisters earlier.

I picked up her hand and planted my lips to the back of it. "We were talking about how precious you are."

"Oh, Caleb—"

Her eyes grew watery as she stared up at me. I got the feeling she had to struggle a bit to accept my answer, but now I understood how her emotions worked, and the tears pretty much confirmed she did, indeed, believe me.

"It's all good, baby. It's all good between your grandmother and me. She just needed some reassurance that I was more than happy to give to her. She also insisted I call her Aunt Ellen from now on."

She took in a deep breath and gave me one of her half-sad smiles—the kind I recognized already as her signature Brooke-is-okay-now smile.

"I have something to tell you later on tonight when we are alone together," she said, still smiling.

"Oh? Is it something I will like to hear?" *I really fuckin' pray it's something I want to hear.*

My heart sped up. I didn't want to hope, but my mind went right to the words I most wanted to hear from her more than anything.

Just three words.

Three words that would confirm what I was feeling went both ways. That it wasn't just my dick talking because the sex was so fucking hot. Sex with Brooke *was* incredibly hot, but I knew I couldn't allow sex to be the main reason behind my ever-growing feelings for her. There had to be some other justification for why I'd felt so strongly about her right from the beginning.

She brought her hand to my cheek and caressed with her thumb, soothing me in an instant. "I think you will like hearing it, Caleb."

24

Brooke

"My son shares next to nothing with me about his life, so imagine my surprise when Winter informed me that he's having the penthouse remodeled from top to bottom." This was Caleb's mother's attempt to engage me in conversation.

It was also her making sure I was fully aware of my place in her world—that of being a paid employee and nothing more. I wasn't offended really, because Caleb had already warned me that she would most likely be prickly with me. She was close to his previous girlfriend's family, apparently, and their breakup had not been well received. Caleb also told me that his relationship with his mother was not a warm one, nor had it ever been. I felt sad for him but didn't really know what to say. It was her problem if she didn't like me being with her son. He was an adult who could choose for himself.

I hadn't imagined she would be thrilled upon meeting me anyway—my reason for being blunt with Caleb in the beginning about us—because I would be a hard sell for many in their high-society, blue-blooded world.

I had no illusions about whose name topped that list of many—Madelaine Blackstone—a classically beautiful woman who dressed impeccably and had perfect hair, makeup, jewelry—everything. She was a very well put together society doyenne who looked too young to have a son Caleb's age. I could see a resemblance between her daughters and her, but not Caleb. He must have gotten all of his looks from his father, because he looked nothing like his mother. Nan had remarked how Caleb looked so much like his father at the same age he could be his clone.

I'd been pleasantly surprised by the rest of his family, though. Lucas and Winter more so, because we'd spent some time together in the last weeks and had bonded already. Today I'd met Willow and her fiancé, Roger, for the first time, and they'd been nothing but kind and friendly to me. Willow even remembered to bring a signed set of her books for me. I had Caleb to thank for that surprise probably, but I suppose Willow wouldn't have gifted me the books if she hadn't felt like doing it.

Herman's children all expressed support of their father's marriage to Nan. Each one had told me personally how glad they were to see their dad finally finding happiness with his soul mate. Herman's relationship with their mother had been acrimonious and remained that way even in the years after their divorce, so it was a good thing for the kids to be able to see their dad happy and in love after such a long time.

All in all, I felt pleasantly relieved that my introduction to the large clan of Blackstones was now behind me—even the matriarch who didn't approve of me being with her son.

"I'd have to agree with you, Mrs. Blackstone. One of the first things I asked Caleb was if his penthouse really needed a remodel because I think it is stunning just as it is now." I smiled at Caleb before I answered her. He winked at me, and I took it as a sign we'd discuss his mum later tonight when we were alone. Right now I was going to kill her with kindness.

She nodded at me in a way that felt patronizing and also one hundred percent calculated before she spoke. "It is a shame really, because Janice thought so, too." Waiting for me to take the bait, she smiled sweetly.

But she would have to wait a very long time, because I'd never ask her the question. I knew very well who Janice was. Caleb's ex—none other than Janice Thorndike—the former face of Vogue, and now working in the upper echelons of the fashion world. I'd seen pictures of them out together on Google, and he'd told me she was the reason behind the black eye he was sporting when I'd first met him. He'd also said getting involved with her had been a terrible mistake because of their two families' close friendship over the years. Anything else about Janice I didn't know would have to remain that way, because I really didn't care to know. Most people had a past. Caleb was a bit older than me. I knew he'd been with many women before me, and nothing would change that fact, so the jealousy factor did not motivate me much. I'd learned being jealous of something that cannot be changed was a pointless waste of my time. Caleb didn't want to be with Janice anymore, and his mother's disappointment over their breakup wouldn't make the slightest influence on his feelings there.

Caleb wanted to be with me—showing me constantly how he felt was so much more powerful than just saying the words.

"Mom, please." Caleb scowled at her and shook his head in annoyance. "*I've* decided that *I* want to make some changes to *my* home . . . because *I* feel the time has come for some changes." He turned to look at me with those gorgeous blue-and-gold eyes of his, and said, "And Brooke is just the person to help me with it."

$$$

"IT was perfection, *condesa. La abuela* looked stunning—a total GILF if not for the part about me being gay," Eduardo told me as I bid him farewell at the ferry.

"I think I should call her up and tell her you said that." He dropped the flippant expression and actually looked scared for once. "Ha . . . gotcha!" I rarely got the upper hand with Eduardo and his outrageous comments, so I relished the enjoyment of making him squirm in fear.

"*Ay, Dios mío*, you scared me, *condesa. Abuela* would have my *cojones*."

"Indeed she would, but she might forgive you for helping make her wedding so lovely."

"It was my very great pleasure to help you both."

Eduardo hugged me good-bye and did the two kisses to each cheek ritual he'd perfected, before boarding the boat. I blew him a kiss, and then turned back to Woody where Caleb was waiting inside for me.

I knew a few people were staying the night at Lucas's beach house, but most of the guests had left the island after seeing the bride and groom away via helicopter. Herman and Nan were spending their wedding night in New York before heading off on their European cruise. The new Mr. and Mrs. Blackstone had looked radiant as they left the island this afternoon. It was strange, sending my grandmother away on her honeymoon, but it also felt so very *right* at the same time.

Caleb was taking a call when I returned, so I didn't interrupt him as I drove us to the cottage. He'd asked me earlier if I wanted to go back to Boston for the rest of the weekend, but I'd told him I wanted to stay here. We'd come to an unspoken agreement about our sleeping arrangements during the last month. Most weekdays I stayed in Boston with him, because the penthouse redesign was now my full-time job. That left the weekends for the island and the cottage. I'd also started working from home on Fridays up until today, because I'd been planning the wedding. There was still plenty I could do via the Internet for redesigning the penthouse, so I planned to continue. I didn't know what Caleb would think of my plan, and since he was technically my boss on the project, I really hoped he wouldn't object. I knew he liked having me at his penthouse. I liked being there with him. But I needed to *live* on the island. I just needed it and didn't really have the words to explain why. Maybe it was some kind of emotional healing for me to live in the same house where my mother grew up. I don't know what it was that bonded me to Blackstone Island so deeply, but the need was there, and Caleb would have to understand and accept it—if he wanted to be with me. I knew what I felt for Caleb, and I didn't want to be difficult. I also knew I didn't want more pressure to acquiesce to a man's control.

Meeting his mother just this afternoon pretty much cemented the fact that I didn't really fit in to the Blackstone billionaire world—even more so now than I'd felt it before. I was an island girl, and I was going to stay an island girl.

"Offer thirty-nine point five and see if she accepts. I feel forty is our threshold on this, but at the same time, I want to make sure she bites hard. There haven't been any reasonable offers up 'til now, so let's just see how this first round goes. And not even a whisper of where this is originating, okay?" I shamelessly listened in on his conversation, knowing he was discussing a deal in the millions of dollars as if it were a daily occurrence. It probably was for him, and served as a reminder, yet again, how vastly different my simple life was from his.

"That's right. William J. Brookermann is the principal on the offer. No, with two *n*'s. I already said it's a silent partnership. She cannot suspect, or it'll flop. Good. Of course, yes, put out feelers with the state. I want to know if it's been done before. We'll talk again midweek."

Caleb ended his call and turned to me, grinning like a boy who'd just found a secret stash of sweets.

"Your business call just now pleases you?" I asked him, now curious about his conversation.

"It does. Very much."

"Are you buying something?"

"I hope so." More cryptic answers from him, but I wasn't the kind of person who begged for answers. I imagined if he wanted to tell me about it, then he would. He hadn't announced anything to me about his plan to buy some land and build a house on the south end of the island, either. I wondered if his call just now had been part of it. Whatever his business deal was about seemed to be good news, so I dropped the subject.

I could feel his eyes on me as I drove the winding roads up through the hilly grassland to the point. "What do you want to do tonight?" he asked after a moment.

"Thank you for asking," I paused, "because it saves me from having to tell you what we are doing tonight."

He laughed. "That's my girl using her wicked British wit on me again. I'd tickle you senseless if you weren't driving this ancient vehicle right now."

I pretended shock. "Are you insulting dear Woody again? I love this *ancient vehicle*, I'll have you know. Woody is here to stay." I stroked over the faux wood-grain fascia as if I were petting a dog.

"He can stay, but what if Woody were to get a loving restoration and then a nice big garage in which to enjoy his retirement? You can take him out on his birthday and special occasions."

"Oh, Caleb, not again with buying me a new car. We've talked about this," I scolded gently. I knew he meant well, but I still felt uncomfortable with the money issue.

He sighed as if conceding to me, so I knew he wasn't really angry. He was just really stubborn when he wanted something. "Well, what if *I* buy a car for use on the island that belongs to *me*, and you can drive it? How does that idea sit with you?" He put his lips to my ear. "I need to know you are as safe as you can possibly be, or I will worry all the fuckin' time. A thirty-six-year-old vehicle is too old to be safely reliable anymore. Please don't make me worry, baby." He kissed below my ear before moving back into his seat.

Very stubborn. "Can we discuss this further after I explain what we're doing tonight?"

"Will what we're doing tonight help you agree to driving the new car with every imaginable safety feature already installed that I'm buying for use on the island?" he fired back. *Stubborn, but totally adorable.*

"Enjoying a soak in my huge claw-foot tub together, and a *massage* from you just might."

"I like that plan, especially where we'll be having our *discussion*, baby," he said wickedly.

$$$

"I want you to redesign my master bath to have a huge bathtub incorporated," he said softly.

"Oh? Because . . . ?" This was a change from what we'd talked about.

"Because I want to do this with you all the time." Caleb had me leaning back against him in the hot water, his arms holding me captive, but only in the very best way. He trailed his fingers up my arm to cross over to my throat, and then down to shape the fullness of a breast before circling the nipple and playing with it until it was tight and throbbing. Caleb liked to keep up the touching long after the sex was over. It was just one of his sweet ways. One of the many.

But the sex was probably not over yet, because I could feel him hard again, his big cock lying flat against my lower back. I wondered what his next move might be. Would it be as thrilling as what we had done before the bath? Which was me on top, riding his magic tongue with his cock down my throat as I came all over his mouth. He'd lifted me off him before I could find my way back to earth, arranging me half on my side and half on my back. With determined movements he'd gripped one leg and held it straight up for leverage.

Then he'd fucked me hard, with those deep-blue eyes drilling into me as intently as his cock had until he throbbed out his own orgasm.

I was so out of it afterward, I wasn't even aware of him preparing the bath we were in right now. Caleb had gotten everything ready and then carried me in here to get in the water with him.

"You weren't so keen about having a bathtub before today," I reminded him.

"That's because I never had anyone I wanted to take a bath with before."

"So, I am your bathing buddy now?"

"Yep—bathing buddy, shower buddy, bed buddy—all of those." He thrust his pelvis into my back so I could feel exactly how hard and ready he was for more.

"You are insatiable."

"You make me insatiable and have from the beginning. I can't help it. Especially when I have your tight naked ass pressed up against my cock. What do you think I am, woman? An alien?"

"Sometimes I do, yes." I turned slightly so I could meet his eyes. "Sometimes I think you can't possibly be a real human man because of how amazing you are, and how kind and generous—Caleb, I want to tell you something important—"

He stopped me with two of his fingers pressed to my lips. "Wait—before you say whatever it is, I have a request."

"All right," I said, curious. "What is your request?"

"I'd like to give you something first. I've had it for a few weeks, but then I wasn't so sure if you would welcome it, so I've held back from giving it to you to wait for the right time. But, I'd like to give it to you now, before you tell me your *something important*." He tilted his head at me. "Please?"

"Okay, Caleb." I absolutely adored him like this. He could be so demanding and dominant during sex, and then transform into the sweetest, most romantic gentleman imaginable. I don't know how he did it, but the combination was pure magic for me. "I can't seem to say no to you."

"I can't give you my gift from inside the bathtub, either."

We both laughed as he helped me out of the tub. I loved this part, too. Caleb liked to dry me off and get me settled after we showered. He was very good as he drew the supersoft Egyptian cotton towel over my skin. He gave extra attention to my breasts and even dropped a few soft kisses as he worked. "You're so beautiful, standing here like this for me," he said on a whisper.

Caleb was very good at just about everything, and I didn't even try to stop the few tears that fell as I watched him take care of me. He didn't react at all to my crying, which oddly, only served to help me to fall even harder for him. The only concession he made to having noticed my tears was when he finished with the towel at my cheeks before helping me into my robe.

$$$

HE handed me a red velvet case with *Cartier* embossed on the top. "For you," he said with an unreadable expression as my heart bounced around inside my chest.

Dressed in my robe, I sat beside him and accepted the box with shaking hands. I lifted the lid to find a link bracelet in white gold with the classic Cartier *C* diamond clasp. The bracelet had three charms attached. A lighthouse with what looked like a diamond at the top to represent the light, a little house with a round window filled in with a red stone, and finally a heart-shaped padlock with a tiny key linked to the lock handle.

"Oh, Caleb, it's so beautiful. Thank you. Thank you for such a perfect gift." I leaned forward and kissed him. "Where did you get this?"

"I found it when I was in Abu Dhabi, and I thought you might like it."

"I more than like it. I love it. How did you know I always wanted a charm bracelet?"

"Well, I didn't, but I hoped you would," he said. "I'm really glad you love it—so does this mean you'll drive the new car I'm getting for you?" He gave me his melting little-boy grin.

"You aren't going to let the car thing go, I can see. All right, I agree to the car, but right now I want you to help me put this gorgeous bracelet on, and tell me why you chose each charm."

"Thank you," he said while gently closing the diamond *C* clasp around my wrist. "It started when I was looking for something that would remind you of me when you wore it. I know the *C* is for

Cartier, but it's also the first letter of *Caleb*, so you should think of me when you see that part." He winked. "The little house with the round window is your cottage of course, but the little red stone in the window reminded me of a meatball . . . so you got a cottage with a meatball window. That should be self-explanatory." He chuckled. "The lighthouse is the Fairchild Light to represent how you are a south-end island girl." He kissed me sweetly. "The padlock is my heart . . . to which there is only one key. The key is you. You are my key, Brooke Casterley."

"That was the most beautiful explanation I've ever heard . . ."

"Look at the back of the padlock, and you'll see my initials are engraved there. I had yours added to the shaft of the key."

In beautiful antique script were the initials *C.J.W.B.* on the padlock, and on the key were mine, *B.E.C.* "So I won't ever forget that you are the heart and I am your key?" I asked.

"That is correct, beautiful."

"What if I told you that you are the same for me, Caleb? That *I* am the heart and you are *my* key?"

"Am I, Brooke?"

I nodded my head up and down because I needed a moment to compose myself from the onslaught of emotions bubbling up. "You are inside my h-heart, Caaa—leb. You're in here s-so very deep, inside a p-part of me I thought—I thought—wouldn't ever be c-capable of f-f-feeling this way." I splayed my palm over my heart and struggled to get the rest of the words out. "But my heart does work. You healed what was broken inside it and brought that part back to life. I know now what I was feeling. I didn't recognize it right away because I'd never felt it before, but I figured it out when you went away on your trip. I missed you dreadfully, but more than that, I saw how much you cared by having your people looking out for me while you were away. That's when I knew for sure. So, at the same time you were choosing this beautiful gift for me, I was realizing I had fallen in love with you." I took his face in both of my hands, rubbed my thumbs over his cheeks, and felt the stubble on his jaw beneath my fingers. "I love you, Caleb Blackstone, who is so very deep inside of my heart."

He closed his eyes for a moment as he took in my words. I heard a rush of breath come out of him and realized he'd been waiting to hear me say it. But now, finally faced with hearing those three important words from me, he was stirred up. I could feel him trembling beneath my hands as I touched him. As clear as day for me to see—telling Caleb I loved him was profoundly meaningful to him.

Loving him had made me realize something. It wasn't about one's station in life. *I love him—every beautiful, generous, thoughtful part of him.* And it was so easy to do so, as if he'd been made for me. I was now seeing it must be the same for him. *He loves me completely.* It hadn't made sense to me before, but loving *him* had opened my eyes to the startling fact. Love simply was.

Caleb didn't say a word when he swept me up into his arms and kissed me. He kissed me the whole distance as he carried me up the stairs. He didn't stop kissing me while he stripped me out of my robe, nor while slipping out of his jeans, which he'd donned after our bath. He kept on kissing me once we were naked on my bed together, and he'd put himself inside me.

When we were as close as two people could possibly be, he said it back to me.

"I love you, Brooke. Only you."

He didn't hold back after that with any of the words he spoke to me.

Neither did I.

25

Brooke

Monday morning came all too quickly for both of us, I think. Resurfacing back to reality after our emotionally binding weekend was like coming down from floating in the clouds to walking barefoot in the desert. But since we were doing it together as a couple, it was okay.

As I was settling the cottage for my days and nights away in Boston, Caleb's phone started blowing up. He took call after call, growing more agitated with each one in a way I'd never witnessed coming from him before.

"No response is the best way to handle it, Calvin, and if you want the funds for your subsidiaries to continue flowing from BGE to your press, then shut this whole mess the fuck down as quietly as possible. Make it go away and you will be rewarded." He tapped into his phone.

"What? Hell, no! Those shithead parasites aren't getting a statement from me. Seriously, Georgie, you know me better than that by now.

Fucking figure it out. Use the full resources of the company that you have at your disposal, and don't give me a reason to find someone else to head up the department. Hanging up now." More taps into his phone.

"I don't care. Why should I, exactly? It's private information they are not entitled to know. Todd, I shouldn't even have to say this, you are the head of fucking PR—do your job and *relate* to the public, for fuck's sake! I already told you what to do, but you didn't like my suggestion." He ended the call abruptly, and on to the next.

"Hey. Yeah, I am done with these goddamn paparazzi circus performers. I need you to reach out to LeRoy in security for setting up a plan for round-the-clock surveillance. Two, with one on call should be sufficient. Twenty-four seven, when out of my sight—at least until this all cools down, or some new sensation pops up in the world to distract the vipers away from her."

I glanced up from watering Nan's potted fern to find him tracking me. He mouthed "Love you" to me as he listened to whoever was speaking to him. He held out his hand, beckoning me to come to him. He took hold of my hand when I came into his reach. "I'll be in around eight thirty. Thank you." His call ended, he pulled me down to sit beside him on the living room couch. He took hold of my chin and gave me such an intense look, I knew something was wrong.

"Who was that on the phone?"

"Just now? Victoria. Before her, it was a series of crybabies in need of some slaps upside the head, unfortunately."

"Caleb, what has happened?"

He still had hold of my chin, which he maneuvered toward his lips for a soft kiss before pulling back again and delivering the same intense blaze from his eyes as before. "I need you to remember all of the things we said to each other this weekend. Those were real words, real feelings, real emotions—the real fucking truth about us. Okay?"

I felt myself break out in a sweat. "You're scaring me. What is this all about? Caleb—I don't know what—"

"Shh . . . it's going to be fine," he soothed, "don't be scared, baby. I'm handling it. All I need from you right now is to trust me to take care of everything to keep you protected. Because I won't let anyone or anything hurt you or take from what we have together."

Protected from what? "Please tell me," I begged, feeling like I might be suddenly sick. Oh God. My first thought was Marcus's family. Could they have found me via my connection to Caleb? *Probably yes.*

"I love you, Brooke," he reminded me, his voice roughly insistent.

"I know you do. I love you, too." *Caleb loves me—don't forget that.*

His jaw tensed. "The paparazzi got wind of the wedding this weekend. They also have photos. Probably sourced from a caterer or someone who facilitated on Saturday, and now the photos have been leaked with lots and lots of speculation. Celebrity news in every format knows about you and me. I had hoped we could have a long time of incognito and quiet before we were faced with this kind of thing. But, that time has evaporated, I'm afraid."

"What are they saying?"

"Here's CNZ's top story of the day." He handed me his phone with a screenshot and photos from the website of a popular celebrity-news TV show. Real Life Cinderella Story—Blackstone Billionaire Claimed by the Maid's Granddaughter the headline read. There was a picture of us together at the wedding. Caleb and I dressed to the nines, standing in the doorway of Stone Church, taken just at the moment when he'd kissed the top of my head. The lighting in the photo made it look as if my dress were white instead of the multicolored gold lace it was actually made of. The photo was misleading and suggestive—as if we were the bride and groom, coming out of the chapel newly married. If I were seeing it from a bystander's viewpoint, I would certainly think so. Done purposefully to appear as if *we'd* had the secret wedding instead of Herman and Nan. The truth wildly stretched to make a nonstory into a headline, which would sell more papers and magazines. *Fucking hell.*

Oh, my God. "Caleb, I don't know what to say." And I really didn't, because it was shocking to think the general public was seeing my picture, and reading my name, and . . . watching me. *Do they know?* Did the Pattens know where I was? Marcus's family had stayed away, but they had to suspect I knew things about them. Or did they think they were untouchable? I wondered if I should be afraid.

"You don't have to say anything, Brooke. I dreaded this happening eventually, but hoped we could have a more gradual introduction of you and me as a couple to the public. The paparazzi dog me all the time, and I fucking hate them. Unfortunately, the wedding tipped them off, or more likely somebody on the island offered the tip for money." He grimaced disgustedly. "It happens all the time."

"So, your phone calls just now were to stop the stories?"

His expression softened in sympathy—for me. "I wish I had that power, baby, oh how I wish." He tucked a loose piece of hair behind my ear. "No, I am afraid we have been outed. It's out there for public consumption now. The paparazzi is going to stalk you and follow you around and write things that are not true about you in the media. They will take your picture and ask you questions when they catch you off guard. The more controversial the story or unflattering the picture, the more valuable it becomes to them, because it sells more papers."

"But, I don't want attention like that, Caleb. I don't want it—I can't bear to be followed around and pictures—"

"Shhhhh." He pressed me against his chest, his hand holding me securely at the back of my neck. "It's okay. Remember what I said when I started this conversation. I love you, and you need to trust me. I am handling it."

"But how does that work, Caleb?" I asked sadly. I couldn't imagine what he could say to calm the panic rising up inside me.

"I've already put in motion to have security on you every second I'm not with you. You shouldn't go into your office today or maybe this entire week. You can work from the penthouse and have Eduardo come meet you there. I can call your boss when we get to my office."

"Bloody security guards?" I couldn't even imagine that scenario.

"I'm afraid it's necessary, baby. I'm so sorry, but it wouldn't be safe for you without security, and I won't take that chance. You're too precious, and there are too many fucking lunatics in the world."

"Like someone might try to kidnap me for ransom or something?" Where had all the oxygen gone? I felt suddenly sick.

"Oh fuck, don't say that. Nobody is going to get close enough to have the chance to do anything to you. I will make sure. Brooke, baby . . . it's okay. You've just gotten a rude introduction to how the media feeds off celebrities just because they have fame, or in my case, wealth."

"You're angry about what they've said about us," I said from against his chest where he was holding me so close to his heart.

"What? Angry? No! I'm not angry about the picture or what it suggests. I love you, and we are together. End of. They would've gotten hold of it eventually. I'm so sorry, Brooke, but it's just one of those not-so-pleasant consequences that come with being with me."

I didn't say anything. I couldn't really. The shock of what he was saying had barely registered in all parts of my very befuddled brain. Caleb rubbed a hand up and down my back while he held me.

The silence drew out, becoming uncomfortable as the seconds ticked on. Finally, I pulled myself out of his hold and looked down at my lap. I couldn't meet his eyes.

"Brooke?" His voice sounded thready.

"Yes?" I kept my head down, still unable to look at him.

"This is the part where you are supposed to say something like, 'I know you love me, Caleb, and I don't care if the world knows about us because I love you, too.'" His voice carried an edge, and I could tell my silence had made him feel as if I were rejecting him.

I lifted my eyes to find him looking very concerned, and maybe even a little hurt. "Oh, Caleb, I know you love me, and I love you back. I am frightened of people invading my personal space . . . and knowing things about me. *I like my quiet life.* I want to keep my quiet life as it is." If he only knew how terrified the thought of photographers snapping my picture and strangers following me around made me feel, he might be a bit more understanding. *Smothered. Suffocated. Controlled.* Those were the feelings I hadn't felt since I'd come back to the island. Those were the feelings associated with Marcus and his terrifying instability. *Breathe.*

But this wasn't the same thing at all. It *felt* the same, but I had never been safe with Marcus. I was safe with Caleb, though. Caleb wasn't trying to control *me* but keep me safe. Safe.

And safety was on the island.

"I know you do, but I can't promise your life will ever be the way it was before, at least not for a while."

"Caleb, I can't—"

"What? You're saying you can't be with me now?" The look he gave me ripped into my heart.

I took a shuddering breath. "Not publicly, Caleb. I can't go back to Boston right now. I'm staying here. I'll work from the cottage this week." I knew I was babbling senselessly, but I couldn't still the panic building inside my chest.

"Brooke, there is no way I am leaving you here unprotected, or letting you out of my sight right now. No fuckin' way, so you can just forget that idea, baby, and let it go right on out of your pretty head." He glared at me in a way I had never seen from him before. "You're coming back to Boston *with me* until I can get your security situated," he insisted, reaching for me.

"But I didn't choose this," I snapped, pulling back from his hands. "I didn't choose this." This time the words came out as a faint whisper.

He froze, his eyes widening as he stared me down. "I know you didn't *choose* this, and neither did I, but I'm trying to make it livable for us both." His scowl was replaced by a softer grimace as he reached for me again—more slowly this time, but not taking no for an answer, either—pulling me to his chest.

I allowed him to hold me and listened to him telling me the many reasons why I had to swallow my fear and go back to Boston for now. He said it would take time to make a secured home for me on the island—and it broke my heart. I didn't know how to tell him what I knew would hurt him. I was scared and feeling like a selfish bitch, but that didn't stop me from complaining.

"But, Caleb, you said you would come and be in my world with me. You told me," I reminded him, knowing it would change nothing about this situation.

"I know I did, and I will, Brooke, but I need some time to make that happen, and right now there's a nest of pit vipers trying to dig out a story about you, and the *only* way I can shield you is to take you back to the city, where I have the resources in place to keep them the fuck out."

"It's not permanent, Caleb, you have to understand that I will go for the short term, and only because of safety reasons. I won't live with you in Boston permanently. I wish I could, for your sake, because your home is there, and your work. But I *know* that I can't. It's very h-hard for m-me to explain, but I n-n-need to live here on the island." I shuddered and gasped for air that seemed in very short supply.

"I understand, baby," he said quietly.

"You do?"

"I do. I understand that's what you need, and because I love you, I want to give you everything that you need. We can live on the island if the city is a deal breaker for you. It doesn't even affect me that much because I can come and go via chopper in mere minutes, but—and this is one huge-ass but—I can't do it overnight. It is going to take some time to get a suitable place for us here, with security that is acceptable, and especially to limit the access of every fool who thinks they can approach us."

I nodded into his chest, breathing in his scent to help stabilize my overtaxed emotions. "Thank you. I'm sorry for all of this trouble. I wish I could feel differently, but it doesn't change how much I love you." It didn't change how much I loved him, but his words just made me love him more. He wasn't trying to make me yield to his demands, but make our new life livable according to *safety* and my needs. *I understand that's what you need, and because I love you, I want to give you everything that you need.* My mother never got that from my father.

He sighed, and it felt as though it was a sigh of relief. I recognized his body language loud and clear. "You will probably never know how much I needed to hear those words from you right now, baby." *Yep. I was right.* "And I don't want you to be a different person—ever. You are just how you should be, and there is nothing to be sorry for."

"None of this mess changes the fact you are a remarkable man. I cannot even begin to understand why you aren't running away from me at a fast clip, but you aren't. You stay with me and tell me you love me and say you will make your home here—with me—and it feels like I'm in a waking dream. This couldn't possibly be real—"

"It's real, Brooke. It's real."

After a few more minutes of silence he asked, "Ready to go?"

"I'm ready," I lied.

As I drove us to the helipad, I ruminated over everything. I knew it would be hard for me to see stories and pictures of me in the gossip magazines, and I made a vow not to read them. The thought of things being written about my personal life made me physically ill. This paparazzi issue would be a tough nut for me to crack. I would do my best and I didn't want to let Caleb down, but I couldn't deny the worry now settled in my heart.

I didn't know if I was strong enough to make it through unscathed—and I guess I was about to find out.

The closer we got to the helipad at Lucas's place, the more I realized the many concessions Caleb had made in order to spend his weekends with me on the island. He was doing his best to accommodate my wishes, except for where the ferry was concerned. He told me Blackstone Island Ferry wasn't going to cut it for his commute, and he didn't want me taking it, either. He cited the time delay was unacceptable for him when his helicopter could make the trip in a quarter of the time. I didn't complain. I'd miss seeing Will, but it was wonderful to make the journey to the mainland in mere minutes, instead of an hour or more depending on the sea conditions.

Caleb's pilot was a huge ex-soldier named Spence. He didn't say much, but Spence was reliable. He was always waiting for us when we pulled up to the helipad, just as he was now. The helicopter was fired up and ready to go when I parked and locked up Woody. Caleb helped me navigate through the extreme wind blasting down off the rotors, and got me settled into my seat and our bags securely stowed.

As he buckled me in, I watched his hands working determinedly in securing the straps, which would make this journey a safe one for me. A kind of a metaphor for what he was trying to do for me in his life. I trusted him completely.

He gave me a quick kiss before strapping himself into his own seat. Caleb didn't seem to have any doubts, and I liked that he was so confident about having me in his life. His confidence would have to do for the both of us right now, because I didn't have mine down yet.

The time to face my new life in the spotlight had come, no matter how much I despised the idea. I was with Caleb now. Everything else could be sorted out with time and patience.

The time to ponder my new situation was very brief.

Because just a short fifteen minutes later, Spence set us down on top of the Blackstone Global Enterprises building in the middle of downtown, corporate Boston.

Caleb

"Caleb, you cannot be serious about this girl. She's the illegitimate grandchild of our former housekeeping staff, for Christ's sake." My mother stood in my office, in her Prada and Gucci armor, somehow under the impression her disapproval of Brooke would influence me to break up with her. *Delusional* was about the only thing that came close to explaining the state of my mother's mental health right now.

"I assure you I am totally serious about Brooke, and for the record, she is the grandchild of your sister-in-law, who is married to my *very* rich uncle. And here's another news flash for you, Mom, we're not in the fifties anymore when people cared about pedigrees. The illegitimacy aspect doesn't pull much weight when there's money to factor into it—mine and Herman's should be enough to smooth over any offended sensibilities." It was a challenge to keep my cool with her attitude. She'd waited three days since the news hit, before descending upon me to throw in her two cents about Brooke. Like I needed her up my ass right now, in addition to fending off the relentless press, who fought for scraps like hyenas over a carcass. It was exhausting.

"Your father would be devastated by this," she said, shaking her head at me.

"Seriously, Mom? You believe that Dad would disapprove of Brooke if he were alive?"

"Yes, Caleb, I *know* he would."

"I disagree. You're wrong about this. One hundred percent wrong. He told me to hold on to the things that make me happy with all of my heart. Since Brooke is the only woman who can ever make me happy, I'm holding on to her."

"He told you that, son?" she asked, her tone much more diffused than when she'd first started in.

"From his deathbed, yes, he did."

A look of pain came over her face, and I could see she was still grieving. "He had some regrets at the end of his life, but he would not condone your relationship with Brooke. The Blackstone name was too important to him." She shook her head slowly. "No, he wouldn't approve, Caleb, not after all he did to make certain you were given the best of everything life had to offer."

"But isn't that what any parent does for their child? Want them to be happy and try to give them the best of everything?"

She was frustrated with my logic, I could tell.

"It will never last. Your relationship with Brooke will not stand the pressures of society. She won't be able to rise above her scandalous past—"

"*She* doesn't have a scandalous past, Mom!"

"Brooke will never be accepted as one of the tribe," she said tightly.

"Brooke doesn't care about social affairs, and frankly, neither do I. If I don't go to another event, where the *tribe* struts around dressed to kill, attempting to blow Chanel-scented smoke up my ass, then I'm good with that. I can still give to the charity without attending."

"You need a wife who understands how to move in the world you were born into, son."

"Someone like Janice, you mean?"

"Yes, exactly. The Thorndikes are just as devastated about this as Janice is. Alicia told me how shocked they were to find out you were in another relationship so soon after breaking off with Janice. It doesn't sit well with them at all."

"Well, don't get your hopes up there, because Janice is definitely *not* a candidate for my future bride. It didn't sit well with me when I was betrayed by their daughter. I'll spare you the ugly details and just leave it there. And they *are* ugly." She grimaced. "Furthermore, there is only one person who will ever claim the title of Mrs. Caleb Blackstone, and her name is Brooke Casterley."

"Caleb, for heaven's sake. We all know Janice, and have for years. I am sure she is not capable of anything any other woman scorned would do given your hasty breakup with her."

Mother dearest, you have no fucking idea. Obviously Janice's parents were clueless about the mental nastiness and manipulation she was capable of. I should've taken pictures of my bathroom before Ann cleaned it. James had received a few texts from her, since I'd blocked her number. Even James had been surprised at the things she'd told him about me. "She still believes you'll marry her," he'd shared with me the other week. "She says you're only biding time with your 'English slut' until you come to your senses and beg her forgiveness for breaking up. She's fucking delusional, my friend." I couldn't agree more. Thank fuck I got away from her when I did.

"Janice is nothing to me and never will be."

"This is very disappointing, Caleb, and if your father were alive, he'd tell you the same."

No, he wouldn't.

"It's happening, Mom," I fired back angrily. "The best thing for you to do is let the notion of Janice and me as a couple go. She was never even a consideration for me."

"So, you truly are going to marry this girl with no family, no money, and no social status of any kind?" she asked, exasperated.

"When she is ready, yes, I am. And I will expect *all* of my family to welcome her into our *tribe* with enthusiastic acceptance and kindness. If you can't do that for Brooke, then you won't have me in your life, either." I let her know I was dead fucking serious. "If you don't believe me, just wait and see what happens."

I never thought I'd see the day where my mother gave up on any of the standards she held. But after I said that last bit, the fight just went out of her. Surprising. It was strange to witness, because I'd never seen her lose the veil of aloof confidence she always carried around. Ever. Surely this wasn't the last I'd hear of it.

$$$

THE Autumn Ball occurred every year on the Saturday after Thanksgiving at the Massachusetts Club in Back Bay. This year would be the 108th black-tie, formal-dress charity ball, and also marked the first public event for Brooke and me. It was, in all respects, our coming-out party. After tonight, there would be no more speculation, or predictions about our relationship, because it would be undeniably confirmed.

The past three weeks of paparazzi battling had been taxing at times, even for me with my wealth of experience in dealing with their pain-in-my-ass antics. Brooke hated them with a passion, but she'd hung in there and stayed in Boston with me where I did my best to keep her off their relentless radar.

In a way, she was their Cinderella-story darling. The initial CNZ headline plus the picture taken of us at the wedding hadn't brought any bad press to our door. Brooke's beauty, and the lack of a past—due to her youth and never being in the public eye before now—was a definite draw for the gossip rags. Poor-but-beautiful working girl catches the eye of bachelor billionaire, and they fall in love with each other. Add in the fact she was British and I was American, it became *the* Cinderella story everyone wanted to read.

Brooke said she didn't care what they found out about her, because there was nothing to hide. All of the people involved were dead, so they couldn't be hurt by anything written about them. Her mother and father, of course, and even her monster of a husband didn't play out so badly in the press when they were dead. The public was sympathetic to those who had suffered. I only cared about Brooke not being hurt by the stories they reported, but so far it was just the usual history of her life up until now. The press loved the theme of her grandmother being the "maid" and marrying into riches. Herman and Ellen's story pushed all the feel-good buttons people had inside them, and I understood why it sold so well for the media.

There had been only one negative back draft from the relentless media attention focused on our relationship. Her picture with me had sparked the memories of the many who had witnessed Aldrich's altercation with Brooke—the ruined designer suits, the inappropriate advances he made toward her, and how she'd fought back by breaking his nose. It was an easy episode to remember for the people who saw it happen, or if they were one of the lucky few hit by the flying shrimp cocktails. The story was passed around to the extent that the details made it back to Mrs. Aldrich, who then sued her disgusting, cheating-ass husband for divorce. Hearing that bit had made me really fucking happy, I had to admit. Aldrich deserved it for how he treated women in general, and I hoped his wife got a helluva big settlement as a reward for putting up with the asshole for so long.

Regardless of the fairly easy time we'd had overall with the paparazzi, my fears for Brooke's safety were by no means erased. My team was on high alert now, as much as ever. Plenty of freaks in the world obsessed on celebrities and tried befriending them. In some cases they stalked and hurt them—their twisted minds justifying their needy, psycho behavior. There was also the worry she could be taken and ransomed, which scared me the most. I trusted very, very few in my immediate circle, and those in it were either my family, or had earned their way in through years of proving it to me. James still wasn't convinced Patten's family would stay away from Brooke. He hadn't found anything that could prove they'd act on approaching her, but we were both aware that she knew a little too much about their criminal activity. It was a slight cloud hanging over us, but I had the luxury of unlimited resources to keep any unwanteds the fuck away from her. The Pattens knew how to hide their shit, though, so we both took comfort believing they thought themselves impenetrable.

I'd made some progress on securing a place for us at the south end of Blackstone Island. My old friend, Asher, had pointed me in the right direction with a twenty-acre plot that abutted Brooke's small property to the south. I'd made offers on other surrounding parcels as well, so we could have a secured oasis, with a great view, and the privacy I required. It would take some time to build a house, but the wheels were already set in motion. I really didn't care where I lived; as long as I had Brooke with me, it would be home. *She made it home.* She wanted to live on the island, so that's where we would live. It was that simple of a decision for me.

Brooke was my most important priority now. My life had changed dramatically in just two short months, and I knew I could never go back to how I'd been living before. Every decision I made now was done with Brooke's input or with her happiness in mind. The more I thought about what my dad had told me on his deathbed, the more I believed him. Despite my mother's conviction Dad would've disapproved of my Brooke, I didn't accept the idea. He would have adored her. He would've told us to go off and be happy together, and make him a grandfather.

Someday.

I pulled up a new text message.

How is my sweet, beautiful girl feeling?

I hoped she was doing better now than this morning, when she'd woken up with a bad headache. I figured she would have let me know by now if she wasn't feeling up to going out to the Autumn Ball.

Much better. Headache is gone. Winter and I are having our makeup and hair done. The bedroom is a beauty salon right now. When are you coming home?

I was thrilled about the fact Brooke and my sister had hit it off. They had common interests, and seemed to find endless topics to talk about. They shopped for clothes and decorator items for the remodel. Winter had introduced Brooke to some of her colleagues at the South Boston Youth Center where she was interning for her master's degree, and now had Brooke signed up to volunteer once a week. Brooke really loved helping the kids, and I could see the potential for her to make an even bigger impact on the center in the future. I'd not forgotten the story she'd told me about the woman who had helped her so much after she'd escaped her abusive marriage. *Marni Cole.* I wasn't crazy about the neighborhood where she went to volunteer and made sure she was fully protected when she went there, but so far everything was settling into a good routine she seemed to enjoy.

C: I have to pick up one thing and then I'll be home. Can't wait to take my Cinderella to the ball. xx

B: I can't wait to be taken by my Prince Charming to the ball. xoxoxoxoxo

We still did the thing where we mimicked each other's words. Somehow it never got old or felt cheesy, even though it totally was.

C: I'll "take" you after the ball, baby.

B: Is my prince sexting me?

C: Yes he is. Send me a picture please.

She sent me a picture all right—wearing a strapless black bra with her hair in giant rollers, and blowing me a kiss.

B: That's the best I can do with others in the room. Lol. Use your imagination.

C: Sexy. I always use my imagination when thinking of you. See you soon, beautiful.

B: See you soon, handsome.

I opened my desk drawer and pulled out the velvet box I'd been hiding inside there for weeks. I'd bought the gift on a whim along with the bracelet when I was in Abu Dhabi for the conference. I'd spent one evening browsing the shops in the hotel complex where the sessions were being held, when I discovered it in a window display.

A ring.

And a very unusual ring at that.

Giving a ring to Brooke seemed like it would have been too much, too fast, at the time. So, I'd held on to it, knowing eventually the time would be right. The ring had been an impulse buy, because it was so perfect for her—for how we'd met—and I hoped she'd understand my thought process in choosing it. I hoped she would want it on her finger.

I'd be finding out soon enough.

I headed toward the elevators leading me down and out of the building, to where Isaac was waiting to take me home . . . to my very own Cinderella.

Brooke

Have you turned around, Caleb?" I called from the hallway into the living room.

"Yes. I'm behaving myself, baby. You can come on out. I'm dying to see you."

My gut danced in nervous glee over attending this ball tonight with Caleb. I'd never gone to anything like it before, and hardly knew what to expect. I liked the fact the Autumn Ball was to benefit charity, and I loved my burgundy silk ball gown, but beyond those two points I wasn't so sure. Caleb just kept reassuring me he would be beside me every second, and that everyone would be displaying their best behavior along with their frocks. The Autumn Ball was always well attended, and thoroughly covered by the media, both local and national. Caleb wanted us to attend as a couple, to hopefully end some of the fascination the press had about our relationship. It was completely nuts to me why they would care so much, but care they did.

I stepped out slowly, testing how to maneuver in yards of silk and tulle. The dress I'd found was a work of art. Deep, wine-red silk, with a sash waist and a full-tulle skirt. The skirt is what sold me on the dress when I first saw it, because it was embellished with three-dimensional velvet cascading flowers. It was a Cinderella dress indeed.

Caleb had turned away from the door as I'd requested. He was wearing a black velvet jacket I'd never seen before, and he smelled delightful. Even from across the room, his unique manly scent, combined with the delicious cologne he used, tempted me. He always looked good, too.

When he'd arrived home to get himself ready, he had to use the guest room to shower and dress, because Winter and I had commandeered our bedroom for the beauty makeovers. He didn't blink an eye over being deposed from his domain. He'd taken one look at the plethora of girly supplies in his bedroom and bathroom, and surrendered to us without a fight. He was so easygoing about such things. Just one of the many qualities of Caleb I adored. I couldn't imagine my life without him now. He was a part of me.

I loved him so much.

"You can now turn around," I said finally.

He pivoted on his foot and swept his eyes from top to bottom, and then back up. "You *are* Cinderella in that dress. I am speechless right now. Every man in the room will be envious of me tonight."

"Will they? And why do you say that, my handsome prince?"

"Because I am the lucky bastard who gets to take you home at the end of the ball and help you out of your pretty dress."

"Ah, thinking ahead as usual, I see."

He stalked toward me, something small I couldn't make out in his hand. "I'm very good at forward thinking, baby. I didn't make my fortune on a string of lousy predictions."

"Indeed." He stopped right in front of me where I could enjoy his intoxicating scent. "Do you have any predictions for the near future?"

"Oh yes," he said wickedly. "For example, I see Cinderella being kissed thoroughly before she gets taken to the ball tonight."

I couldn't hold back the smile. "Cinderella likes your prediction."

He tipped my chin toward his lips with one finger and descended. I had to resist the urge to bury my hands in his hair and go to town as I usually did. I loved seeing his hair mussed with a just-fucked flag proudly waving, but this wasn't the time for it. Instead, I melted into his demanding kiss and let him get me all stirred up. "You are fucking gorgeous, Brooke. I don't know if I can let you out of the house tonight," he said.

"You will disappoint a great deal of people that way, I'm afraid," I reminded him, even though I'd gladly stay home tonight if it were an option.

"Not me they want to see, baby. They want to meet Cinderella tonight." He nibbled on my bottom lip.

My turn to sigh. "I hope you've remembered your promise to stay with me at all times. I'm nervous, Caleb."

"There's nothing to be nervous about, and everyone will love and adore you." He placed something soft into my hand. "I have a very special gift for you. I've been waiting weeks to give it to you, and now is the time."

"Oh!" I looked down at what I held, to see a small black velvet box. A jewelry box. My fingers trembled as they worked on opening the lid. I gasped. *Oh, bloody hell.*

The most unusual ring I'd ever seen—an art piece which had to be one of a kind. A large, dark-pink stone, resembling a pearl, set in masses of pink and white stones—possibly diamonds—to form the shape of a flower. "Caleb . . ." I breathed. "This is stunningly beautiful."

"Do you really love it?" he asked. *How could he doubt I would love this?*

"Yes. I really do. Tell me about this gorgeous ring." I was almost afraid to ask what the ring meant, but knew he'd tell me anyway because he was always honest about everything he did.

"It's a peony—like the flowers I sent to you. The red stone is a forty-carat cabochon tourmaline. The rest of the stones are diamonds, rubies, and pink sapphires. I found it in the jewelry store window in Abu Dhabi, and went in there and bought it five minutes later. There was no question it was meant for you from the moment I saw it."

"How did you know it was meant for me?"

"Everything about this ring reminded me of you . . . of how we met."

"The meatball lesson?" I asked him.

He nodded and smiled. "After I went in the shop and they told me it was a peony, well . . . I knew it was fate at work again." He took the ring out of the box and held it between two fingers. He slipped the empty box into his pocket. "Will you wear it tonight, Brooke?"

"Y-y-yes," I stammered.

He slipped it onto the ring finger of my left hand. The engagement ring finger. I flipped my eyes up to meet his. "My whole life changed the moment I saw you, Brooke. I knew it then. It felt like the shades were drawn open, letting the sunlight in after being shut in the dark for years. That's exactly how it felt for me."

If I could love him any more, I would. He made gestures like this one all the time, rendering me speechless with his thoughtfulness in choosing the perfect gifts. "I love the ring. And I love you, Caleb."

He took both of my hands and kissed me sweetly before pulling back to catch my eyes with his. "I realize you're not ready right now, but I want you to know my greatest desire is to spend the rest of my life loving you—as my wife."

I gasped as he went down onto one knee in front of the picture window, the city lights of Boston a stunning backdrop beyond us. "Brooke Ellen Casterley, will you be my wife and marry me when you feel you are ready?"

The swirling vortex had swept me up again and whisked me away to another time continuum—I was certain about that. It took me a moment to find my voice and to see through the veil of tears, which had welled up in my eyes, but I managed somehow. "I—I will, Caleb, my love."

He did something I'd seen him do before on a few occasions . . .

He closed his eyes for an instant, and then looked up as if sending a silent prayer heavenward. It was a show of relief and gratefulness. My Caleb was so *relieved* I'd said yes.

To own such power over another person was fearsome in a way. To have the burden of their happiness along with your own was a kind of terrible, beautiful treasure.

Priceless . . . but so fragile at the same time.

$$$

MY beautiful ring winked at me throughout dinner at the Autumn Ball. Caleb and I hadn't said anything officially, but it was right there in living color for people to see, and if they put two and two together . . . well . . . we wouldn't lie.

Like most of our entire relationship, this *engagement* was a whirlwind of love and emotions with Caleb.

Jesus, you've just become engaged to Caleb Blackstone!

Just thinking about it felt like a guilty pleasure. But Caleb always had felt like a guilty pleasure to me. I needed to pinch myself that he was real *and* wanted to marry me. He was right, I wasn't ready just this moment to get married again, but knowing Caleb was committed only to me, certainly put me on the fast track to becoming ready. When I'd told him that part, he'd beamed with happiness and said to just let him know when I *was* ready, and he would take care of the rest.

"What are you smiling about?" he asked.

I turned to him. "Thinking about how good it feels for me when you are happy."

"I love you so much," he whispered so nobody could hear, "and I wish I had you all to myself right now so I could show you without words."

As usual his sexy verses turned me into a puddle of goo. Usually it didn't matter, but right now it did. Sitting down to a formal dinner, surrounded by Boston's ultrarich high society, was definitely not the time or place for wanting to shag my fiancé blind, especially with people watching us from all directions.

Rather a problem with Caleb's effect on me, though. He was very good at turning me on at his will. "You've given me something very wonderful to look forward to when this evening is over," I whispered and licked my lips.

He groaned softly. "You're killing me, baby."

$$$

MY headache decided to return with a vengeance after dinner. I was regretting the clam bisque and the champagne already. Neither were probably the best choices for me. I should've known better than to indulge in champagne when I'd had a brutal headache just this morning. It was so delicious, but the aftereffects could be downright deadly. Due to the hectic days leading up to Nan and Herman's wedding and then the sudden move to Boston, I hadn't had time to see the specialist regarding PBA. Caleb had put in a call to the head of neurology at Mass General, who was a friend of a friend—he had connections everywhere it seemed—but I still needed to set up the consultation appointment to begin the process of a proper diagnosis. It had been shelved for now, but Dr. Google had provided a little more on the topic for me to digest. I did wonder if my headaches had anything to do with my accident. *Stress maybe?*

Being on the receiving end of expressions of thinly veiled hatred did not help my headache any. The Thorndikes had been throwing them my way ever since we'd been introduced earlier. I knew who they were, of course—the parents of his ex, Janice. I hadn't seen her yet, but I figured she would make an appearance at some point before the night was over. Caleb had been so stiff and cold when one of the hosts brought Mr. and Mrs. Thorndike over to meet me. I could tell their hostile reactions toward me had wound him up tightly, and I dearly hoped he wouldn't lose his temper over it.

I rubbed my temples with the tips of my fingertips.

"Are you feeling all right, baby?" he asked.

I nodded. "I'm fine, it's just my headache from earlier has decided to return."

"We can leave if you're not well," he said.

"No, Caleb, there's still the silent auction and the awards to come. We absolutely cannot abandon the night just yet. I'll be fine, and I still want to be taken for a spin around the dance floor with my handsome prince." I gave him a smile. "I'll take something for it if you'll get me a glass of iced water."

"Consider it done," he said with a kiss to my throbbing forehead. "Stay right here and I'll be back in a flash."

I watched my man head off on his mission, admiring how handsome he looked in his tuxedo, and so full of love for him I could barely contain it. My eyes landed on my peony ring, and I felt my stomach flutter as I recalled the image of Caleb down on one knee proposing. I did love my ring. The stone looked like a wine-colored pearl—so unique and beautiful—I was afraid it would be damaged if I wore it all the time because it was a piece of bejeweled art rather than a typical engagement ring. It had to have cost a fortune.

As I waited for Caleb to return, I indulged in some people watching. It was fascinating to imagine what people were feeling or thinking about as they went about their evening at a charity gala such as Boston's Autumn Ball. For example, Caleb's brother Lucas was definitely brooding from across the room. He appeared to be people watching, too. I followed his line of sight to Victoria and her fiancé, Clay Whitcomb, who I'd met a few weeks ago. If I had to make a guess, I'd say Victoria wasn't in a much better mood than Lucas was, based on her body language and how she turned away from Clay while he was speaking to her. Victoria and Clay seemed like an odd pairing to me, but I didn't know either of them well enough to make a judgment; it was more of an impression.

Winter and James had come together tonight, but she'd told me numerous times they were *just good friends*. I wasn't so sure about James's interpretation of *good friends* and her interpretation being even remotely on the same page, though. James Blakney wanted Winter Blackstone with a desperation that was clear as day to anyone with two functioning eyeballs. Well, everyone except for Caleb, that is. He didn't see it, and brushed their relationship off as very close, lifelong friends. I just nodded my head and rolled my eyes at his explanation. It wasn't our business anyway. Winter and James were the only ones who needed to be concerned about the status of their *friendship*.

Caleb's other sister Willow and her fiancé, Roger, were in another corner, conversing with Judge Blakney and his wife—James and Victoria's father and mother. Everyone was, indeed, connected somehow, just as Caleb had told me. The Blakneys were an odd coupling as well, just as I felt Victoria's was with Clay Whitcomb. When I'd met the judge and his wife earlier in the evening, I'd been hit with the most powerful sense of déjà vu, making the hairs on the back of my neck prickle. Something was very wrong there. I knew it down deep in my bones that Judge Blakney was a cruel man, and that Mrs. Blakney was trapped on the receiving end of his cruelty. I knew it—because she looked exactly like me when I'd been with Marcus. I very much wished there was something I could do to help her.

It was déjà vu all over again, as Mr. Yogi Berra had so eloquently coined the phrase.

When Caleb didn't return with my water, I decided to go search out some on my own. The pounding in my head was only getting worse, and I really needed to take something quickly.

It wasn't like him to forget about me.

And then I discovered the reason.

Janice Thorndike had arrived.

Although, *this* Janice Thorndike didn't resemble the many pictures I'd seen of her. She definitely wasn't the stunning, svelte, cover-worthy model I knew her to be. Her face was stretched in an ugly sneer, her dark-auburn hair spilling wildly over her thin, pale shoulders. In a word, she looked enraged. Caleb's stance looked angry from behind, if I had to describe how he appeared as I approached where they argued in a corner alongside the bar. He had his back to me, but Janice didn't. She trained her eyes on me with all of the poisonous venom of a cobra ready to strike its prey. My only thought was to get Caleb away from her because she looked downright fucking dangerous.

"I know what you did, you scheming bitch. James told me about the fucking condoms you poked holes into," I heard Caleb say to her. "Do you really think it would matter to me, if she became pregnant as a result of your twisted games, Janice?"

She grinned evilly in my direction, knowing I was watching and listening.

"I'd fucking rejoice if it were true, because I love her, and I'm marrying her."

"Don't lie, Caleb. You're not marrying anybody other than *me*."

"Caleb?" I gasped out his name, needing to understand why exactly they were talking about damaged condoms and possibly pregnancy.

A wave of ice-cold fear settled over me instantly.

Again, the reminiscent feeling of déjà vu filled my head.

My body's recent slew of ailments and pains no longer mystified and confused me. They all made sense to me now. I'd never taken birth control pills before, so I'd chalked my symptoms up to starting on them.

A new medication for me, one that essentially produced the same hormones as when a woman was pregnant.

But I have been pregnant before.

I knew what pregnancy felt like. And I understood that my new birth control pills wouldn't have done a thing for me if I'd already been pregnant when I started on them. If Janice *had* damaged the condoms Caleb and I used the first few times we were together, then . . . it *was* possible.

He turned to find me standing behind them, shocked at what I'd overheard most likely. "Brooke," he said calmly, "this is Janice Thorndike, someone who used to be my friend at one time. Now, I don't recognize her anymore, because she's become a complete stranger to me."

"Fuck you, Caleb," she screeched. "And fuck your English cunt whore, too."

"Janice, meet my fiancée, Brooke Casterley," Caleb said.

I just stood there, gaping at the two of them in utter astonishment. Frozen in place as my emotions collided with the logic of what had happened to us. My hands went protectively to cradle my belly. Caleb and Janice both tracked the movement of my hands with their eyes. It was as if we all comprehended the stark truth in the same few seconds—a brief increment of time that stretched out painfully in slow motion and perfect illumination.

Caleb faced me, then turned a ghostly shade of white. "You *are* pregnant—"

"Noooooo," Janice screamed as she grabbed a champagne flute and smashed it against the bar counter.

The sounds of breaking glass and shouting erupted amid the scramble of bodies rushing toward me. I didn't feel the pain where she slashed at me with the broken glass. I was in automatic defense mode, my goal to protect rather than fight.

Protect my baby at all costs.

I registered the hard floor beneath my back with Caleb hovering over me, his white shirt collar dark with blood as it dripped down from a wound in his neck. *Caleb was hurt.* I felt the pressure of his hands at my side along with a throbbing dull ache as he shouted, "Call 9-1-1. Call 9-1-1. *Call fucking 9-1-1!*"

I was wet where his hands were pressing into me.

It was my blood?

My blood . . . probably blending into the color of my gorgeous ball gown almost perfectly.

I tried to speak, but no words would come. I wanted to tell Caleb I loved him and had no regrets about anything.

Being loved by him was the best thing to ever happen to me.

I could hear him speaking to me even after everything grew dark.

"I love you, and you're going to be okay." He cried the same thing over and over again in a chanting prayer.

My Caleb cried out his love for me so I could hear him. So I'd never forget.

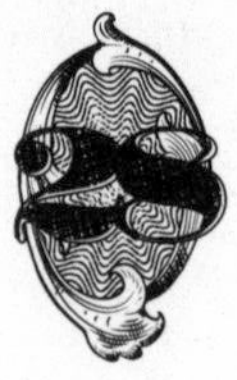

Caleb

I wouldn't let anyone touch my neck until Brooke was wheeled into surgery.

At which time they had to force me to leave her side.

I shuddered to recount the last hour of terrifying agony. My brother's presence was the only thing keeping me from losing my motherfucking shit in the middle of the ER at Mass General. I barely comprehended what the doctor had said about Brooke's injury assessment. My only focus was on her, so thank God for Lucas being here to relay the details to me after the doctor had left.

"She's going to be okay, bro. The surgery is minor, doc said. They're going in as a precaution because a small piece of glass showed up on the ultrasound, and they want a pristine wound before they stitch her up."

"She's pregnant. I heard him say around seven weeks give or take." I couldn't believe it, but it was confirmed before they wheeled her away. One of the first questions they asked me in the ambulance was the possibility of pregnancy. I had to tell them yes. The look on Brooke's face when she overheard me with Janice—she hadn't known she was pregnant, either. This was a complete surprise for all of us.

"Yeah. You're going to be a father, big brother." He slapped a hand down on my thigh. "Your turn to get stitched up. The nurses need to do their job now."

I let them sew up the gash in my neck and was never so afraid in all my life. What if Brooke didn't want to marry me now? What if she wanted to leave me or wanted an abortion? I didn't know the answers to those questions yet, but I knew she wasn't ready to get married right now. Or be pregnant again.

I'd done the same thing that Patten had done to her.

If you try to force her into a corner, she will run from you as far and as fast as she can, and she won't look back, either. Fuck. Her grandmother's words hit me brutally hard right at that moment.

Would she be able to forgive me? Would she see this as the same entrapment she'd gotten from Patten? Could she even still love me after this fucking nightmare was behind us? Would it ever be behind us?

Question after question played in my head like a song on repeat. And I knew no fucking answers to *any* of them.

I asked them to point me in the direction of the hospital's chapel. It had been a long time for me since I'd set foot inside a sanctuary of worship. Didn't matter, though, because it all came back to me. Catholic roots spread deep.

I fell to my knees and prayed.

And the fear of losing the most important person in my life and even our innocent child before I'd have the chance to know him or her absolutely slayed me down to the most humble soul on earth to ever plead for mercy.

$$$

SOFT fingers worked their way through my hair. I knew those fingers, and I recognized their familiar pattern of rubbing and gently tugging on sections at a time. My girl had told me before how much she liked having her hands buried in my hair . . .

"Caaa-leb?"

My eyelids snapped open. "Baby! Oh, my God, how are you?" I jolted awake instantly and feasted my eyes on her. She looked terrible lying in that hospital bed. Pale and weak and worried—and so perfectly beautiful to me, I knew nothing would ever compare for as long as I lived.

"Am I pregnant? I m-mean, was I? Am I st-still?" Her face twisted into a mask of fear as she began to cry.

"Oh, God. Yes, you are. The doc guessed you're about seven weeks along."

She let out a moaning wail and cried even harder. "I was so afraid I wouldn't be when I w-w-woke u-up."

Pure, unadulterated, blessed relief rolled through my body as I leaned over her and held her the best I could in the circumstances. *She wants our baby.*

"Shh, don't worry. Our baby is fine, because its mother is so brave. You protected our child from being hurt. It was your right side where she cut you . . ." I lost it. I just lost my ability to hold it together for a second longer, and sobbed like a bitch. "I l-love you so m-much. I'm so f-fuckin' sorry for everything that's happened to you because of me. I—I am s-s-so s-sorry, Brooke."

It took me a while to come up for air from my emotional breakdown. It was her hands in my hair that grounded me enough to resurface. That she was comforting me at a time like this when she was the one who'd been hurt meant more to me than any words could ever express.

"Caleb?"

"Yes?"

"Do something for me?" she asked in a low voice.

"Anything. Whatever you want, baby. What can I do for you?" I pulled back so we could see each other.

"I need you . . . to tell me . . . your greatest wish. If you could have whatever you wish for right now, what would it be?" She lifted her hand with the IV still stuck in her vein and cupped my cheek. "Be truthful and tell me what you want most in the world."

And the surprises just keep on coming.

Not at all what I expected her to say. I understood clearly that this was not the time to fuck around by hedging or lying. Brooke was dead serious about me giving her the straight-up truth right now. She asked me to tell her what I wanted . . . and so I did.

"I want to marry you the minute you are well enough to do it. I want you to have my name and my ring on your finger, with the legal documentation to back it up. Then I want to take you away to a place that's beautiful and warm and private for about a month. I want it to be somewhere very special, where we do nothing but make love, eat, sleep, talk about our future, plan for the birth of our precious baby, and any other fuckin' thing we want to do."

"Then let's do that," she said softly.

Brooke

December

We married in Stone Church, one week later on the second of December. Only Nan and Herman were there to witness our moment. Herman, in fact, married us. As mayor, he had obtained the proper credentials years ago and on occasion officiated the joining of two people together in matrimony.

After the nightmare events that played out at the ball, Caleb and I were both in agreement that our wedding should be exactly what we wanted . . . and what we needed it to be.

A private ceremony at dusk in the little stone chapel set along the bay with the blazing sunset hovering over everything was indeed what we needed.

I chose a blush silk batiste gown with long sleeves in French lace and no veil. Instead, I had four peonies woven into my hair, which I wore down because Caleb liked it best that way.

Caleb dressed in a black Brioni with a silver patterned tie and a vintage silk pocket handkerchief from his father. He looked so handsome it made my eyes hurt a little to look at him.

The old wooden floorboards inside were strewn with white rose petals perfuming the air to mix with the vanilla-scented candlelight, which was the only lighting.

After signing our names to the proper documents, Herman read us our vows, which we repeated to each other with nothing but love and promises forged into every word. We exchanged platinum wedding bands we had chosen together and would wear forever. Everything was just as it should be.

Caleb and Brooke pledging themselves to one another until death . . . becoming Mr. and Mrs. Blackstone.

$$$

AFTER the vows we celebrated with cupcakes and champagne.

Just one sip of the champagne for me, but I sure enjoyed the sugary goodness of that cupcake. Nan took pictures for us using Caleb's phone, and then it was time for us to say good-bye.

"I love you, my darling Brooke. I was given the greatest gift when you came to me. Nothing could make me happier than I am right now, seeing you and Caleb so in love and so happy together." *And about to make you a great-grandmother*. Nan didn't bother holding back her tears and neither did I. Nothing more needed to be said, because we both knew.

"I love you, Nan."

"I know you do, my darling. Now off you go to start living your beautiful life together," she said to both of us before the final hugs and kisses were exchanged.

Caleb drove us to the Blackstone Island Airport in the new Range Rover Autobiography he'd bought for *island use* as he referred to it. I'd never part with Woody, but I did love driving the new Rover, which delivered an exceptionally smooth ride over the bouncy lanes. It was a short trip to the airport.

A chartered Gulfstream was lit up, waiting to take us to Hawaii for our honeymoon, our bags and everything we needed already stowed.

The only thing left for us to do was board the plane.

"Please wait for me, Mrs. Blackstone," he said. "Stay right where you are."

"Yes, darling." I mocked him a little, but only because I knew it wound him up when I teased him. In only the sexiest way, he'd once told me.

Caleb came around to my side of the Rover, and opened my door. Then he helped me to step down while bunching the skirt of my dress in one hand, so I didn't ruin it.

Still in our wedding clothes, we both needed to change into something more comfortable for our eleven-hour flight to Hawaii. The Gulfstream had a private master bedroom, so I imagined we'd make good use of it. Eleven hours was an awfully long stint to be up in the air, and we should fill our time effectively. *Fill* being the operative word.

"This is what I wanted to do," he said as he swept me up into his arms. "Carry my bride over the threshold—in this case it's the threshold of a jet plane, but it'll work."

"My husband is very strong to lug me around so effortlessly," I said, looking up at him as he carried me onto the plane.

"My wife is a feather when it comes to me having to lug her around," he quipped before planting a decadent kiss on my lips.

At the top of the stairs, we were greeted by the flight staff and the pilots who offered their congratulations on our marriage. Caleb didn't set me down until we'd made our way to the back of the plane and into the master suite. He shut us inside and locked the door, a wicked smirk lighting up his handsome face as he worked.

"You're not even breathing heavily after carrying me all that distance."

He pushed up against me and stared down. "You'll be witness to my heavy breathing in a bit, Mrs. Blackstone, but first we need to take care of a few things."

"What sorts of things?" I asked innocently.

"Well, we need to choose a wedding photo to share with the world, for one thing," he answered.

"Yes, that's true." I nodded.

"We should probably send a text to our close family and friends first, though. They'll have their feelings hurt if they find out our news from the paparazzi before we can tell them."

"You are so smart, Caleb. You have thought of everything." I sat down on the bed and pulled him down to sit beside me. We scrolled through the many photos Nan had taken, until we decided on the one we wanted to share. Caleb sent it off to Victoria with instructions to forward it to the head of PR at Blackstone Global for release to the press with the simple message:

> Caleb Blackstone and Brooke Casterley were married this evening in a private ceremony at Stone Church chapel on south Blackstone Island.

The picture was of us in the doorway of the church, the interior backlit with the candle glow, and the scattered rose petals clearly visible upon the floor. Caleb's lips were pressed to the back of my hand as I smiled up at him with love.

To our close friends and family, we sent a different message:

> We took the advice of a very wise man, and decided

to hold on to our happiness, and each other, starting tonight. With much love, Caleb & Brooke Blackstone xoxo

After the second text was sent, Caleb powered off his phone and pulled me into his arms.

He showed me how much he loved me, as he had done from the very beginning when we'd first met.

My gentleman lover with the dirty mouth and the romantic sensibilities, who couldn't remember what a meatball was called, and who knew nothing about shopping at Target before he met me.

My filthy rich billionaire, who concerned himself with villages in Africa in need of fresh well water more than how to make the next dollar.

My husband who loved me and who would be the father our future children adored and respected.

My wonderful, amazing, perfect man.

EPILOGUE

Caleb

February

"You have always been just like your father. I never understood his fascination with the *help*." My mother waved her hand in a graceful circle toward Brooke and Ellen. "JW's philanthropic notions with his charities and good works to help those less fortunate were deeply in him. You've followed right in his footsteps, Caleb." I knew what she was doing. Her skills at delivering an insult while making it appear as if she was simply being charming were almost legendary. I decided to call her out on it.

"Okay, since I am just like my father, is that why you sold off his treasured Blackwater without ever mentioning to me you were selling, because you knew I would object?"

"No, Caleb. I sold Blackwater for the reason that it was mine to sell. Your father gave it to me to do whatever I saw fit." I could hardly believe it, but I'd seen the documents to prove that she was, indeed, telling the truth. Why would Dad give her Blackwater in the first place, though?

"Why keep the news of selling from me?"

"I didn't really. I just put it up for sale and didn't discuss it with you. It's not like you showed much of an interest, Caleb. It'd been years since you even went there, until you met Brooke that is."

She waved her hand in our direction again, as if she were bestowing her grace upon poor peasants begging for a favor. It annoyed me greatly. "Do not go there with Brooke." I was barely able to keep a lid on my temper. You would think with how incredibly, seriously wrong my mother had been about Janice that she wouldn't even consider showing anything but kindness toward my beautiful girl. But that would mean conceding, and in her twisted view, it put her on the losing side. Very fucked-up ideology to liken us to combatants in a battle, but sadly those were the rules she played by—and they were ironclad. Losers were given no quarter and even less sympathy. No second chances.

Janice, for instance, had been shunned by the tribe and would never be welcomed into Boston's inner circle of society again. Despite the actual fucking restraining order preventing her from coming within two hundred feet of us, I'd made sure her wings were clipped. It was either agree to leave the country or face a messy trial inside a Boston courtroom. A courtroom with plenty of drooling media hacks lying in wait to deliver the most unflattering picture of the day to the eager public, whose sole entertainment was watching celebrities go off the rails—she figured her psycho shit out real quick. Janice might be crazy, but she wasn't stupid. She chose Hong Kong.

My mother did not heed my warning tone and turned away to take a sip from her wineglass. "I don't understand what the fuss is with selling Blackwater. The old place brought in a fortune. All's well that ends well."

"What the fuck, *Mom*?" I exploded. "I want an explanation, and I want it now." I stabbed my finger down on the table. "Why did Dad ever give Blackwater to you in the first place?"

She scowled at my f-bomb. "Language, Caleb, remember how you were brought up, please."

"How I was brought up . . . hmm . . . that's interesting, my dear *mother*, because I don't really remember you being very involved with me. Dad was, of course, but I only remember nannies and babysitters reading to me, or giving me baths, or any of the normal things mothers do for their children." I wished I didn't have to ask her the rest, but I needed to know. "Why have I felt, for my whole goddamn life, that you resented me—that you could barely tolerate being around your own son?"

"Caleb, this is not the time, nor is it the place, for this discussion." She looked around the room at all the faces. My brothers, my sisters, Herman and Ellen, Brooke, James, my cousins—all of them waiting to hear from her. Everyone was uncomfortable and yet frozen in place. I felt the same. All of the ugly was about to come spewing out in front of everyone, and I did not care.

The fuckin' bell had been rung. Fuckin' loudly, too. There was no unringing it.

"Madelaine, you need to tell him the truth," Herman said. "JW is gone, and the boy deserves to know."

Every eye in the room turned toward my uncle, including both of mine, as all of the hairs on the back of my neck tilted straight up.

Along with the axis of the earth.

"What *is* the fucking truth that's been kept from me for my whole life?" I yelled back at her.

She flinched in her seat.

The only thing holding me from going into a total meltdown was Brooke's hand rubbing on my back in gentle but steady circles, grounding me from absolutely losing my motherfucking shit in front of everyone I cared about most in the world.

My mother straightened her back and lost the hauteur that she usually carried around on her face. I knew the *truth* I was about to hear would change everything.

She turned to me and said it calmly.

"The truth is, Caleb, you are not my son."

$$$

RELIEF. I felt relief for the first time in thirty-one years where my "mother" was concerned. I didn't have to wonder what I'd done to spurn her love. Now I understood. It finally made some goddamn fucking sense to me. I blocked out everyone else in the room. I knew they were there, but I didn't care anymore. The truth is all I cared about, because I had nothing to hide from any of them.

"My father?" I was almost fearful of asking.

"Your father was your father, Caleb. You are his son, but you are not mine." More relief poured over me at knowing my whole existence was not a lie. I was a Blackstone after all.

"H-h-how did it happen?"

"Shortly after we'd married I found out he had a lover. One of the cleaning staff, a girl named Melody Rainford—a student on a work visa from England. Yes, she was British," she said in a tone I did not care for. But I held my tongue because I wanted her to tell me the rest. "He made her pregnant and you were born. JW was completely infatuated with her, and I am quite certain he would have left me and married her, if she hadn't died just three weeks after you were born."

I lifted my eyes and stared daggers at my mother—no, wait—I stabbed *Madelaine* with the question I dared not ask.

"No, Caleb. I am not a murderer, despite what you might be imagining right now. It was a postpartum aneurysm that killed your mother. They are a tragic complication that does happen sometimes, and the result is usually fatal. Your father was devastated to lose her, but he wouldn't part with you. He loved you because you were his son, and he wanted you to be raised as his son in the eyes of society, with all of the benefits that would come with his name."

I couldn't imagine the terrible emotion my father must have experienced when my birth mother suddenly died, leaving him with a newborn to raise. I looked over at Brooke and felt the stab of fear punch right through my gut. *If I ever lost her there would be nothing left of me.*

"He came to me humbled and begged me to take him back. We struck a deal, your father and I. I would claim you as my child, and he would never stray again during the course of our marriage. He would also give to me certain assets that would belong only *to* me—so I would never be under his thumb for money again and always in control of my own personal wealth, even if he lost everything he owned. The deed to Blackwater was one such provision. Fortunes are lost every day in the oil business. I had to make sure what I was getting would stand the test of time and hold its value."

I couldn't fault her explanation. *A fortune promised in exchange for claiming me as her own. Secrets kept . . . for a price.*

"He moved us to Houston for two years so our friends wouldn't question your birth after it was announced I was expecting. Everything was arranged, even your birth certificate was altered. People were paid to forget what they'd seen, if they were even aware. Good servants understand the value of turning a blind eye and your father made sure they were well compensated. By the time we returned to Boston, you were a little boy in the care of your nanny, because I was pregnant with twins and too ill to mother you. Nobody noticed. You looked just like JW, and so your parentage was accepted without doubt. People see what we want them to see, Caleb. And what they saw was a growing, happy family with a mother and a father.

"Your father did all of that for you, Caleb. He kept his promise to me, and in spite of what you might believe, I did love him very much and our marriage grew stronger after our tumultuous beginning *because* of our agreement. I did my best for you—the best that I was capable of giving you. I did not interfere with your relationship with your father or with your brothers and your sisters. You loved them all unconditionally, and they you—I could see that clearly.

"He didn't want you to know. Even on his deathbed, your father made me promise never to tell you, because he was afraid you would lose respect for him. He was afraid for *all* of his children to lose their respect for him. JW was not the perfect man you've always believed him to be. He was flawed . . . as we all are. Until right now, I have kept my promise to my husband, and I never once betrayed him or h-his w-wishes," she stammered slightly, "and regardless of what you *think*, Caleb, I have always thought of myself *as your mother*."

She stood up from the table with all of the poise I'd known her to have throughout my life and tilted her head in my direction as an acknowledgment. "So you know the truth, son." She addressed the rest of the people in the room. "Please excuse me, but I must say goodnight to all of you. Thank you for dinner, Caleb and Brooke, but I find myself suddenly very tired." Then she walked out with her head held high. We heard the front door open and close a minute later.

We are a mother and a son who are not a mother and a son.

I didn't feel the devastation I thought I should be feeling, because it was all shades of gray, wasn't it?

A father in a desperate situation trying to make the best he could out of it.

A wife who had been betrayed in her marriage asked to cover up her husband's mistakes.

A child completely unaware of anything different from what he'd always known.

Because really, my childhood had been good. I'd been a happy kid. I'd *felt* loved. I never remember feeling like I was set apart within the family, so I couldn't fault her for excluding me in any way that had been recognizable to me as a child. She'd sent my brothers off to boarding school when they were ten, same as me. My sisters, too, when it was their turn. So, she'd hidden her resentment well. I guess my dad had loved me enough for the both of them. I was curious about my birth mother, though. She had been a British girl like my Brooke. Melody Rainford—a pretty name. I wanted to know more about her.

As I came out of my mental fog, I felt Brooke touching me, letting me know she was still with me as she rubbed my back with one hand and held my face with the other. She tugged on my cheek so I would turn to her. "Caleb, my love, how are you?"

"I am surprisingly well." I gave her a small smile because I really felt it. "If I have you, I am fine."

"You have me."

"I love you, Brooke."

She smiled back at me and offered up her lips to kiss me sweetly. "As I love you, my darling, and I want you to look around and see the whole roomful of people who also love you without question. It is a forever love, Caleb, that they all feel for you and you don't ever have to doubt, okay?"

I regarded each of them. Lucas and Wyatt who looked completely shell-shocked; Willow and Winter with tears leaking out of their eyes; Herman and Ellen who seemed peacefully calm; my cousins who looked about on par with my brothers; James offering his unwavering support without question. Brooke was absolutely right, though. Nothing was going to change my relationships with any of them. They were still my brothers, my sisters, my uncle, my cousins, and my friend—my *family* would always be my family. Even Madelaine was still my mother—she was the only one I'd ever known and ever would know. Sadly, there was no changing that fact for either one of us.

We'd both have to deal with it and go forward. In time I hoped we'd be able to meet in the middle and find some peace. I'd had no choice in any of it, but I needed to remember that she *did* have a choice all those years ago. She could have told my father no and yet she hadn't. She'd taken on the role of mother to her husband's bastard love child for better or for worse.

It was all a pretty heavy concept for me to delve into right at this moment, but at least I didn't feel like something was missing anymore. That odd sense of feeling lost but not really. All my life I'd sensed I was just a little bit off course from the rest of my family but with no real reason to justify why I should feel that way.

Still a savage mind fucking, though.

For everyone—not just me. I couldn't forget that.

I stood up from the table and knew it was time to share with them all the real reason I'd wanted them to come tonight.

"I realize that was a helluva lot for everyone to take in just now. Not at all what I was expecting tonight when I invited you all here to share in a new venture. So let me just get this out there first, and then we can begin the lovefest, okay?"

Someone laughed.

Lucas broke the tension with, "I'll always be your younger and much hotter brother!" in a salute with his beer bottle from across the table, and I knew it would all be fine.

I lifted my chin to let him know I appreciated his timely interruption and then focused.

Deep breath.

"My lovely wife has helped me to find a world I was missing out on before she rescued me." I squeezed her hand and looked down at her sitting so elegantly and beautiful in her turquoise dress with our son growing stronger inside her every day as she waited for me to share her genius idea. I could never pay back fate for the gift of her into my life. I knew I would be forever in fate's debt, so this was just one small way in which I could begin to even the score.

Everything I needed to live was right beside me.

She whispered, "My Caleb, I love you so very much."

"I know you do," I told her before returning to finish what I wanted to say to the rest of them. "A world where good efforts are made helping those who desperately need it. Not many have the resources and financial blessings I was born into, so I wanted to give something back. Blackwater has been sold off, yes, but not to just anyone—and not out of this family. The silent partner on the deed is really a nonprofit we set up called the Sanctuary at Blackwater. And I'm not talking about a sanctuary for wildlife. It was recently approved for a business license from the Massachusetts Department of Health and Human Services, and will begin moving forward with operations as soon as a governing board has been appointed. That's where you all come in." I focused my eyes on my sister. Winter was born for this job. I hoped she would take on the position of director, but if it was her choice not to accept, then I'd be okay with that, too. This would be a labor of love from all angles and only for those who felt so inspired. I merely wanted to offer my family the first opportunity to become involved with the project before going out into the community.

"Begin operations as a place for . . . ?" Winter asked hopefully.

"Women and children who need sanctuary," I told her.

$$$

BROOKE'S eyes never left mine when I made love to her after everyone had gone. I needed the connection to her more than ever after the news I'd gotten tonight. She grounded me in a way that I realized was necessary for my future survival. Whatever had happened in the past didn't define me, and it didn't change me as the person I'd become. Only Brooke had been able to do that.

With our bodies flush as we lay side by side, I spoke to her belly, which was now slightly rounded with our little John William growing fast inside her. "How are you doing in there, son?" I asked.

We did this daily. I spoke to him, told him about my day, read the financial reports aloud to him, and generally made a nuisance of myself with his mother.

"He says he's very proud of his daddy for being so generous and caring to help those who need it." Brooke always answered for Johnny, and somehow I believed her words were his words. The whole thing was ridiculously believable to me.

"That's nice of him to say so."

"He's a very nice boy . . . a great deal like his father from what I can tell."

"I love you, Brooke. And I love you, Johnny," I called down to him in the direction of her belly. "Just think, he already is beginning to know the sound of our voices—"

Brooke raised an eyebrow in question at my abrupt pause.

"I just figured out why I fell in love with you the moment I first heard you speak to me at that cocktail party."

"I think I know why, now," she said.

"Tell me your theory, baby."

"You liked my accent because your mother spoke to you in the same British accent when she was carrying you inside her for nine months. Your subconscious memories recalled that long ago someone who sounded a lot like me loved you with all of her heart."

"Do you think that's possible?" I asked.

"I do, Caleb—and now you have me loving you with all of my heart."

I kissed my sweet Brooke and thanked her for saving me in as many ways as I could show her. It would take the rest of my life probably, but I was up for the challenge. I had nothing else more important to do . . . than love her.

ACKNOWLEDGMENTS

My first thank-you goes out to Ruth and Jan for their helpful push. This journey would never have happened if not for your encouragement. You both are an incredible inspiration to me in this business. To my agent, Jane Dystel . . . I am continually amazed at the things you can accomplish . . . and ever grateful for it. Thank you for always having my back. To my editor, Maria Gomez at Montlake Romance, thank you for taking me on and supporting me at every turn. To Luna and Franzi, who read every page of this manuscript as it was born, falling in love with the story, and begging me for the next chapter. I don't think I can ever express what that meant to me, especially at a time when I was struggling with so much doubt. You believed in me. To Darren, for reading faithfully, even though romance books are not your thing. You never complain, and your input is invaluable. I love that we can work this gig together. To Marion, for helping me to make it through that last leg of the book race—to its polished and complete end. You are always a joy to work with. Big love and immense appreciation to the ladies of *Raine Miller Romance Readers* for bringing daily inspiration to so many people, and for your love and support not just for my books, but for me personally. You are the ones who keep me tapping away at my keyboard—don't ever forget that! Thank you, thank you, thank you. I can't ever say it enough times.

xxoo R

READ ON FOR AN EXCERPT FROM

FILTHY LIES

A BLACKSTONE DYNASTY NOVEL

BY RAINE MILLER

AVAILABLE FEBRUARY 2017

Editor's Note: This is an early excerpt and may not reflect the finished book.

PROLOGUE

Winter

The day I turned fifteen years old I knew I loved James Blakney. There was a look in his eye that told me he'd finally noticed I existed in a realm beyond best-friend's-much-younger-off-limits-don't-even-think-about-it-little-sister. Call it womanly intuition, despite the fact I was barely qualified for being an actual woman at just fifteen—and only in the biological sense—but still, I knew my own feelings.

I shared those feelings with no one.

James came to my birthday that year. To the gathering at Blackwater on the island where my family summered and vacationed as often as my father could convince my mother to spend time at the old estate perched on the coast. We were in the pool playing chicken fight when it happened. Wyatt was carrying me on his shoulders while Lucas carried Janice Thorndike and the two of us squared off. Janice was one of those people we were forced to tolerate because our parents were close. She was a manipulative attention whore most of the time, and it being my birthday didn't change that fact for her one iota. Why she would go out of her way to humiliate someone who was much younger than her—and during their birthday celebration no less—was beyond me.

But she did.

Janice yanked on the tie at my neck that held up my bikini top and announced to all within shouting distance to have a look at my tits when it fell down. I was mortified to the depths of my soul as I frantically tried to cover back up after jumping from Wyatt's shoulders down into the water. Awkwardly struggling with my chest submerged, I turned away from everyone and pulled myself together as best I could through hot tears. I think my brothers were either too freaked out or oblivious to what had just happened because neither said anything to me as I made for the edge of the pool to leave. Maybe they figured I didn't want any more attention drawn to myself—which I most certainly didn't—but a little compassion would have been nice, too. Brothers can be stupidly dense.

James met me at the steps with a towel and told me Janice was a jealous bitch who wished she looked as good as I did without her bikini top.

"You saw?" I asked him on a sob.

His striking greeny-brown eyes burned right into me before he answered. "You have nothing to be ashamed of, Winter, and you didn't do anything wrong. You can't help that you're beautiful and sweet." The way he looked at me told me we'd moved beyond our big-brother/little-sister type of relationship in that moment. It wasn't him being pervy with me, either. It was simply James being my champion when I desperately needed one.

"Thank you," I mumbled, still mortified that he'd seen my naked boobs, but strangely aware the incident had given me the gift of James Blakney's attention at the same time.

"Don't let this ruin your special day, Win. You are perfectly lovely in *every* way," he said before grinning at me in a way that could only be described as a little bit wicked. My skin pebbled along with my nipples as I stood there like a mute. James winked as he took a swig of the Sam Adams he held before going back over to his group of friends on the grass as if nothing had ever happened.

And just like that I fell in love with him.

Not even my twin sister, Willow, was privy to the innermost secrets of my heart in regards to James Blakney. In my dreams he was mine alone, and I didn't have to share him with anyone else. Or be humiliated because I'd set my sights far too high on a man who could never possibly be interested in a young girl like me. And that right there was the division between us. James was a *man* at twenty-three, and I was merely a young *girl* at fifteen. Those eight years spanning between us was gargantuan—far too great of a distance to cross.

Then.

But I've always known him. James has been around and in my life for as long as I can remember. He met my oldest brother, Caleb, at St. Damien's when they were ten years old, and they've been friends ever since. I was two then. Willow and I went to St. Damien's eight years later when it was our turn to be shipped off to boarding school—and our twin brothers, Wyatt and Lucas, were sent off five years before us. In the Blackstone family, children were always schooled away from home, because it built character and toughened them up for the real world. Even though the "real world" was so far removed from our lifestyle it was laughable. Things like twenty-year-old mothers who worked the streets so her children could have food and a place to sleep; or homeless vets struggling with wartime PTSD manifested in drug abuse and suicide were the *real* world.

But those types of things weren't the "real world" examples my parents were referring to.

Boarding school was just one of the many requirements that came with the territory of growing up rich. James understood completely, because he was raised in much the same way. The Blakneys owned a beach retreat on Blackstone Island not far from my family's ancestral estate, Blackwater, and so our lives had been spent at the same gatherings and social functions for as long as we both could remember.

As the years went along I loved James from afar, watching him grow more serious . . . and more cynical. I think his fiancé dumping him at the altar five years ago to run away with a senior partner in his father's law firm had a lot to do with the change in his personality. Leah Allison turned out to be a money-hungry bitch who'd left a trail of destruction in her wake. She broke my James's heart. And she did it publicly in a way that was cruel and unnecessary, and on the very day they were to be married. With the guests already arriving at the church! I'll never forget the look on James's face when Caleb led him out of there.

Crushed.

I didn't know *all* of the reasons for his devastation at the time. It was more than just Leah leaving him hanging at the altar. It was worse than that, I would discover in time.

I couldn't have known all of the machinations that went on behind the scenes in our world when I was barely eighteen years old, but I'd learned enough to get an idea that a lot of it wasn't nice.

Despicable was a much better adjective.

James had been twenty-six when he found out there were lots of secret deals and plenty of depravity in plain sight if you knew where to look.

I think that discovery was part of my interest in choosing to study Social Work at Boston University. I wanted to live my life differently than the people in my "social" circle. I didn't desire to be impoverished, but I didn't desire to waste my money on frivolous excess, either. I wanted to use it to help make a difference for people who desperately needed someone to care, and had no one.

No one at all.

After his wedding-that-didn't-happen, I'd heard that James had promptly started drinking and stayed drunk for about a week before pulling himself back together. With fierce resolve to overcome the betrayal of those who'd done him wrong, a mask descended over his handsome face. James lost his carefree manner and the easy smile he'd always had for others, and most importantly, for me. He became more closed off and far less engaging in person after Leah worked him over. The change in him was permanent.

I missed the old James terribly at first, but I didn't have a great many encounters with him during the years I was an undergrad at BU. I was busy being a student, and James was busy separating himself from his father's firm. There was some drama over that decision at the time. I remember my parents discussing it, but in the end James made his own stamp in the legal community, establishing himself as the go-to guy for contract law in New England. James R. Blakney & Associates, P.C. was retained by my dad for Blackstone Global Enterprises as soon as James had set up on his own. Nothing had changed now that Caleb was the one heading up BGE since Dad's death. In fact, James probated his will—a complicated undertaking for anyone faced with settling the billion-dollar personal fortune our father left to us—and he handled it all without a blip. On top of being a close family friend, James knew the conditions of my trust fund. He knew what would have to happen in order for me to gain access to it before my thirtieth birthday, too. He was the one who explained it to me and my sister at the reading of the will. Lucas and Wyatt weren't at issue because they were already sitting only a year out from thirty when Dad passed away.

It would be fair to say I hate Leah. Not so much for being with James in the first place, but for wounding him and leaving him a changed man. For that reason alone she is on my unforgivable sinners list. But I've also done something to hurt James. Something that could make him hate me, even though it would kill me inside if he did.

I stole from him.

I took advantage of James in a weak moment. I knew it was wrong, and yet I didn't care when I was crossing over a dangerous line with him. I indulged nearly a decade's worth of craving to experience the magic of being loved by James Blakney. Loved? Probably more like fucked. But it was done in a loving way so I did not care. Carelessness indeed. I knew the risks and took my chances anyway.

Still, it was so very wrong of me to let it happen, because the circumstances were too close to how he'd been betrayed by Leah. My betrayal is even worse because the effects will be passed along onto others.

And now?

I'll have to face up to the consequences of what I've done.

To James.

To us.

To our unborn child.

ONE

James

Three Months Earlier
Boston

One reason and one reason only could be responsible for my presence at my father's law office today. That reason was the woman who gave birth to me. My mother had asked me to see him, and so I agreed, even though I'd rather take a swim in the Charles River. The fact that I would prefer immersing myself into a polluted-as-fuck body of water over meeting with my dad spoke volumes.

The truth? I love my mother . . . but I honestly couldn't say the same about my father. Harsh as it was to acknowledge, my pragmatism told me I wasn't the first son to feel this way about a parent. History was filled with examples.

I dreaded this meeting with him because I knew whatever message he wanted to deliver to me personally wasn't anything I would want to hear. Nothing he ever imparted was good news, but this felt like walking into an ambush. To say we had a *stiff* relationship was a polite way of describing it. I kept myself guarded because I had to. Having your father sitting on the First Circuit Court of Appeals would probably do it for most people. The fact I practiced law in the same city required the appearance of family solidarity even if there was none. I had a fuck-ton of valid reasons for feeling the way I did.

So, guarded it would be. Even though I'd been in his company at family dinners and holiday occasions, I hadn't been here in his office since the day I'd left it five years ago. The feelings of anger and disgust simmered just below the surface where I'd forced them to stay. After this I'd need a release to bring me back down to level. I knew where I'd be heading tonight. Annnnnd wasn't the irony just fucking beautiful considering where I was right now?

"He's ready for you now, James." Patricia's smile held a touch of sympathy. She probably knew the reason for my summons. My father, the judge, only hired the best, and every lawyer with half a brain understood a smooth running office existed in direct correlation to the skills of his or her legal secretary.

"Thanks. Oh, before I forget, tell your son to get in touch with Marguerite at my offices if he's interested in an internship." Patricia's oldest son was a first year law student at Suffolk and probably a smart kid if he was anything like his mom.

"Oh, that's so kind. I know Chase will jump at the opportunity, James." She smiled her genuine thanks before leading me into my father's inner sanctum.

He tracked me with his eyes as I entered the room. I had to work fucking hard to keep a lid on my emotions and stand there impassively. I was on enemy turf for as long as this meeting lasted. I thought of my mother and that helped to keep my feet planted, otherwise I'd be out the door and down on the street where I could breathe again.

"Sit down, son."

I settled into one of his soft leather chairs and leaned back with an expression of relaxed comfort. An acting performance that should probably earn me an Academy Award because it really felt like I was being ass-fucked on a bed of jagged nails. I probably was about to be but just didn't know it yet.

"Thank you for coming today. I realize your mother had to persuade you."

I kept my eyes forward and ignored the calculated barb. "How is Mom?" I deflected.

"Your mother is very well as she always is." It was probably a lie, but I'd learned long ago my parent's relationship was not my battle to fight. "The reason I've asked you for a private meeting is to share my news. You need to know what's coming."

I stared back and said nothing. There wasn't a thing on earth that could've compelled me to ask him for the information. I was unable to pretend that much with my father. All of my energy was taken up just by my presence here in the first place. I knew my silent disinterest rankled him. And I fucking loved that it did.

"Ted Robinson's recent cancer diagnosis has ended his political career."

"You know what they say about karma," I answered. All I could envision in my head was the darkly beautiful goddess that was Karma swooping in for her well-deserved dues, because Ted Robinson shared space on the same list with my dad. Cut from exactly the same cloth. "Besides, he has *Mrs.* Robinson to care for his every need now so he can certainly take some comfort in that."

Bitch, please.

The idea of Leah nursing her sick husband back to health was so outrageous even I had to call bullshit on my own inner monologue. Robinson would abso-fucking-lutely have private in-home nursing care, because his adoring wife certainly couldn't soil her hands cleaning up his piss and puke.

"It's time to let go of whatever happened in the past, James. It's done. Move on to the new."

Let go of whatever happened in the past?

My jaw twitched involuntarily, probably from how hard I was gritting my teeth. I *had* moved on to the new, as he put it. What the fuck did he think that was five years ago when I severed ties with this law firm and started my own? James R. Blakney & Associates, P.C. was something pretty fucking new. I shrugged and shook my head slowly. "So what, you're running for public office now?"

"I've been approached by the party, yes." He unclasped his hands and placed both palms down onto his desk. "I will accept their invitation to throw my hat into the proverbial ring. I have every intention of representing Massachusetts in the US Senate one year from now."

Of course you do.

I figured this day would come in time. My father's ego pretty much predestined a political career at some point. "Congratulations," I managed to grind out.

"The senate is just the first step in the overarching plan though."

"Overarching plan?" I loathed when he spoke in riddles like he was doing right now. So arrogantly smug in his passive aggressiveness it grated on my already stretched patience.

"Yes. The senate campaign announcement will come early January when everyone is breathing a collective sigh of relief the presidential race debacle has finally been put to bed—try to deflect some of the negative into a positive. Four years isn't a horribly long time to have to wait for a candidate they can really get behind and safely propel into the White House."

Whoa. Was he saying what I thought he was saying? "You're serious."

"Deadly serious."

"You're going to run for President of the United States." I didn't pose it as a question. I blinked at him, hoping to wake up from a really bad fucking dream—unable to accept the idea, grasping at straws of denial instead. "But aren't you getting ahead of things? The White House is a long way from a judgeship on the First Circuit."

He stone-faced me, taking me straight back to when I was a kid and about to get served my punishment for some irrationally perceived infraction. There were a lot of those moments in my childhood to draw from. A flicker of fear crept inside my heart.

"I-I m-mean, you have to w-win the senate seat before you can declare a run for P-President in four years." I wanted to cut out my tongue for stammering and showing my weakness in front of him.

"The senate race won't be even a small problem. It's already done. All I need to make it stick is the cooperation of my beloved *family*." His lip curled up on one side in a definite tell of distaste as he spoke the last word. Jesus Christ, he must hate us all.

"How so?" I wouldn't have anything to do with his campaign. No fucking way. I held my palms up. "This has nothing to do with me. Your campaign is yours—as in *not mine*."

"Oh, but it is in a way, *son*. You'll have to do your part to help present the right image to the voting public. Every aspect of our lives will be scrutinized—every predilection . . . " He folded his hands and focused his dark eyes on mine, finally getting to the crux of the issue.

"Even I can't change who I am . . . *Dad*. You might think you can clean me up for your precious campaign, but you can't. You *are* responsible for my transformation after all."

Maybe he was responsible.

But maybe not.

The darkness had always been there from as long as I could remember, just not acted on until rather recently in my life. Now? I needed it to survive. The control was essential for me. The fact my father had knowledge of my sexual proclivities was a far worse burden to bear on my part. The fact I liked to tie up women and spank them while fucking was gonna be his.

"Don't be so dramatic. It's a simple solution. Your sister is already on the right path. She understands her duty to her family. The only loose end in my equation is you." He did that lip-curl thing again. "You will also do your duty to this family, and you will do it quickly."

I shook my head at him. Denying what I knew he was asking of me. "I'm not hearing this."

"You *are* hearing this. I can't run a campaign for the highest office in the land with a thirty-something son unmarried and frequenting an underground sex club. Discreet you may be, but this upcoming level of scrutiny isn't what you've been used to thus far. I might be able to get the past whitewashed somewhat but my powers aren't infinite here. A pretty wife and a young family will do a much more convincing job than a cover-up could ever manage. The Internet makes things very goddamn complicated for all of us."

Ain't that the fuckin' truth.

"*Married* doesn't work for me. I mean, just look at what happened the last time I tried to put a ring on it. You orchestrated that catastrophe like a pro, I might add."

"Ancient history, James," he said with a dismissive wave of a hand.

"It doesn't feel so ancient to me knowing my own father arranged for my *marriage* to disintegrate at the fucking altar in front of a church full of guests."

"She wasn't the right wife for you—obviously—and beneath this family. Can you deny you're better off without her now?"

That last part stung like a bitch because he was right on that one point. I *was* better off without Leah in my life. But what was worse *was knowing* how I'd been played by the people who shouldn't have ever dreamed of playing me. At the time it had been beneficial for Leah to leave.

Beneficial for him and for Ted Robinson.

My father cared only about himself, and that wouldn't change until the day he took his last breath on this earth. Rage got the upper hand over my self-control and I jumped up from the chair. "Why do you feel entitled to dictate the who and the when I should marry?"

He shrugged. "Because I can, and because it behooves me to have both of my children happily settled with families of their own. Family values will be the impetus of my campaign. Family. Values." His frustration was beginning to show. "You are going to get some."

"And how do you suggest I do this?"

He made a sound of disgust. "Do I really have to spell this out for you, son?"

"Since it's me you're asking to do this, yeah you do, *Dad*."

He settled back into the luxurious leather and let me have it. "Marry a girl from a good family and make her pregnant. I *am* assuming you can figure that part of it—" He paused, his expression changing to one of interest. "Or get her pregnant *first*, and then marry her if you prefer."

"I'm not doing any of—"

"In fact, a surprise pregnancy might work even better to endorse our support of traditional values with a thoroughly modern interpretation." He tapped his lips with an index finger and looked genuinely pleased for the first time since I'd entered his office.

"Have you lost your mind? I'm not having a child because you dictate it's time for me to have one to benefit your fucking political ambitions."

"Careful now," he warned. "You *will* do exactly as I've outlined. And you *will* settle down and get to work on creating the picture-perfect family I need standing in support of the legacy I am building. It's not like I'm asking you to do anything you wouldn't do eventually, James. People grow up and get married. They have children. It's the only reason marriage exists. Why are you struggling with this?"

I had to fight off the urge to shudder out my revulsion. The image of myself standing on some podium somewhere having to cheer on my father in support was just too fucking much to have to stomach this early in the day. I didn't think I could do it.

"You will not fuck this up for me."

"What if I don't find someone?"

"I suggest you do if you want to be involved with the choice. If you can't manage to find a suitable bride on your own, then one will be found for you. A *suitable* bride, James. Not one of your playthings from the club. Wealth is not as important as an upstanding family background for showing we can relate to solid middle class—"

"Just listen to yourself," I said disgustedly. "How in the hell do you—"

"Before you ask the question, just know that I *can*, and I *will* if you disregard my wishes. I am able to make just about anything happen to suit my needs, and I won't hesitate to follow through if you fail me."

"So you're just taking over my life to serve yourself?" I could hardly wrap my head around this conversation we were having right now.

"You're thinking too hard, and I am weary of this conversation. I am expecting some forward movement on this issue by Thanksgiving. Your mother so looks forward to having her children home for the day."

Yeah, and she is the only *reason we come.* "That's only three weeks from now."

He ignored my comment. "Bring your prospective bride around to meet us so we can get to know this new future daughter-in-law who will be mother to my future grandchildren." The smile he gave looked a bit maniacal. "Children who will have been born to enjoy the honor and privilege of visiting their grandfather in the Oval Office someday."

Please, God, don't ever let that happen.

He then returned his attention to whatever document was in front of him and acted as if I wasn't still in the room. My father was finished with me for the moment, and so I'd been effectively dismissed.

I didn't remember leaving his office, but once I felt the warmth of the autumn sun seeping through the clouds as I stood among the foot traffic moving in both directions around me, I figured I'd made it out somehow.

I shouldn't have felt chilled since the sun was out. But I was cold. Cold with fear and worry. Cold with the kind of winter fury that would take ages to melt away.

Winter fury.

Just . . . Winter.

From the moment my father had started dictating his sordid plans for me I knew who I wanted. There was only one person. The only girl it could ever be for me—even though it would be so wrong of me to bring her into the shitfuckery that was my life.

It would be wrong . . . but it would feel so right.

Because Winter Blackstone was my Kryptonite. This I knew. One small slip of indulging in my desires to be closer and there would be no turning back. With my father's edict burning a hole in my heart, I was being handed a reason to go there with her.

But I can't.

I was fucked, and I knew it. This was a huge problem. I knew myself, and I knew how hard the struggle would be in resisting the temptation of her. For me, the allure of Winter Blackstone was something with which I was well familiar. Her unaffected beauty, her kind and generous heart, her gentle way of listening and knowing just the right thing to say in any situation, made her approachable and easy for people to love.

Love?

Did I love her?

Of course I did. I'd known her since she was a toddler, and she was a dear and trusted friend. But, if I was honest . . . Winter was much more than that for me and she had been for a long time. She possessed all of the qualities I could ever want in a wife. She couldn't be more perfect for selling to the media along the lines of something like my father's political campaign. YOUNG HEIRESS CHOOSES SOCIAL WORK OVER HIGH SOCIETY. The news agencies would eat her up and crown her their darling overnight.

You're still fucked because she's off-limits.

This was my truth. Because I could *never* be with Winter in the way I wanted to be. I could never have her. Not how I'd dreamed of having her when my innermost fantasies took over within my twisted headspace.

Winter was too good.

She was too sweet.

She was just too perfectly innocent . . . for the likes of me.

ABOUT THE AUTHOR

Photo © 2015 Christine Arnold Photography

New York Times bestselling author Raine Miller finds as much happiness in writing romances as she does in reading them. Ever since she picked up her first romance novel at thirteen years of age, she's been hooked. *Filthy Rich*—the first book in her all-new series, Blackstone Dynasty—is Raine's latest contemporary romance.

Raine lives with her handsome husband, brilliant sons, and two very bouncy (but beloved) Italian greyhounds.